SKITTISH *to* LOVE

LAINE FARO

ISBN 978-0-578-80082-0 (Paperback)
ISBN 978-0-578-80083-7 (Hardcover)
ISBN 978-0-578-80084-4 (Ebook)
Library of Congress Control Number: 2020923797

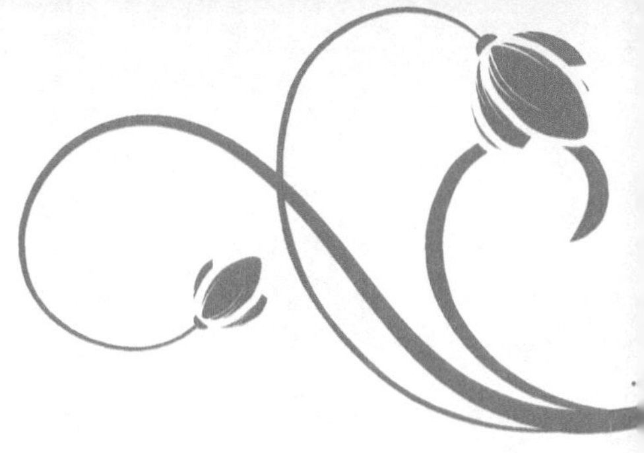

DEDICATION

To all those who commit their time to helping others. It is a true calling to work with others who need a little or a lot of help.

Thank you Kinzi, from Colorado Therapeutic Riding Center Inc., for answering all my research questions. We need so many more companies, like the one you work for, to help those who need the help, horse therapy included.

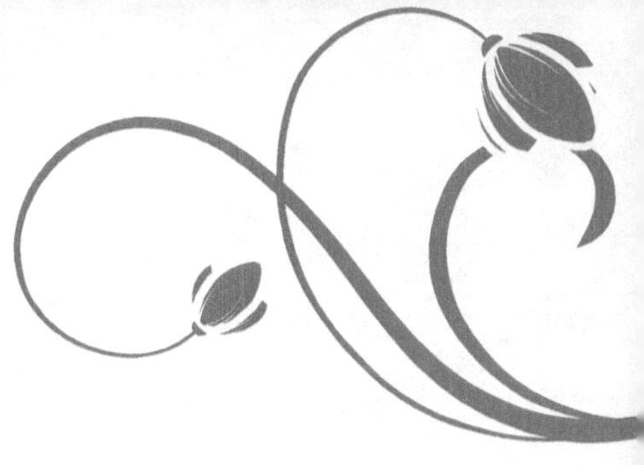

WARNING

For those of you who are sensitive, get anxiety or panic attacks, and have had traumatic sexual assault; there is a graphic rape scene. It is obvious as to where the scene will be.

PREFACE
THANKSGIVING

The song "Can't Take my Eyes Off You" by Frankie Valli comes to mind each time I look at Rose. The lyrics run through my mind and I wonder if this is real as I can't look away. My eyes, heart and soul always find her in a room. Her long, caramel brown hair flows over her shoulders. I want to reach out and touch it, I'm sure it will feel like silk. I watch each of her long fingers twist through the strands when they fall over the front of her crimson red blouse.

"Michael, I asked you a question," Mom says as she catches me staring at Rose. I lower my eyes to the plate of food I haven't touched, then glance at Mom and see the knowing smile on her face.

"I'm sorry Mom, I was thinking about Chestnut. What did you say?" I ask. I'm hoping she doesn't call me out on the small fib. I can see Rose's cheeks blushing a soft pink out of the corner of my eyes. She looks at me, waiting for me to answer the question.

"I asked you if you had any kids coming out to your place over the holiday." Mom raises her glass of wine and takes a sip as my mind takes a moment to process the question. I'm thinking of Rose riding one of the trails with me. I would lose my way on any trail if she was in front of me. I'd be watching her shapely backside swaying back and forth as she moves with the horse.

"No. I don't have anyone until the first week in December," I say looking back to Rose. Her cheeks are no longer pink, but she lowers her eyes when I look directly at her. I know she's going back to Colorado this weekend and take her semester finals in a couple weeks then starts her last semester of college. I wish she could stay and visit a little longer this trip. I feel an intense need to know everything about her. "It will give me more time to work with Chestnut. I can't figure out why he won't let me near him. Anytime I open his stall door, he raises up on his hind legs. He will let all the girls in to feed him and put water in his stall, but no one has been able to touch him." Chestnut has been boarding with me since his owners brought him in October and none of us have a clue what is wrong. He has no physical injuries.

"I can come out and look at him again. Anna should look at him too, she did wonders with Cocoa," Nick tells me. I remember the confusion in finding out what was going on with Cocoa for months. Anna found the reason why Cocoa wasn't healing after just a few days being around him. It turned out there was a piece of paint still in the wound Cocoa got from a storage shed that hit her during the last tornado in the area. Anna suggested they ultrasound the area and they found three pieces of paint still under the skin from the metal they removed.

"Nick, that would be great. I'm at the end of my rope trying to figure it out. I feel so bad for him every time we enter his stall." I look over at Rose and see the interest in her eyes. Rose asks Anna if she can come along. "We can always use another set of eyes," I tell her. I look at Mom when I hear her chuckle. I know what she's thinking. The woman is already planning Lily's, Nick's, and Seth's weddings in her head.

All three come over the next day and I see the miracle that is the De'Amedo sisters. They hum a classical tune, which calms Chestnut down right away. Anna gives him carrots and suggests sugar cubes and vegetables be given as rewards or treats.

"It appears Chestnut needs treats and lots of love. He doesn't have any physical scars, but I'm thinking he probably got trained with human dominance and overpowering," Anna says as she rubs him from neck to flank without Chestnut acting out. "He seems to like us humming to him too. We play music for Cocoa whenever no one is around. Ask Nick about the sound system he had installed for the animals. It might really help," she says as Rose continues to hum the tune to the horse. I would love to make her hum for me.

"I'll call you with the information as soon as I get back home. For now, be amazed by how calm he got when they started humming to him. I think Chestnut will be better with your training techniques. He might take a little longer, but I'm sure your non-physical discipline method will work." Nick says while he pats me on the shoulder. I appreciate the information from the older brother I look up to.

CHAPTER 1

CHRISTMAS

I gave everyone Christmas day off so they can spend time with their families. I can take care of feeding and watering the horses on my own for one day, but now I feel rushed coming over to Mom and Dad's. Chestnut is getting better, but still requires extra time for each training session and daily care. I had to make sure he was fed and watered before leaving for dinner.

Rose decided to fly in for Christmas and I'm beyond excited to see her again. With all the kids grown and out of the house, my parents have plenty of room for out of town guests, so Rose is staying with them while she's here. I offered to pick her up at the airport, but Dad said it would be foolish for me to get her only to drop her off at their house. I see his point, but I really wanted the extra time with her. I haven't spoken with her since Thanksgiving.

I can hear the boisterous noise as soon as I get out of my truck. I see Patrick's black truck at the end of the driveway, which usually means he has plans with a lady later and wants to be able to get out quickly. His truck is so big he can get pinned in very easily with all the vehicles that come for Christmas. Nick and Anna brought her cherry red Mustang again to get Patrick riled up. She still hasn't let him drive it, even though Anna knows it's his dream car. Gabby must have driven because Seth's truck

1

isn't out front. When Gabby's ex-husband was stalking her, they were always in Seth's truck. He made sure he was with her all the time except when she drove her car to work at the vet clinic. Any other time they were in his truck. Joseph's white truck is right in front of the stairs leading up to the double door entry to the house. Mom and Dad have the employees, who have no one else in the area to celebrate Christmas, over for a good home cooked meal, good conversation, special gifts for children, and a yearly bonus envelope for each employee. Joseph volunteers to pick up anyone needing a ride.

As I open the door, I hear Merry Christmas being shouted from people in the living room along with paper crinkling and screams from the children opening their gifts. Mom is in the kitchen, so they hug my Dad and say thank you. I scan the room and don't see Rose. I head straight for the kitchen. I can pick out the smell of spices from Mom's side dishes and the sweet smell of fresh fruit. Holiday smells are wonderful, I would usually stand and take in the smell, but I need to see Rose. I walk through the kitchen to kiss my mom and say hello to everyone in the room. I hear the dishes clinking in the other room as I look around. I don't see her, and I start to panic that she didn't make the trip after all.

"She's in the other room helping with the table," Mom says with a wink. It's scary how in tune Mom is with all her children. She seems to know who the perfect match is for each of us.

I make my way through the kitchen and push the door to the dining room open. I dodge people with platters, bowls, and trays of food they are placing on the server. We always do Christmas dinner buffet style; it makes it easier on the kids and their parents. The employees come early to open gifts, eat dinner with us, and then they go home before the family opens their gifts. I don't see Rose right away and feel uneasiness take over. I turn around to head back to kitchen and smack right into her carrying a tray of fruit.

"I'm sorry," I say as I catch one side of the tray. None of the fruit drops to the floor, but it no longer looks the same as it did when it was put together. The fruit is bunched up on the side I caught.

"No, I'm sorry. I think I came around the corner a little fast," she says. I see her cheeks start to blush before she lowers her head. "Thank you for catching it. I would hate to go back in the kitchen and tell your Mom I dropped the fruit." Her hair is a little longer and darker than at Thanksgiving. Rose has light red gloss on her lips, but I can't see any other make-up on her face. She's beautiful without it.

"You know she wouldn't get mad at something so trivial, right?" I help Rose arrange the fruit after she puts the tray down on the far end of the server. Our fingers touch while we are arranging the strawberries. I feel a spark of electricity go straight to my heart each time our fingers touch. She keeps her head lowered, but I can still see her flushed cheeks.

"I know. Your mom's great but I'd feel bad for wasting the food," she says. I see the gold flecks in her hazel eyes when she lifts her head. She pulls her hands back and moves toward the table as we hear Mom yell that dinner is ready. I follow behind Rose and pull out a chair for her, but not before admiring her curves. She's dressed very festive today. The red cashmere sweater hugs her curves. Rose's hair lays straight down her back and once again, I want to reach out and see if it feels like silk. The forest green slacks tighten across her backside as her body meets the chair. I see red and green wreath earrings dangling from her ears, the same colors as her clothes. As I move around the end of the table to take my seat, I see her cheeks match the crimson red of her sweater.

Everyone comes in and takes their seat. I take a seat across from her so I can see her face as we talk. With a knowing smile on her face, Mom sits at our end of the table which puts her right between us.

CHAPTER 2

"So, Rose, Anna tells me you have one more semester until graduation. What classes do you have left?" Mom asks, winking at me. Mom turns her body towards Rose and shows her she is truly interested in what Rose has to say. I remember Rose talking about taking her finals for the semester after Thanksgiving. I'm sure I've heard Anna talking about her baby sister becoming a nurse at another family dinner. While I listen to Rose talking to Mom, I realize I don't know that much about her even though I find myself falling for her. I will have to change that fact while she's here.

"I'm taking four classes this semester. Two of the classes emphasize on public health. One focuses on health history and physical assessment while interviewing the patient and the other specializes on what key issues are a concern with public health and advancements currently available. The other two emphasize on primary health care for families from obstetric through adolescence. I'm really excited about those two," Rose says with a smile that lights up her entire face. She blushes when she glances across the table and realizes I've been looking at her for the entire conversation.

"That sounds like you will have your hands full these next few months," Mom says while she reaches over and squeezes her hand.

"I'm still working at the local clinic to finish my hours there, too. I'm ready to finish school and get a job." She mentions working at the clinic like it's nothing. She must be taking at least twelve hours of classes and homework at this level of college can't be easy.

"Don't let her fool you," Anna says from the seat next to Rose. "She's terribly busy all the time. Luckily, she works for some great doctors for her required clinical hours. It does help that she also loves the work." Anna puts her arm behind Rose and pulls her in for a side hug. I catch something pass over her eyes when Anna mentions the doctors. I forget about it as soon as Anna starts praising her little sister. "My baby sister here is an over achiever. She's getting her Master's in a year. She went to classes every summer to get ahead and has a GPA higher than me, and I graduated top of my class." I watch Rose's cheek bones redden from the praise her sister is giving her. I didn't know she's getting her Master's. I thought she was getting her four-year Bachelor's degree. I'm impressed, but also intimidated by her obvious intelligence.

I start to think maybe she's too smart for me. She probably doesn't want to date someone with my mental challenges. I continue to listen to Anna brag about her sister and see Rose's cheek go from a soft pink to a dark crimson red. It's great to see the support and praise her family is giving her. They are definitely proud of her. It reminds me of my own family.

"So, what are you going to do after graduation?" my mom asks her.

"I'm actually coming back here to interview at the Women's Health Clinic in Oklahoma City and the Women's Center in Tulsa," she says looking first at my mom and then her hazel eyes find me staring at her. I get excited thinking she may live close by. But then I hear her next statement and my excitement disappears. "I'm also interviewing with the Colorado Women's Health Center in Denver. They specialize in obstetrics and gynecology. That is the field I want to work. I want to work with women's issues more than any other field. Some of the locations have crisis centers I can volunteer at or have programs that I can help with," Rose says with such conviction in her voice I start to wonder why she's wants to volunteer. I hear the passion behind the words and wonder why she is dedicated to this field. I remember Anna saying that their parents died when all three sisters were in their teens. Maybe she wants to work in a field to help others that may have had the same struggles she had without a mother around.

"You sound like you have everything under control, I'm impressed! Some of my boys knew what they wanted to do at your age and others didn't have a clue," she says looking down the table at Patrick. He either didn't hear her or chose to not respond. Patrick is the youngest of the boys and runs a third of the family ranch they gave him. He went from football quarterback who won the state championship his senior year of high school to a bull riding champion. When he was injured and couldn't keep riding, Mom and Dad gave him a share of the ranch to run as his own. Joseph runs the other third. I chose to buy my own land and make something of myself in a different field.

I look down the table and see people stuffing food into their mouths, people smiling and telling stories of their own. Each child is jumping in their seat, waiting for the desserts to be served. We aren't all family by blood, but this loud, rowdy crowd will always be considered family. Christmas is always such a good time at the Corsco's house. I can feel the love my parents share with everyone. I return my attention to Rose after looking at everyone from my Dad at the head of the table, to the parents trying to wrangle their kids, to my brothers and some of their partners. Anna has made Nick so happy and the vet clinic Nick expanded for her is doing very well. Gabriella is finally able to share her entire life with Seth with her ex-husband is in jail after stalking and tormenting her. I can see the love each couple shares with the other. I want my own love story and I know I want Rose to be in that story.

"I knew in my teens that I wanted to help people. When I started looking at colleges and degrees I could get, I discovered that women's health was a field I could specialize in. Brady sat down with me after I got information from several colleges. I found I could stay close to home and get the degree I wanted. Brady was happy I found an in-state college which would lower tuition costs." My mom laughs along with Anna and Rose. "Brady was happy with all of us sisters. We all went to schools in Colorado. He wanted to make sure none of us got stuck with a huge financial aid bill after we graduated. Mom and Dad left some money and Brady invested it, so we would have it for school, but it didn't cover all the expenses for the four of us."

"Your brother is the lucky one to have such amazing sisters. We are very happy you are part of our family now." Mom squeezes her hand then raises her glass. "I know the whole family isn't here today, but we are happy to share this meal with the ones who are. Merry Christmas everyone," she says as we all raise our glasses and wish everyone a Merry Christmas of our own. "Now who is cleaning this mess up today?" Mom asks with a chuckle.

"I think it's my turn," I stand up and start collecting dishes to take into the kitchen. I overhear my mom ask Rose if she would mind helping because she doesn't trust a man in her kitchen. I lower my head and smile. My mother, the match maker is at work, again. Rose stands and collects a stack herself. I hold the door as I walk ahead of her through the door to the kitchen.

"Be careful of the kitchen," Gabriella is telling her before she follows me all the way through the door. "I'm sure Cate has a match making spell in that room." Rose's eyebrows are scrunched together when she enters the kitchen. I heard Gabriella and know exactly what she means, but I don't think Rose would understand so I don't say anything. If it's true, I don't want to risk changing the outcome.

"If you want to get the food bowls and trays, I'll start rinsing and loading the dishwasher," I say as she stacks her pile of dishes next to me. She turns and goes back into the dining room for the next load without saying a word. I turn on the radio and start scraping food into the trash then stack the dishes in the sink to rinse. I look up from the plate in my hand and watch her carrying several items at a time. She can see the surprise on my face. She holds the trays and bowls like a pro. I'm impressed.

"Did you ever work in a restaurant? I've never seen anyone carry so much and have it look so easy." I watch her set each bowl on the kitchen table then place the trays on the counter next to me. Her cheeks turn a soft, rosy pink as I watch her. I'm falling in love with her pink cheeks. She shows her emotions, every time, with the color of her cheeks.

"I worked at the local diner in Greeley before I started my clinic hours. I didn't want Brady working himself to death when I could help pay for some of my necessities," she says. She starts looking around the kitchen. "Where does your mom keep the storage containers?" she asks, turning around and looking straight into my eyes. I can see the golden flex as she looks at me, waiting for my answer.

"They are in the cabinet directly behind you. Do you want to switch jobs with me?" I ask her. I know what size containers the leftovers need just by looking at the food. My mom said it is a gift to eye it and get the right container each time. I've been able to do it since Mom let me start helping in the kitchen when I was seven. I'm looking at her curves swaying as she walks around the kitchen when she turns. I think my cheeks are blushing now as she catches me.

"No, I think I can get it." Rose walks over to the cabinets at the back of the kitchen. I'm watching her get the containers out when I see her look at the table and count how many containers she needs. I get distracted by the skin on her back that peaks out when she leans over to pick out a larger container for the meat. I feel the water dripping down my arms. I have to make myself concentrate on my own task as she gets the containers out. She has a good eye. I glance at the table and counter and realize I would have gotten the exact containers that she has in her hands. Rose turns around and catches me watching her, again.

"I'm seeing what containers you're getting," I say as I turn around and place the plates in the sink. She walks over to the table and I hear the scraping noise of the food getting pushed into the storage container from the serving bowls. I start rinsing each plate and place them into the dishwasher. When I was a child, we all had to take turns hand washing the dishes. Dad surprised Mom with a dishwasher when Joseph and Nick were in junior high. Mom said it was a good lesson for all her children to learn, but now we could start using the dishwasher. I start loading the silverware into the bins as she comes over to starts working on the trays of food. I look over my shoulder to follow her movements. I feel a stab into my finger as a sharp knife cuts into my thumb.

"Ow," I yell. I turn my head and see blood flowing down my fingers as I lift my hand to the sink. I turn on the water to rinse the blood off but can't see exactly where the cut is. I forget Rose is next to me until she reaches over the sink to see my hand. I can feel the electricity bouncing off each of us. My head forgets about the cut as my heart takes over.

"What did you puncture your thumb on?" she asks as she grabs a paper towel off the counter next to the sink. She looks down in the dishwasher. She is holding my hand up and wrapping the paper towel around my thumb as she shakes her head back and forth. My mind is telling me to forget about the pain and enjoy her hand holding mine.

"I think I hit a steak knife when I was putting the silverware in the bin," I tell her. She looks around me and sees the knives pointing up. I feel stupid as she lifts the door of dishwasher. She hears the latch click and then she looks into my eyes, moving her body closer until our bodies are almost touching. I'm feeling a little lightheaded, but that can be the shock of cutting my thumb, right?

"Come sit down at the table so I can see how deep the cut is," she says and starts walking me to the table holding my hand. I know I shouldn't be happy about the reason she is holding my hand, but I feel the same electrical currents going from my hand up to my heart. I think I'm a goner. She's it for me. Nick and Seth said the same thing about Anna and Gabriella. They knew the first day they met that they were on the fast track to love.

"I think I nicked the top of my thumb. Really, I'm fine," I tell her. "Mom has bandages under the sink. Just get me one and I'm sure it will stop bleeding." It's like she doesn't hear me. She takes the paper towel off slowly. She looks the cut over and dabs the paper towel over it when the blood starts up again.

"I think you might need a stitch if it doesn't stop bleeding. Let me get you some ice to put on it then we'll see if I can bandage it up. Keep it above your heart," she tells me. I see her move around the kitchen like she lives here. She finds the storage bags, takes one and places several pieces of ice in it. She gets the mallet from another counter where my mom's mallets are for thinning out meat. She wraps a towel around the bag of ice and starts to smash it with the mallet. I can't believe how easily she is smashing the ice. I'm quick to make note to never piss her off. She looks totally in her element, in the kitchen and taking care of me. "Okay Michael, place this over the tip of your thumb. It may hurt," she tells me. She pulls a chair closer to mine and looks at my hand.

The ice did hurt when I put it over my thumb. I didn't cry out like I wanted. I can't let her think I'm a wimp over a little cut. I look at her face and notice a few freckles on her nose, despite her olive colored skin. Her hazel eyes have gold flecks shining through. I see the highlights blending into her caramel brown hair. She's wearing it down today. As she leans over my hand and removes the ice, a few strands fall over her shoulder and lays on my arm. I have my answer, it does feel like silk against my skin. I would take the pain my thumb would feel just to run my hand through her hair.

"Michael, it looks like you're lucky. The bleeding has stopped. I'll put a bandage on it." She moves to the cabinet where the bandages are and pulls out a few different sizes then sits back in the chair next to me. She contemplates which one she should use. I can see the wheels turning in her mind. I would slap anyone of them on and call it good, but not Rose. "I don't see one that will cover the top of your thumb so I'm going to use two. One will cover the tip and the other will wrap around your nail to hold the first one in place. If it starts coming off, let me know and I'll get one from Anna's place," she explains. I feel the electricity move up my arm as her skin touches my hand.

"Thank you, I could have done it myself," I say, looking straight into her beautiful eyes.

"What's the point of having a nurse in the family if she doesn't take care of those she cares about," she says smiling at me. Her teeth are a sparkly white. I notice she isn't blushing. Her face is so close to mine. All I need to do is tip my head down and I could taste those glossy lips. I start to process what she said and get confused. I raise one of my eyebrows as I pull my face back.

"Why would you go to Anna's for the bandage?" I ask her. Anna is a vet, so I don't connect the two.

"Brady had Lilla, Anna and me, put together first aid kits for our cars and houses. Mine is in my kitchen. He said you never know when we would need it. I remember all of us putting every shape and size bandage in the kit." She gets up to take the ice pack to the sink. "I think I should finish loading the dishwasher. The hot water will start the bleeding again, plus I don't want you to get that thumb wet." She turns toward the counter and opens the dishwasher door. I see that patch of skin as she bends over, loading the rest of the utensils. I'm sad to see the skin disappear as she stands up and loads the glasses into the top rack.

"Thank you. I'll finish packaging up the food on the trays." I look at the table and see all the food neatly stacked in storage containers, ready for the refrigerator. She brought the bowls over already so there really wasn't much for me to finish. I catch the song on the radio as I place the last container on the top shelf of the refrigerator. Mom must have been in a sentimental mood while cooking today. Frank Sinatra is singing "You're Nobody 'Til Somebody Loves You." I see Rose mouthing the words as she sways her hips to the music. I'm a little surprised she would know the song. Sinatra is a classic and well known in this house, but I picture her listening to Shawn Mendes or Ed Sheeran, not a member of the Rat Pack. As I listen to the words, I realize I want to be her somebody.

"We're all done," Rose says as she dries her hands on the hand towel my mom leaves over the cabinet door below the sink. Rose gives one more look at the counters, table, and stovetop. "It looks like we can go in and open gifts with everyone." We're walking towards the living when we hear the phone ring.

I'm walking behind her enjoying the view of her hips moving from side to side. Her long hair is swaying back and forth with each step. Rose goes over to the ladies sitting at the small table we use for playing cards. I take the one chair left in the room. The gifts are piled high under the tree, which Mom decorated with red and gold ornaments this year. She changes the color scheme each year. Mom is walking around the room with the phone next to her ear, saying that she was so excited and happy for them. I catch Rose look over at Anna with her eyebrows raised. When Mom gets off the phone, I get the answer to the questioning look they exchanged.

"That was Lily. She says Merry Christmas and that she's engaged. Brady asked her to marry her a few minutes ago. She's going to send a picture of the ring in a second," she says. Mom is giddy with excitement. This is the first of her children to get engaged, even though Nick and Anna live together. Seth has been with Gabriella for almost two months, but they aren't officially living together since they both have their own places. Lily was married before and here she is getting married again.

"Damn straight he proposed! When he was here for Thanksgiving he asked for her hand in marriage. Of course, I said yes and that he better propose soon. No daughter of mine shacks up with a man that she isn't married to," Dad says. He's sitting in his chair with his chest puffed out. He thinks he's in charge of the family and what he says goes. I know, secretly, he knows Mom is in charge. All us kids know who really runs the Corsco family.

Mom's phone beeps and the picture Lily promised shows up on her screen. The girls look at it first. Mom is speechless, Gabriella comments on the size of the stone, Anna says how beautiful it is, and Rose squeals and gets teary. The guys take a quick look, not really interested. Mom saves it to her phone. Rose is now sitting next to Anna and talking quietly, tears running down her face.

"Rose, are you okay?" I ask, everyone looks at her. I didn't mean for the whole room to look at her and now her cheeks are that crimson red they turn when she is really embarrassed.

"She's fine. We both knew Brady was giving Lily our Mom's engagement ring. It overwhelmed her when she actually saw it on Lily's finger," Anna says, hugging Rose as she sniffles and dabs her cheeks with the tissue Gabriella has handed her.

"I knew he was proposing today, but I didn't know it was with your Mom's ring. That's so sweet. Your brother is a good man and you both should be proud of him," Mom says as she walks over and gives Rose a motherly hug.

"Alright, we have gifts of our own to open. Who's first?" Dad asks. He tries to lighten the mood anytime a female starts to cry. I've come to discover, my dad in his own way, is a sensitive man. He wants to fix the problem, but in most cases can't.

CHAPTER 3

I'm in the stables cleaning up after the kids that were here today. I love to see the smiles on their faces while riding, I think I get a little therapy of my own by seeing the kids enjoy themselves each day. Who would have thought after my terrible accident with my horse, I would be running an equine therapy program? I also board and train horses, but my true joy is the equine program I put together a few years back.

I'm looking forward to a couple of days off from the kids, though. I need to work with Chestnut some more. Anna and Rose really started his recovery when they came along with Nick at Thanksgiving. I asked Nick's help to see if he could figure out what was wrong with him. Anna's suggestion to install a sound system into the stables really worked miracles with Chestnut and some of my other horses. Nick still makes regular visits to check on Chestnut and he knows when Nick comes to visit, so does Anna. She has spoiled him with carrots and sugar cubes. He won't listen to anyone but Anna when she's here.

I check with my site manager before heading up to the house. I built my house and stables at the same time. I always had a dream of running my own horse training business, but after my accident I researched adding the equine therapy to my business. It meant I needed a lot more staff, so I added a few cabins on the property. I wanted my employees, and their families, to live close by for my convenience and theirs. I have a few high school kids

14

that clean the stables and feed all the horses as part of the local 4H program. All of them learn Cooling Out, which is cooling down the horse by walking them, brushing, and sponging them off and giving the horses small amounts of water. They also work with me on bit training. The horse needs to be comfortable with a piece of metal in their mouth for training to move forward. I let them ride the horses after one of my staff saddle breaks them. Most of the kids love the chance to ride and I appreciate their help. I've seen a few water fights after they are done sponging down the horse and as long as it doesn't upset the horse, I let them have their fun.

I have three wings to the stable; boarded horses for those families who don't have their own barn, horses here for training, and the therapy horses. The therapy horses take over most of the stable. I've turned on the sound system already. All the horses seem to quiet down nicely in the evenings with the music. I took Anna and Rose's suggestion and play classical piano music every night. I'm heading up the hill to my house when my phone chirps. I take my phone out of my shirt pocket and open the email.

February 4 @ 6:13 pm

Hi Michael,

I'm so happy that it's the weekend. I only have a half day shift tomorrow and then I'm off Sunday. Thank you for updating me on Chestnut. I'm really attached to him. Are you giving him carrots and sugar cubes?

How did the kids' camp go this week? I have no idea how you manage it. Do you still have nine horses boarding with you? Last time we spoke you were training five horses. How is that going? Did you ever buy the horse from Ft. Worth for the equine program?

I'm off to my night shift at the clinic. I'm only working until nine. If you're up when I get off, why don't you call me?

Rose

We have been emailing and texting a few times a week since she went back to Colorado after Christmas. We mostly discuss her classes or work. She always asks me how Chestnut is doing and if I'm still giving him treats. Chestnut is responding great after we figured out he had been trained with a firm hand. We work with him on a reward basis and let him tell us what he needs to move forward. With any horse, I evaluate them to see what training method will work best. Each animal is different, but I never use a firm hand with any of them. Working the horses using the equestrian therapy has given me insight about the differences between an ornery horse who likes to do things on purpose to get a rise out of you and a stubborn horse that doesn't want to follow the program. Chestnut likes working with the female employees at Corsco Equestrian Healing and will do about anything to get a sugar cube.

I respond to the email and tell Rose I'll call her around nine thirty her time, which is ten thirty my time. We've never called each other but hearing her cheerful voice again will be a treat. I fix myself a simple dinner of herb chicken and a salad before going into my office to finish up some paperwork for the next class.

I run programs for teenagers and adults who suffer from PTSD or trauma along with programs for kids with mild to moderate autism. I try and alternate programs, but it doesn't always work out that way. I just finished up a kids' class. The kids come with a parent or guardian that can stay or if the child has Asperger's, a mild autism where the child is high functioning, they can take the time for themselves. I have half day and full day programs, depending on severity of their autism. My paid staff have different degrees in therapy. Steph has a Masters in Child Psychology. He usually heads up the trouble youth programs. Jerry is a retired Navy Seal and has a Masters in Mental Health specializing in trauma. He runs the adult programs for our PTSD clients. Carrie is working towards her Masters in Child Psychology specializing in trauma. She heads the program with the younger kids suffering from PTSD, either from abuse, neglect, or trauma. I've known Carrie since grade school. She would show up in class with ripped jeans, before they became popular, holes in her shoes, and no lunch. I remember the day she was taken out of class and didn't come back for a week. She got placed in a foster home and came back with new clothes, new shoes, and a lunch box full of healthy food and milk every day. I don't mind that she doesn't have her Master's yet because she only has a few months to go. She does have her Bachelor's in Child Psychology. She lived it and that's always the best education. She understands the kids she works with because she went through it. She also helps me with the autistic programs. Then there is Zoe, she came in the door, applying for the position with the Autistic Therapy Program, and took over like she was perfectly handpicked. She told me not only does she have a degree in Mental Health for Special Education, she also has an adult son with severe autism. She takes the lead in all the autistic programs. I have a great crew and I know it.

I finish checking how many will be in the adult session next week. I'm happy it isn't too large, so it should run smoothly with a lot of specialized work from the staff. I look at the security screens and make sure all the horses are in their stalls for the night. It seems that everything is in order, so I head out of the office and back into the kitchen. I place my dish in the sink and grab a beer from the refrigerator. I think there is a basketball or hockey game on tonight, so I head into the living room and look for the remote. I always seem to misplace it and find it in the cushions of my couch or recliner. One time I found it under my recliner, so I check there too. It isn't in the usual spots, so I check in the kitchen and sure enough it is on the kitchen table. I must have set it there earlier. No one else lives in the house to move it on me, but that is one of those things I had to get used to after my accident. My memory has holes in it, some days I'm great, other days I forget which program is running or who's in charge of the group. All my staff is aware of my memory issues and work with me on my bad days. I find the basketball game while I start thinking about talking to Rose tonight.

My phone chirps with a text message, right at nine o'clock and I'm suddenly nervous and excited at the same time.

Rose: Hi Michael. Off work and heading home. You still up?
Michael: I'm still up. It's only 10 pm here. Give me a call
when you get settled at home.
Rose: Okay. Give me 20 mins.

I go to the kitchen, rinse out my beer bottle, throw it in the recycling bin, and grab a glass of water. I'm nervous and know my mouth will go dry while I talk to her. I know I talked with her during the holidays, but there were people around. I'm hoping my memory doesn't do its usual thing tonight. I find I have more issues with my memory loss at night. I head back to the couch and turn on a music channel, not a video site, but just the music. Having music on instead of a TV show or movie on will help keep my mind stay with the conversation. I definitely can't be watching a game, either.

Exactly twenty minutes later my phone rings. I almost spill the water while I'm setting it on the light pine coffee table and pick up the phone. I take a couple deep breaths then answer.

"Hey," I say, without checking the caller ID. I know it's most likely Rose on the other end.

"Hey yourself," Rose says. Her voice is exactly how I remember it. Sweet and quiet. Not quiet in volume, but quiet in the sense that she doesn't come across as aggressive or even confident in what she is saying.

"How was your shift at the clinic?" I decide to take the conversation in a safe direction.

"It was a little slow for a night shift. It usually gets the parents bringing in their kids because they couldn't get them into their primary physician during the day. Sometimes they don't want their workday interrupted or they couldn't get away," she says sounding annoyed. "Tonight, we had a few kids with colds and flu, some sports injuries, and a woman in labor that thought she didn't need to go to the hospital to have her baby." She is laughing after that last one. She sounds a little tired, even though she's laughing.

"How does a pregnant woman think she doesn't have to go to the hospital to have her baby?" I ask her. I remember our neighbor's daughter watching us when Mom went into labor. We didn't see Mom again for a couple days, then she'd bring a new brother or sister home with her.

"This is one reason I want to work with women. I can't tell you much, because of patient confidentiality, but she didn't see anyone. I can't believe there are people, in this day and age, who never seek medical attention. I know it costs money, but it's your health," she said with such passion, it reminds me of the conversation she had with my mom at Christmas. They had talked about price gouging for all medical services, especially hospitals.

"You and I are the lucky ones who can afford medical care. I see it a lot in the therapy side of my business. Sometimes the insurance will pay all or a part of the therapy, but most of my clients pay out of pocket or get grants. Insurance companies don't think working with horses is a form of therapy. They state it is an elective treatment and not a necessary cost." I feel her frustration. "My staff and I have had to come up with very inventive diagnostic descriptions to have the insurance companies pay for my client's programs," I tell her. I know my clients with PTSD really struggle with their insurance companies paying for treatment. I really work with them to get their cost down. Most of the adults in the program wouldn't be able to come if the insurance companies didn't pay a large portion of the cost.

"That is horrible. I understand the insurance companies are a business and they need to keep their costs down but having this woman in tonight not wanting to go to the hospital made me so frustrated. We got her to go without the cost of an ambulance. I hope she has an easy birth and a healthy baby, so she can be discharged quickly. I wonder what environment she is going back to with a newborn," she says. I hear ice clinking in a glass over the phone line. I imagine sweat dripping off a glass as she sets it down. I then see a drop of water on her bottom lip that I want to lick off. I start to picture her throat muscles moving up and down swallowing her cold drink. I shake my head and realize she is still talking, and I've missed what she has said. "Okay, that is enough of my insurance rant. What did you do today?"

"I finished up the week-long kids program today. They enjoy the horses so much; they hate when the week ends. I think the parents hate when the week ends too. The kids being safe and with us for the program gives the parents time to get some things done without their kids or, if they choose, be around their kids when they are really happy from being around the horses for the day," I say. I'm smiling as I talk to her about the kids. I love seeing my clients with smiles on their faces, which most do.

"Which class are you doing next?" she asks. I can still hear the ice, which makes me lose my concentration. I tell myself to focus.

"Monday's program is for the adults with PTSD. I gave Jerry the final count this afternoon. It's a smaller group so I shouldn't have to help this time," I tell her, taking a sip of my water and hear "I've Got You Under My Skin" by Frank Sinatra on the music channel I have on. I can still remember her hips swaying to another Sinatra song on Christmas.

"Are you going to work with Chestnut then?" I can hear the happiness in her voice. She really connected with him. I think if she moves to Oklahoma after graduation, I may have to give Chestnut to her. His original owners didn't want him with the training taking so long, so I bought him. He would still stay in my stables, but she could come out and ride him whenever she wanted. Chestnut should be trained for riders by the time Rose would be moving here. I'll have to think about it a little more, but not while I'm on the phone with her. I want to concentrate on her sweet voice.

"I work with him every day. Next week we will try a blanket on his back," I tell her. We slowly work him because of his previous trainer's methods. "He's happy when one of the girls brush him after his walks. He has even let one of them braid his mane." I hear a light, musical laugh over the phone. It sounds so beautiful; I wish I could hear it all the time.

"He's eating up the attention, isn't he?" she asks, still laughing. I can shut my eyes and see her face in my mind. I can see her smile lighting up her entire face with her hazel eyes sparkling a little greener.

"He is. We have him out in the training area with a couple of our older, calmer horses to see how he reacts. So far he's been doing well." I wasn't surprised when he did so well. We have him in between our oldest horses in the stables. I wanted him away from the younger horses I'm training.

"I asked, in the email, if you still have five horses your training and nine, you're boarding." She doesn't word it in a question, but I understand what she is saying.

"It has slowed down a little around here. I have three horses I'm training now. Two were ready to go back to their owners along with four of the boarding horses. Now that the warmer weather is here, we have families coming back from their winter travels," I tell her. I know it means income for the business, but both boarding and training take up a lot of time and supplies. Sometimes, think about not doing one or the other. If it were just me working with all three areas of the business, I would definitely cut back. Luckily, I have staff and the 4H club kids to keep us running smoothly.

"I still don't know how you manage. I realize, coming from me, that sounds funny. I think if I'm not doing something, all the time, I would go crazy. I like having a busy schedule," she says. I understand what she is saying. Stopping at the end of the day, I sit wondering if I should be doing something. I even worry I have forgotten something.

"You're doing everything to reach your final goal of graduating and getting a job in the field you want. When you told everyone what your days look like, I thought the same thing you thought of my schedule. We are both the same in that we are passionate about what we do," I say. I should not have said passionate. Now I'm thinking about how I would like to be passionate with her.

"You're right. I guess we both want the same thing, a meaningful, full life." We both are quiet for a few seconds. I'm not sure what to say. Then I remember the other question in her email this morning.

"You asked me about going to Ft. Worth. I haven't gone yet. It turns out the owner's granddaughter doesn't want the horse sold. I told them to contact me in the next month if anything changes. There was another horse I was looking at in Colorado around the same time. The horse in Ft. Worth was a little older and I thought she would be perfect for the kid's program." I look at several sites selling horses every few weeks. I like to have the horses to be about ten to fifteen years old. Some are retired racing horses or breeding horses who have passed their prime. Others may have owners that can't handle the expense anymore. I also go to auctions where the horses are part of an estate sale.

"I would love to go with you some time. I mean if I move down there," she says. I hear the hesitation in her voice.

"I'll tell you when I'm going on another trip. I'd love the company. Driving hours on end to look at a horse, I may not even buy, gets lonely." I like that she is thinking about being around me.

"It sounds like fun. I remember going on family vacations with my folks. I was young, but I remember the car rides with Brady, Anna, Lilla, and my folks. We would fight over the music choices, play the license plate game and my folks would tell us stories about their childhood." I hear her voice choke up.

"It sounds like you have great memories of your folks." I give her a few seconds and continue. "We never went on road trips because there were too many of us. We had to make a rule that the music could get changed every thirty minutes if there were three or more of us in the car. We did hear stories of Italy from both Mom and Dad, they made it sound so magical. I want to go there one day." I look at the clock on the wall and realize we have been talking for an hour. She said she's working tomorrow, but I don't want to stop talking with her.

"We heard stories of Italy too. Maybe one day we can take that trip together," she says. I hear her yawn on the other end of the phone. "I think for right now I need to get some sleep. Saturdays are always busy. I'm glad it is only a half day shift." I hear the clinking again and know I will have a hard time sleeping without dreaming about Rose.

"Okay. Get some sleep and have sweet dreams," I tell her knowing I will.

"Thank you. You too," she says then my phone goes silent.

We really talked tonight. I had no problems with my memory the entire conversation, which is good. I haven't talked to Rose about my memory issues yet. I need to find out if she is moving to Oklahoma before I say anything. I feel very vulnerable telling people, so I only tell people in my day to day life.

I reach for the remote and turn back to the sports channel. The game is over, but the commentary is still on. I listen to who won the game and decide to turn off the TV. I go into my office and check the security camera feed on the computer. Everything seems to be in order, so I head up to my bedroom.

I detour into the bathroom to heat up the water for a shower. I usually shower first thing after a day with the horses. I should have taken a shower instead of watching the game earlier, but my mind was so focused on Rose, I forgot about it. I step under the stream of warm water and take a deep breath. My muscles are relaxed from talking to Rose, but my imagination runs wild when I close my eyes. I reach for my cedar scented soap bar and soap up the washcloth. I drag the bubbles across my arms and chest. I pass over the erection I now have and scrub my calves, dragging the washcloth upward. After washing both thighs, I let the washcloth drop to the floor and take my erection in my hand. I place one hand on the tile wall in front of me for balance. My breathing is uneven as I picture Rose's pink lips with droplets of water suspended on them. I want to lick the droplets off her lower lip and lean in for a kiss. I'm picturing her leaning into my chest, returning my kiss. I can feel her tongue touch mine. I run my hand up and down the smooth hard shaft. I imagine her hands gliding down my chest before reaching for my hands. I move my hands to rest on her hips as she touches my aching, swollen erection. Her hands squeeze the base and glides to the tip. I feel the precum dripping around my hand as I continue my fantasy. She pulls her hip into me and continues gliding her hands up and down between us. My hips start to thrust harder into my hand. I feel my balls tighten and then cum sprays into the cooling water. I continue to rub myself until the orgasm has finished racking through me, leaving me spent. I shut my eyes one more time to see Rose's smile looking up at me as I whisper her name. I turn the hot water off and cool off for a minute in the cold water.

I climb into bed naked and I think about how cold showers will be my best friend in the nights to come. I fall asleep with her smile on my mind and her name on my lips.

* * *

The next few weeks follow a similar pattern. I get a text from Rose asking about my day and telling me what time she's getting off work. If she gets off work by nine-thirty, her time, she calls me as soon as she gets home. I talk with her at least three or four times a week.

I get excited when I hear my phone go off with a text and I'm instantly disappointed when it isn't her. This time it is Nick asking about when I'll be getting the new horse. I always have him check over any horse I purchase for Corsco Equestrian Healing.

After calling Nick and filling him in on going to Colorado instead of Ft. Worth for the horse, I get the text I'm expecting from Rose. She lets me know she will be off her usual time and will call me when she gets back to her place.

I smile when I hear the phone ring at exactly ten o'clock. We fall into our usual routine. We talk about her studies and if she is ready for the mid-term exams she has coming up. She talks about her shifts at the clinic. I find out how much she truly dis- likes the doctors who oversee her internship. She mentions how both head doctors look down at all females and consider them beneath them. She talks about how excited she is to graduate and find a better place to work. She asks about Chestnut every call. I have not told her about me buying him from the owners yet. I want it to be a surprise the next time she is down here. We discuss how his training is going. I tell her about each weekly program and how they went. It feels so natural talking to her about our daily lives.

"Oh, the horse from Ft. Worth will be staying with the granddaughter. The owner couldn't upset her by selling him. I do, however, have a trip planned to come to Colorado to look at the other horse I think might be a good match for all the programs," I tell her, and I get a small scream in my ear. I take that as a good sign to the answer to my next question. "Do you think I can see you while I'm in town?" I'm hoping to get some real time with her, person to person. I love talking with her on the phone, but I want to see her beautiful smile and her sexy body I'm remembering in my dreams.

"Sure. When are you going to be here?" she asks. I hear the excitement in her voice and I'm ecstatic.

"I'm driving up next Friday. Brady said I can stay at his house if it is okay with you. He knows you come down occasionally," I say. I'm eager to see her. The more time we spend together, the more likely I can see her coming to Oklahoma after she graduates. Of course, I plan on seeing Lily and Brady while I'm in town, but my first thought is of Rose. I know Mom would be terribly upset if I didn't fill her in on what is going on with her youngest child.

"That's okay by me. I will make sure I get Sunday off and come down as soon as I get off Saturday. When are you looking at the horse?" she asks.

"I was hoping you'd say that. I can look at the horse Saturday while you're working. If I decide to buy her, I can pick her up Monday morning." I don't need to be home to run a program, so I can be out of town the whole weekend. I checked with Jerry before committing to a date with the owner of the horse. Jerry usually doesn't need help with his groups, but I always ask.

"I have a paper due that Friday. If I can get someone to cover my shift Saturday, I'll come down Friday after class," she says. I hear ice clinking, Rose cuss, and then she apologizes.

"What did you spill?" I ask imagining her top wet from spilling the drink on herself. I can only imagine her bra showing with the wet material, or her bare breast.

"Just water, but it's really cold when it spills directly on my skin," she tells me, sounding distracted. "The ice cubes fell out." Now my imagination goes wild. I clear my voice and get back on topic.

"That would be great. I should get in late afternoon if I leave early on Friday. Why don't we invite Brady and Lily over for dinner? I can grill up some steaks," I say while thinking about spending two full days with her.

"I'll call Brady and ask what their schedules look like. I know Lily usually gets off after the lunch crowd is done, unless she has a catering job that weekend." I can hear the excitement in her voice. "Brady left the hot tub at his house. Don't forget a swimsuit and then we can relax in it one night," the quiet, shy Rose says.

"I'll pack a swimsuit then," I tell her. I'm now picturing her in a two-piece swimsuit with all her olive toned skin showing. My jeans start to tighten thinking about it. The suit I bring better have a lot of room in the front because I know I will be hard looking at her. I don't want to embarrass either one of us when that happens.

CHAPTER 4

The sun is overhead as I cross the Colorado border. When I get into the Denver area, I know the sun will be in my eyes as it works its way down behind a mountain sunset. This is when I slow down because of the trailer I'm towing. The sky is a beautiful light blue without a cloud in sight. The sunset should be beautiful. Lily has told the family about the multi-colored sunsets over the mountains. I'm looking forward to sitting on the deck and watching it with Rose while I'm in town.

All week our conversations were a little more positive. Rose didn't complain about the doctors at the clinic. She didn't mention them at all in fact. She got someone to cover her Saturday shift, so she's coming to Denver after Friday's class. I ask about her paper and she is confident she'll be getting an A. I don't doubt it. I'm realizing how smart she is during our conversations. The medical terminology she needs to know amazes me. I know, even without my memory issues, I couldn't remember what she so easily talks about during our evening chats. I don't see her having any problems with her Master's Thesis.

I follow the directions Lily gave me when I called her. I left early enough to miss most of the rush hour traffic. Lily told me the highways get really bogged down after three o'clock. I pull into the local shopping center to pick up steaks and salad makings. Rose told me Lily will be making dessert. She didn't tell me what dessert, but anything Lily makes is delicious. The whole family is happy she was able to find a job she genuinely loves. Every week, when she lived at home, she'd be baking something for some cause. Turning her love of baking into a career fits her perfectly. I have to say I miss my sister, but I really miss her baking. I'm expecting to see Brady a few pounds heavier.

I find the produce department and pick up fresh romaine and baby spinach to mix along with baby carrots, cherry tomatoes, croutons, and roasted pecans. I like a variety of flavors in my salads. I'm not as bad as my mom. She slices beets, cucumbers, onions, and celery into her salads. On occasion she will put in black beans, roasted corn, and garbanzo beans. Her salads can be a meal in themselves. You never know what to expect when my mom puts together a meal. With five growing boys and one girl, Mom had to be creative to get us all to eat a nutritional meal.

I head back to the meat department and smell the sweet scent of flowers on the way. I see several bouquets of roses, carnations, and mixed flowers. Lily might tease me about it, but I pick out a collection of flowers to give to Rose. I have never asked what flowers she likes. I wonder if she likes roses, like her name. Our talks have never crossed over to our likes and dislikes. During this visit I will make time to have those discussions. Happy with the flowers I picked, I head over to the meat counter and get three large ribeye steaks. After filling my small basket, I make my way to the cashier. I hear the music, for the first time, playing overhead as I'm standing in line. "No One Like You" by Scorpions is quietly playing over the store speakers. The title alone fits how I think of Rose. The lyrics make me smile as I reach the cashier.

"Hi, did you find everything okay?" the young girl asks me. When she smiles, I smile back. I can't imagine how many times a day she asks that. She looks to be in her late teens, probably a high school student.

"Yes, I did. Thank you," I say as she starts scanning the few items from the basket. She places the basket in the stack accumulating behind her stand.

"It looks like you're going to have a good evening," she says and gives me my total. I hand her cash, which seems to surprise her. I know most people use debit cards now, but I like to carry cash.

"I sure hope so. I'm having dinner with family and a special someone," I tell her. I don't know why I said it, but I do think of Rose as a special someone in my life.

"Well I hope you enjoy your evening and I think that special someone will like the flowers," she says as she hands me my change. I take my bag and flowers back out to my truck. Rose's place is around the corner and I start getting nervous.

I pull up to the two houses, one Lily's and one Brady's, and try to figure out where to park. I see Brady's truck in one driveway, and I realize I don't know which house is Lily's. I pull up in front of both houses and park my truck and trailer in the street. As I exit my truck, my overnight bag in my hand, I hear Rose before I see her. She's yelling my name as she comes running from the house without a porch swing out front. Rose is taking advantage of the mild spring temperatures with her blue jeans and navy-blue t-shirt. Both hug her curves in all the right ways. The curved neckline gives me a hint of cleavage to look at. She's wearing her typical blue running shoes. I noticed when she was down for Christmas, she wore them most of the time.

"You're finally here," she yells as she meets me at the front of my truck. I drop my bag onto the street as she throws herself into my arms. I remember, at that moment, Rose is a hugger. I put my arms around her and lean my head down to smell the flowery scent of her hair. The hug lasts a little longer than I expect. I think I catch her smelling me too.

"It took a little longer because I'm towing the trailer," I tell her as she stands back and looks into my eyes. She looks wonderful with her pink glossy lips and green eye shadow, which brings out the green in her hazel eyes. She told me once how she hated putting on makeup. Her sisters taught her how, but she felt her skin couldn't breathe. I lean down and pick up my bag, realizing I left the food in the truck. "Can you grab the grocery bag out of the truck?" I remember the flowers on the seat of the cab next to the bag too late. She's opening the door before I can grab them.

"No problem. I didn't mean for you to buy dinner but thank you. Brady always picks out the steak. I'm useless when it comes to picking out anything besides chicken and hamburger," she is telling me as she stops and pulls out the flowers. Her eyes sparkle and her pink glossed lips open into an O position.

"Those are for you," I tell her. Her cheeks flush a soft pink. Her eyes lock with mine and I can see the thoughts rolling around in her mind. We have touched on our mutual attraction with a comment here and there, but receiving flowers seem to confirm my definite attraction in her mind. "I didn't know if you like roses, since that is your name, so I got you something that reminds me of you," I tell her. I see a soft resilience like the white Carnation, the color of her flushed cheeks in the Sierra Sunset, and delicate curves in the purple Iris. I looked at the Tulips but decided on a variety of flowers. I know I will be giving her more in the future and will give her different flowers then.

"They are beautiful, Michael. Thank you," she says. I can feel a spark between us as she comes up to me, stands on her toes and gives me a peck on the cheek. We walk up to the house on the right. I look over at what is obviously is my sister's house now. I can see her sitting on the porch swing in the mornings with her cup of tea. She has never been a coffee drinker, even though all of us brothers tried to get her to taste it. She held firm in her flavor choice. She told us coffee always tasted burnt. I see the small garden, I'm sure she planted as soon as she moved in. Lily has always liked fresh herbs and spices in her baking and cooking. I look back up the sidewalk as Rose is entering the house.

"You can put your bag in the room at the end of the hallway. I'll go put these in a vase," she says as she walks to the left and points me to the right. I pass a bedroom on the right that has flowery throw pillows on the bed and a small desk with an open laptop. The desk chair isn't a chair at all, it looks like an exercise ball with a metal ring securing it to the floor. I've heard about them, but I've never seen one. There is a bathroom on the left with blue towels and a scent of Rose's hair. I walk into what must be the master bedroom and set my bag down on the bed. It has a bathroom adjacent I use then head to the kitchen. I didn't expect Rose to give me the big bedroom.

"Rose, you didn't need to put me in the master bedroom. I assume that is your room," I say as I enter the room. I stop short at the doorway. She is swaying her hips to Frank Sinatra's "All the Way." Her hair is in a ponytail at her neck and is swaying back and forth over her shirt. It gives me a flash back to Christmas when I caught her swaying to Frank Sinatra as she washed dishes. I want to come up behind her and sway with her, pressing her hips to mine like I wanted to do in December. She is carefully arranging the flowers and doesn't realize I'm staring at her. The vase is the exact color of the Irises. She must have put the groceries in the refrigerator already because I don't see the bag anywhere.

"I'm not here as often as I would like because of the internship at the clinic. When I first moved in, Brady was in the process of moving his king size bed over to Lily's. I had a few things from Anna's I needed to move right away, so I put my things in the guest room. I'm not here enough to move things around so I stay there." She puts the vase in the center of the large kitchen table.

"Did Brady leave everything else here when he moved in with my sister?" I ask. I glanced around when I walked through the living room on my way to the bedroom. I saw a lot of wood and furniture in blue and tan colors, not quite what I expected from Rose.

"Brady moved the bed because your sister's queen size didn't quite fit his over six-foot body. They also took the grill, so we'll be having dinner over there," she says as she walks to the back door and I follow like a love-sick puppy. The grass is green already, and the deck covers a good portion of the yard. I see the two rocking chairs facing west. This must have been where Lily was sitting each time she told us about the sunsets. "I asked him to leave the rocking chairs. The sunsets are great from here. Lily has a tree that blocks the westward view, so they still come over here to watch the sunsets. He didn't mind leaving them as long as I know they might be here when I come down," she tells me as she sits in one of the rockers and I lower myself into the other. I can picture sitting out here with a beer watching the sunset turn the sky from light to dark colors over the mountains. There is a small table between the rockers, and I can see myself holding Rose's hand and resting it on top of it.

"It's beautiful out here, I see what Lily was talking about. One time she called home; all she did was talk about the colors of the sky during sunsets. She went into detail of which color follows which. I guess I can watch a couple with you while I'm here." I set my hand on the arm of the rocker and my fingers twitch to reach out and grab hers. "So, when are we heading over to Lily's?" I ask as I put my hands in my lap. I had to control my thoughts. I don't want to scare Rose by grabbing her hand.

"Brady should be home in thirty minutes. Lily is home if you want to go over now. You haven't seen her since Thanksgiving, have you?" she asks, still looking towards the west.

"I remember the screaming over the phone when Brady proposed at Christmas, and I've talked to her a few times, but no I haven't seen her since Thanksgiving." I think back to Christmas. Rose and I had just walked into the room when Mom got the call from Lily. We had been in the kitchen doing dishes and to tell you the truth, I was still thinking about Rose when all the commotion was going on around me.

"Do you miss her a lot?" She starts gently rocking as she looks towards me. I see a sadness come over her eyes. I don't know what has caused it, but I know I never want to see it again. Rose is such a positive person and always brings a good energy into any room she enters. I never image her being sad.

"I miss her, but you have to remember she lived in Colorado Springs for a while when she was married to Adrian. Our family got used to her not being there all the time. Why do you ask?" I see the rocker is moving faster. She seems unhappy and agitated.

"I have an interview scheduled in Oklahoma City and one in Tulsa in June. I got to thinking about moving away from the only home I've known and away from Brady and Lilla. Don't get me wrong, I rarely see Lilla, so it wouldn't be a big deal there, but I would miss Brady terribly," she says. I see her fingers are twisting the bottom of her shirt.

"You have to remember, though, you would see Anna a lot. You basically would be switching seeing one sibling for another," I tell her.

"I'd like seeing Anna, but Brady has been more than a big brother to me. He was there as a father figure after our parents died. Raising three sisters couldn't have been easy on him while finishing school and the police academy. He had to deal with a lot more from me than either one of my sisters." I reach over and place my hand over hers. She stops twisting her shirt and places my hand in between hers. "I don't know if I can move that far away from him. I want to graduate and start my life; I just don't know where that life is going to be."

We sit in silence, her fingers curled around my hand. I don't know how to help her conquer her fears and concerns. I want her to move to Oklahoma, so I can make her a part of my life, but I don't want her to be sad away from Brady. Maybe after this weekend she will be able to see her life starting with me.

"Hey you two! Where are those steaks? I'm starving." We hear Brady come through the gate between the houses. Rose slowly releases my hand, pushes imaginary hairs out of her face and gets up to hug Brady as he steps onto the deck. I wait for Rose to finish her long hug then shake Brady's hand. His eyebrows are scrunched down in a silent question to me. I shake my head at him and mouth the word LATER to him.

"Nice to see you again, Brady. Taking good care of my sister?" I ask him. I know he is. Each time I talk to her she sounds incredibly happy.

"As much as she'll let me! You know how your sister is. She's trying to fatten up the squad with her creations." We head back into the house and grab the steaks and salad makings. Brady sees the flowers on the table and sends me a questioning look. I smile at him and move to the front of the house. "She's made some of your favorites, I believe," he says as Rose locks the door. It's a nice neighborhood, but you can't trust leaving the door unlocked even though we are next door.

"She made lemon bars?" I ask, excitedly. We walk around the picket fence that separates the properties. Lily knows I love lemon anything. I used to have lemon meringue pie for my birthday instead of cake until Lily found a recipe for lemon cake. She put a lemon preserve in between two layers of lemon cake. I was in heaven that birthday.

"Better," Brady says. I try and think of what's better than her lemon bars and can't think of anything. We enter through the front door and I'm instantly hit with the sweet smell of lemon as Brady leads the way to the back of the house. I look at the family photos Lily has on the hallway wall. She came to my place one day and took a lot of pictures of me training a couple of horses and me riding my favorite horse. I use a few of the photos on my web site and brochures. The picture of me on her wall was taken two days prior to my accident. I follow Brady and Rose and let the memory fade into the back of my mind.

"Hey sis, Brady said you made something better than your lemon bars. I can't believe that!" I say and give her a hug. She pulls back and smiles at me. I see the impish look in her eyes. This must be good if the look on her face is the judge. I see how comfortable Lily is, not just in wearing jeans and a t-shirt, but in her mannerism and stature. Brady has been good for her. We all wanted her to come home after her husband died while on a deployment, but she held firm and started a new life for herself.

"Hi Michael. I find lots of new recipes now that I'm baking for a company. You'll have to wait until after dinner though." Now she's taunting me. If it's lemon, I'll stay quiet and wait. She hugs Rose hello and then we walk out to the deck, so Brady can start the steaks.

"Michael these steaks look great. I shouldn't have expected anything less from a family who raises cattle," he says. I walk over to the grill to talk with Brady while Lily and Rose sit in the rocking chairs that look exactly like the ones next door. The steaks hiss on the hot grill as Brady, quietly, asks what was going on when he came over.

"Rose was talking about interviewing for two jobs in Oklahoma. She's not sure if she can leave here. This is the only home she knows, and she'd miss you a lot. I know she is a sensitive person, but there seemed to be more going on in her head. She said she put you through more than your other sisters and didn't know if she could leave you." I saw his shoulder straighten and heard a small gasp. I knew they were close because of their parents dying, but I knew in my gut there was more.

"I'm glad to hear she's interviewing outside of Colorado," Brady says. "She's always so happy and cheerful. I never know if it's a show for everyone around her or if she really is that great all the time. I make myself believe the later." Brady flips the steak and asks Lily and Rose to make the salad. The steaks will be ready in fifteen minutes. After the they are in the house, he looks me in the eyes, and I know he is struggling with something.

"What is it? I reminded her that Anna is there, but that didn't seem to be enough," I tell him. I hear the steaks sizzle as the fat drips onto the flame and the women are giggling about something in the kitchen as I wait for the answer.

"I know you care a lot for my sister. I saw the flowers on the table you brought her. I don't want to sound like the over-protective brother, but with Rose I feel like I have to shield her from the bad in the world more than my other sisters," he tells me. "It's not my story to tell. Rose will have to tell you in her own time and her own way. I will tell you this though, she is better now." He puts the steaks on the platter and turns to head back into the house after turning the grill off. He stops and faces me. "I'm trusting you. Treat her right if she moves to Oklahoma," he says and then disappears into the kitchen. I only have more questions now.

We all sit around the table in the kitchen. My sister doesn't have a formal dining room, but the kitchen table fits us perfectly. Brady and I sit across from each other, which puts Lily and Rose next to me. I feel the energy coming off of Rose. I move my legs to get comfortable on the chair and rub Rose's leg by accident. Now that I know she is that close to me; I will accidently rub her leg some more during dinner. I shake my head to get back to the conversation that is happening around me. I look down at the table to clear my mind and recognize the plates and bowls. Mom bought them for Lily's first home. She feels every household should have a matching set of dishes. She told all her sons that there is no excuse for bachelors to piece together a kitchen. She considers it a failing on her part in raising us. I have a set of blue stoneware dishes and bowls. I also have cobalt glasses. Solid blues and browns make up most of the colors in my house.

Brady is asking Rose how her classes are going when I join the conversation. I know exactly what she is going to tell him because of our evening phone calls. I hear the same excitement in her voice and this time I get to see her eyes light up. She bounces in her chair when she tells him about the paper she turned in this morning. I can see the passion in her eyes and the dedication in her voice when she talks about the cases she sees in the clinic. She will make a great nurse for any office. I'm hoping she takes one of the jobs in Oklahoma.

"Michael, do you remember the case I told you about a few weeks back?" she asks me. I look at her with confusion because we have talked about so many of her cases. "The one where the pregnant woman came to the clinic to have her baby," she says.

"I remember that. You said she hadn't gone to any doctors the entire pregnancy because she didn't have the money and she didn't think she needed to." I shake my head with the thought of that poor, young woman. That was the night I knew how passionate she really was about advocating for women's health.

"I couldn't believe it. She tried talking the doctors into letting her have the baby in the clinic. Both doctors had to explain the complications that can happen while delivering a baby that the office isn't equipped for. She thought she had to push, the baby would come out, and then she could go home after with her baby. I don't understand how any woman can be that naïve about their bodies." She takes a bite of steak and I hear her soft moan. "Another great steak, Brady."

"Thank Michael, he picked them out. I don't think you can go wrong with a ribeye though." Brady asks her when her finals are before confirming her graduation date. "Michael, I hear you and your parents will be joining Nick and Anna for Roses graduation ceremony."

"Yes. We will all be flying up. Mom and Dad can't really handle sitting that long in their truck. Don't tell them I said that though. We thought about the time we can save flying, too," I say. Lily laughs at my statement about Mom and Dad. They run their ranch even in their late fifties. Yes, they have people who work for them, which helps but they are still out there every day right alongside the younger employees. They have less land and cattle to worry about since giving a third of the ranch to Joseph and a third to Patrick when they were ready to take on the responsibility. We all chip in if Mom and Dad need help, too.

"I thought Mom and Dad could stay in our extra bedroom and Nick and Anna could stay next door that way you can spend some more time with Anna," Lily says looking at Rose. "The couch in the living room can fold out to a bed for you Michael," Lily says. "Rose will you be out of your place before graduation?" Lily asks.

"My lease is up the week of graduation. Finals are the week prior, so I'll be home for a couple days, then graduation," Rose answers Lily. I'm listening to hear when graduation is. I'm thinking about coming up a couple days sooner than the rest of the family.

"Do you need to borrow my truck to move your stuff back down here?" Brady asks. I never thought about that. I know she has her own place and doesn't live in the dorms. I'm thinking of driving up to help when the thought melts away by her next comment.

"No. The apartment was furnished when I moved in. Everything I need to move will fit in my car, but thanks for the offer." She takes her last bite of steak and moans again. I would love to hear that moan in a different setting. My knee rubs against hers and my jeans start to tighten. I force my mind to other things. Brady doesn't need to know that I'm fantasizing about his sister at his dinner table.

"Okay. Let us know when you're back then. We can go out to celebrate," Lily says. "I know exactly where we should go." I look at Lily and she has that look again, like she knows a secret. Brady smiles at her across the table.

"My last final is in the morning of Friday May 4 and graduation is Sunday May 13, so I should be home Saturday or Sunday after finals. I'm not sure when my internship ends. I might have to work that weekend," Rose says then takes her last bite of salad. She ate all the items I picked for the salad. It's nice to see a woman actually eat and not pick at her food. Rose is a little heavier in the hips and thighs, which I find extremely attractive.

"I think Mom and Dad talked about coming in Friday or Saturday. Neither wants to be away from the ranch that long. They trust the foreman to keep the ranch going, but they feel better if they are there," I tell them. "They will probably leave the Monday after."

"I'll call Mom and let her know the exact dates. Rose will you be able to pick up Nick and Anna? I think they said they will be coming in Thursday night. I'm fairly sure Cal will be covering for Nick and Anna is notifying her clients she will be out of town for the weekend." Lily seems to be informed of everyone's schedule already.

"I'll be home, so no problem. When are you coming in Michael?" Rose asks. I'm running the dates through my head and come up with a date quickly. I want a few days with her, no family around except Brady and Lily. I'm excited she will be home for a week prior graduation to give me a variety of dates to work with.

"I was thinking about coming in Tuesday, so I can help with any celebration arrangements. I'm sure Lily has already started to plan a party of some sort. Tell me I'm wrong," I say looking straight at my sister.

"You aren't wrong. I was planning on talking to Rose about what she wanted tonight if you must know," Lily says swatting my arm lightly. "So, Rose what do you want to do to celebrate?" she asks.

"I don't want anything big just a simple BBQ in the backyard. It's only going to be family since the only friends I have work at the clinic and are heading to their own celebrations with their families," she says. I see a hint of sadness cross over her eyes. She never talks about any friends, but I thought it was because of the advanced classes and shifts at the clinic. I need to remember she is twenty-three and should be having girls' night out and other times with friends away from school and the clinic. I'm sure Anna and Gabriella will be more than willing to take her out for girls' night if she moves to Oklahoma.

"I was actually thinking the same thing. Tuck, our chef at work, offered to make up some beef and pork BBQ. We can come up with the rest of the menu. I know Mom will want to make potato salad and coleslaw if you want those. Anna offered to put together a vegetable and fruit tray. She still isn't much of a cook, so she knows she can't mess those up. I can bake a few things and the guys don't need to do anything except put the tent up in the backyard and get the chairs out there," she says looking at Brady and me.

"Hey, I can cook and bake in a pinch. I can make some baked beans and I have a great recipe for deviled eggs," I tell my sister.

"You make deviled eggs?" Lily asks, and the entire table is looking at me.

"I asked Mom to teach me how to make my favorite dishes, okay! I know how to make a lot of her Italian dishes too. I have to eat you know!" I say, defensively. Lily has been away from home a long time now and when she is home only the women are allowed in the kitchen to cook. It's Mom's rule. She has taught all her boys a few basics, so they can manage on their own, if needed.

"Okay. Mellow out. I'm just surprised. I think it's great you cook. Rose learns a few recipes each time she comes down from school," she says as she smiles at Rose.

"Without a mom to teach me, I had to ask someone. Your mom offered to teach me a few recipes whenever I'm down there.

I would love it if you made deviled eggs. I really like them, and no BBQ would be complete without them." She's looks at me and I can't figure out what is going through her mind.

"How about the beans? I have several different recipes, it depends on if you like spicy, sweet, or tangy." I'm thinking I would like Rose any way.

"I like sweet with brown sugar. I usually pick up the country brown sugar at the store. I'm not one for spicy. Can you make sure the BBQ isn't spicy?" she asks Lily, who nods her head. "Tangy is good too. It reminds me of fruit medleys." Rose gets up and grabs my plate to take to the sink. I get up to help but Lily tells me to sit. Lily takes her plate to the sink along with Brady's. They come back for the steak platter and the salad bowl as I hear the water running in the sink.

"I hear you have a few interviews set up after graduation. Where are you thinking about going?" Brady asks, looking at me. He's trying to get this issue dealt with tonight.

"I have interviews in Oklahoma City, Tulsa, and Denver. All three are women centers of some type. I have the one in Denver the week after graduation and both in Oklahoma the first week of June," she answers Brady's question. We can both hear the change in her voice as she talks about Oklahoma.

"I think that's great Rose. You can hang out with Anna if you get one of the jobs down there," Lily says. She didn't hear the conversation Brady and I had outside, so we don't think she picked up on Rose's voice change.

"Yeah, I know. I'm not sure I'll get either of those jobs," Rose says. You can hear the doubt in her voice. She is graduating with honors and has completed more hours than needed for her internship. I'm sure she will get job offers anywhere she interviews.

"Are you worried about moving away," Brady asks straight out.

"I've never lived anywhere else," she says when her and Lily sit back down at the table. Lily reaches out and takes her hand. Of all of us here, she is the perfect person to help.

"Rose, I know how scary it is. I got married right out of high school and had to move away from everyone I knew to be with my husband. He was in the service and I went where he went, except when he went on his oversea deployments. I had to stay behind, alone, when that happened. I made friends with other military wives, but it's not the same as family. I know I could have gone home when Adrian was overseas, but I needed to prove to myself I could have a life away from my family," she says. I'm watching Brady to see how he reacts to Lily talking about her previous husband. Brady took Lily's other hand and looked at Rose.

"Rose, that's how I met Lily. All of her family wanted her to come home after Adrian died. She still wanted to prove to them and herself that she could be independent and take care of herself. That's when she bought the house next to mine and as they say, its history after that," Brady says with a lot of love in his eyes for the two important women sitting next to him.

"You know my history Brady. I never worried being up in Greeley because I knew you were two hours away. What if I have problems in Oklahoma?" she asks him. I don't know what is really being asked because I have no idea what happened to Rose.

"Anna is right there, no more than thirty minutes away from either job. You can always call me, too. You can ask Anna to find someone for you to talk to down there," he tells her. I look at Lily and she seems to know what they are talking about. "Rose, you have only flourished while in Greeley. I am so proud of the woman you have become despite what happened." He covers Lily and Rose's hand with one of his own. "You can do this sweetie. I'm sure of it. But if you go down there and decide, after the three interviews, you want to take the job in Denver I will support your decision." Rose gets up and gives Brady a quick hug then she flees the room. I hear a door close near the front of the house.

"Can either of you tell me what just happened?" I ask, looking at both of them.

"Like I said outside, it is her story to tell. I'll make sure she talks to Anna before coming down for those interviews. Lily can you talk to your parents to see if she can stay with them while she's in town?" he asks.

"Wouldn't she want to stay with Anna?" I ask Brady.

"She probably would, but I think being around your mom and dad would do her some good. Your mom can teach her a few dishes to cook and besides, she'd love some girl time. Anna will be busy working too." He has a point there. I wish she could stay with me, but that wouldn't be appropriate and after what happened I think she needs to be with a female. I'm starting to think I know what happened, but I won't assume anything. I'll let her tell me in her own time.

"I'm sorry everyone," Rose says when she comes back in the room. I can see by her puffy red eyes that she's been crying. "I didn't mean to make such a big scene out of this." She sits back down.

"How about we go look at the sunset then have dessert," Lily suggests. I think it is a great suggestion. I think Rose needs a little more time to pull herself together after whatever just happened.

"That sounds like a great idea. Michael you are in for a treat. Sunsets around here are amazing and so is the dessert waiting for you," Brady says while he stands up and pats Rose on the shoulder.

"I'm sure," is all I say as I walk out of Lily's house. We walk around the fence and go through Brady's house to the deck Rose and I were sitting at a short while ago. I hear the radio that Rose never turned off. I can't hear the lyrics, but I hear the music. Another Frank Sinatra song is playing. I hesitate at the doorway to hear which one of his hits is playing now. I catch the chorus of "Come Fly with Me" before closing the screen door behind me. I'm thinking Frank Sinatra might be my go-to music whenever Rose comes out to my place.

* * *

Lily was right. The colors of the sky blending seamlessly into the next are fantastic. It is a clear night with a hint of billowy clouds above the mountains and the sun rays shooting through looking like golden rays. A few airplane trails hold the colors of the sky. The red and orange hugging the mountain as the purple and dark blue sweeps over the sky above us is breathtaking. The mountain ridge holds onto the golden yellow as if it weren't ready to have the day end.

We sat there in quiet until I look up and see the stars now filling a black sky like diamonds on a felt cloth. Lily didn't do it justice when she explained all the colors. I barely listened to that conversation, but no one can explain what I saw with words.

"Wow," is all I say. I catch myself whispering the old children's wishful saying. "Star light, star bright, first star I see tonight. I wish I may, I wish I might, have this wish I wish tonight." Rose reaches over and squeezes my hand as she's looking up at the starry sky. I don't feel stupid for being caught. I'm hoping she makes a wish along with me. I have only one wish at this instant and I will make a wish every night if it gets her to move to Oklahoma.

"I haven't heard anyone make a wish on a star in a long time. I should have thought of that since Brady and I catch almost every sunset," Lily says looking up at the stars now, probably making a wish now.

"What do you have to wish for?" Brady asks her. "You have the job you love, the house you bought on your own, and let's not forget the love of a very special man," he teases her. Lily doesn't answer him, instead gets up off her chair and sits on Brady's lap. She places her head on Brady's shoulder and wraps her arms around his shoulders. I feel like I'm intruding on an intimate moment.

"Okay, where is my dessert? I think I have been exceptionally good about not demanding what it is," I say. Lily starts giggling. She knows how to torment me with desserts.

"I wouldn't want you to suffer any more than necessary. Let's head back to my house," Lily says after standing up and giving Brady a kiss. I wish I could be kissing Rose right now. She has gotten her emotions under control and continues holding my hand as we walk out the gate and around the fence. Rose steps in front of me to enter the house first. My hand feels naked without the heat of her hand curled around mine. It does give me the chance to look at her denim clad curves, though.

Lily heads to the refrigerator to get the surprise dessert my mouth has been watering over for hours now. I see Brady getting down cups and glasses as Rose reaches around him to get the dessert dishes. I'm standing in the middle of the action not sure what to do.

"Michael, do you drink coffee?" Brady asks me as he puts water in the coffee maker that is sitting on the counter right in front of him. I know he is the coffee drinker in the house, so he must have gotten a cup for Lily to have tea.

"I do, but I'm afraid I would be up all night if I had any this late." I see the glasses he set on the counter. "I would rather have milk, if you have any." I see the look he shares with Lily and then their laughter fills the small kitchen.

"What is so funny?" I ask. I look at Rose to see if she knows what is going on. She's not laughing but she does have a big smile on her face. Rose places the plates and forks in front of each seat. "What?" I shout. Lily places a glass of milk in front of me. I smell the lemon mixing its scent with the coffee. Rose returns to the table with two cups of hot tea. She places one in front of Lily's dish then sits down in the chair she occupied during dinner.

"You haven't heard the story of how Brady and I got together, have you?" Lily says as she brings over two serving trays. The lemon smell surrounds me.

"I assumed it was because you are neighbors. Mom said something about he helped you get your job." I watch her lift the lids off the servers and look at heaven that is lemon for me. The cookies are golden yellow swirls. They remind me of the sugar cookies Mom would buy in the big blue tin for a special treat. I look over at the second dish and see meringue on top of what looks like a regular cupcake. I look at Lily a little confused. How is a cupcake special?

"Don't make that face at me, Michael," Lily says.

"The local nursing home loves these cupcakes better than her lemon bars," Brady says as he picks up a cupcake and reaches back to the center of the table for a couple of cookies.

"I'm sure it's great. Everything Lily makes tastes wonderful," I say. I couldn't help making a confused look, but I don't want my sister to doubt herself. She took the extra time to make something she knows I'd love, and I want her to know how much I appreciate it. She looks at Brady as he eats the cupcake first. He's smiling and moaning with every bite getting meringue all over his lips and nose. Lily is shaking her head chuckling at him.

Rose and I reach for the cookies at the same time. I get a shock up my arm as our hands touch. She pulls her hand away, quickly, then places a couple of cookies on her dish. I place a cookie on my dish and then reach back to get a cupcake. Again, we touch hands. This time she leaves her fingers next to mine. I turn my head and see the pink coloring her cheeks.

"You can have that one," I say to Rose. My hand moves to the one next to it without looking. I can't take my eyes off her. She puts the cupcake on her dish and dips her finger in the meringue. I would volunteer to lick it off, but after the events of earlier I feel like that would be a bad idea. She reaches for her napkin and she realizes it isn't where she put it while setting the table. Silky tendrils fall over her shoulder as she leans down. A few strands of hair have pulled out from the band holding it in place. I see a hint of cleavage as she reaches for her napkin that has floated off the table. I make myself look away before Lily or Brady says something to me. It is his sister I'm gawking at after all.

Lily clears her voice to get my attention. I look at her and Brady, both smiling at me. I've been caught, and nobody seems to mind where my thoughts have gone.

"Are you going to try the lemon cupcake?" Lily asks me. I get my thoughts back to trying the lemon delights Lily has baked for me. I taste the cookie first, knowing I will like them if they are similar to the sugar cookies of our youth. The lemon flavor doesn't overwhelm my taste buds. It crumbles in my mouth and glides down the back of my throat with the sip of milk I take. A hint of lemon stays on my palette. I can imagine eating one of these between courses to cleanse the palette.

"These are great, Lily. They look like the sugar cookies we used to eat." I reach for another and take my time eating it. I don't take a sip of milk until I have wolfed down several more.

"I took creative license with a sugar cookie recipe. For the holidays I put peppermint and spearmint flavoring in the recipe for work and everyone loved them. They sold out every day at the café. I've been experimenting with different flavors to keep the sugar cookie interesting." Lily was holding the cookie up while she talks about other flavor additives. "I saw the blue tin one day at Costco and thought I could always change the shape easily, so here are the lemon cookies I created," she says. Brady lifts her hand to his lips and kisses her wrist and then takes a bite out of the cookie she's holding. Rose and I laugh along with Lily. Lily now has meringue on her wrist from Brady's mouth.

"Lily, the cupcakes are great," Rose says. I look at her and see the meringue on her nose. "What's in the middle?" she asks. I continue to watch the meringue touch her nose with each bite she takes from the side of the cupcake.

"I want Michael to try it first. I'll say what's in it after." Lily looks at me and then the cupcake on my plate. I know I need to take the plunge and try it. I take the wrapper off and lift it to my mouth. I see why Rose got meringue on her nose. It sits on top of the cupcake a third of the height in total. Rose is laughing at me and pointing at my nose.

"You need to wipe your nose, Michael. You have meringue all over the tip," Rose says while giggling.

"You do too." I point to Rose's nose. She lifts the napkin up to her face then cleans off her nose.

"I might as well wait until I'm done with the cupcake. I'll only get more on me after each bite." She looks over at me taking my second bite. Sure enough, I get more meringue on my nose. "See what I mean?" She is laughing along with the rest of us at the table.

"So, Michael. What do you think of the plain old cupcake now?" Lily asks.

"I was so wrong. I apologize," I say as I finish the cupcake and finally clean the meringue off my nose. I watch Rose wipe her nose clean and again I think about how I would take the meringue off. "These are amazing, but messy," I say. "Well worth the mess I think."

"I put a lemon curd mixture in the center. Remember the chocolate lava cakes I made for the church fund raiser?" she asks me.

"The ones you cut into and chocolate goop flowed out of?" I remember having to eat it with a fork and I still had chocolate all over my face. They were a chocolate heaven for any chocoholic.

"Yes, those," she laughs at my description. "These are the same concept, but lemon. I mixed in a little lemon curd to pudding for the centers to have more of a punch. The meringue I sprinkled with lemon zest, again to get a true lemon punch." I can see the excitement in her eyes. She has always loved baking and now it sounds like she can experiment and come up with an array of items for work and home.

"It definitely worked. I was a little skeptical at first, but now I'm a believer of never questioning my sister's creations." I finish my milk and still retain a mild lemon flavor on my tongue. Rose tells me I now have a milk mustache. I wipe my mouth once again.

"You asked if Michael has ever heard how you and Brady got together. I think it's a good time to tell him. My brother seems to need your assistance in cleaning his face," Rose says. I hear a small laugh. Lily reaches over with her napkin and wipes the meringue off Brady's mouth. As she sits back in her chair, I don't see humor in his eyes. The look in Brady's eyes is darker. It reminds me of a wolf looking at his prey. I think, maybe, Rose and I should leave now.

"Oh, that's right." Lily clears her voice and looks at me. I know she caught her fiancée's look and I can only guess what it fully means.

"You can tell me tomorrow. I think we should be heading next door Rose," I say. I start getting up from my chair to put my dish and glass in the sink, but Lily reaches over and stops me.

"I'll get the dishes later. I think you'll get a kick out of the story," she says as I sit back down. "The first day I met Brady, he was leaving his house and on his way in to work. I got to see him in his uniform, so I knew he was a police officer. We exchanged hellos and he invited me to dinner, on one of his days off, to say welcome to the neighborhood. I brought cookies over. Then, I met a lady, Mary, at the deli when I went shopping. It turns out she needed someone at her café and catering business to do baked goods." Brady reached up and held her hand with a smile on his face. "I asked Brady to be my Guinee pig and taste everything for me. He came over for dinner a few days later and tasted the cookies I made. He was the one that recommended sugar cookies when I messed up a fruit cookie I was trying," she says. Her eyes looked sad. Brady lifts her chin up with his finger.

"Remember what came out of that mistake, not the mistake itself." Brady tells my sister and I see her eyes soften with tenderness.

"True." She squeezes his hand and continues with the story. "I wanted to do some fancier desserts for Mary to try. I made a fruit tortilla, butterscotch cannoli, and peanut butter cheesecake. When Brady tried the cannoli, he got powder sugar all over his face. I helped him clean it off. What Brady and I were laughing at, though, was the fact you asked for milk. We discovered we are both cookie dunkers in milk." Rose must have known this story because she laughed at all the right places during Lily telling the story. Brady sat back and let Lily tell the story in its entirety. Her eyes showed excitement, her body bouncing on her seat, and her laughter sounded light and gay. This evening will be the one I convey to my parents. Lily is the happiest I have ever seen her.

"It sounds like Brady got the better deal," I say. Brady gets up and takes Lily's hand. She stands in front of him and he turns her around so they both face the table. His hands are circling my sister's waist and his chin is on her shoulder.

"You're wrong Michael. I got more than sweets. I got the sweetest thing in my life." Brady kissed her cheek and releases her to collect the dishes off the table. Rose gets up to take the teacups to the sink and I follow with my glass.

"I think you're right in that," I say to Brady. We leave the scent of lemon behind and walk towards the living room. I see the wall of photos again. I pass over mine and I'm surprised to see a picture of Adrian on the wall. I would have thought Brady would object. He, obviously, is a good man. I don't know if I would be able to do the same.

"I think I'm ready to head home," Rose says. Oh, thank god. I can finally have some alone time with her. "How about you?" she asks me. I nod my head and hug Lily and Brady then say good night.

CHAPTER 5

We enter the front door and I hear the radio. We left the house earlier and forgot to turn it off. This time I don't hear Frank Sinatra. Instead, I hear Peter Frampton singing "Show Me the Way." Rose must have an oldie station on. I listen to the lyrics as we walk through the living room and enter the kitchen. With today's discussion going to something involving Rose's past she will have to be the one showing me the way into her life and her heart. I won't rush anything with her, but I need to know what happened, so I know the path I will have to tip toe through.

"You're on Oklahoma time, but it is still early. Would you like to sit in the hot tub?" Rose walks over to the flowers on the table and touches a few petals. She's looking at the flowers as she talks to me. "I thought you might be stiff from the long drive." She looks over her shoulder and I can see her cheeks are rosy. I don't know why she won't look at me or what she's thinking to make her blush. I want her to be comfortable around me.

"I would love that. I am a little stiff from my drive," I tell her. I'm actually not that stiff. My muscles have stretched out between standing with Brady while he grilled the steaks and the time watching the sunset. My mind relaxed seeing the sky turn a full rainbow of colors. "I'll meet you outside after we get our suits on," I tell her and turn around to head to the bedroom.

"Wait," she says. I turn back around and see her looking at me with her pink cheeks and gold flecks in her eyes. "You heard all that confusion from earlier. I want you to know it has nothing to do with you, Michael." She lowers her head, and the pink darkens into a bright scarlet red.

"Rose don't worry about it. When you're ready to talk to me about it, I'll be here," I tell her. I walk up to her and place my hand on her shoulder. I'm not sure where to lay my hands that won't upset her. She looks up into my eyes. I know she sees tenderness in my eyes. I want to pull her into a hug, but again, I don't want to scare her off. I squeeze her shoulder then turn around and leave the room to put on my swimsuit. I hear her close the door to her room a minute later. I can only image what she will wear. I'd love to think of her walking down the hall in front of me with a small brightly colored bikini, but I doubt she's going to show that much skin. I can see it in my head. I'd come out of my room with my large black swim trunks and see her exit her room. I can see the string bow through her long hair as it sways from side to side. Her full hips are covered with a small triangle of fabric, showing her beautiful olive skin. Her thighs are rubbing together as she heads out the door in the kitchen. She bends over to turn on the bubbles and I help her take off the cover. She turns, and I see the small amount of fabric covering her modest size breasts. I'm sure my mouth would cover them perfectly. I catch a glimmer of something shiny when I look down to her belly button. She has a piercing. The gold ring gets me hotter for her.

"Michael, are you ready?" she says after knocking on the door. "I have the lid off and the bubbles are waiting for us," her soft voice says through the door I'm hesitant to open. My fantasy ran away from me.

"I have to grab a towel from the bathroom and then I'll meet you out there," I choke out the words. I don't want her to know I have an erection already. I need to get my body and thoughts under control before I see her.

I walk out to the deck with a towel around my neck and a swimsuit that is laying flat again. Brady did a great job in placing lattice panels around two sides of the hot tub. One side faced the deck and one side faces the house. It looks very private and cozy. I see Rose's shoulders peaking above the steaming water. If I'm not mistaken, I don't see any straps. Her hair is piled on top of her head, with a few tendrils are surrounding her face. I place my towel on the hook next to hers and test the water with my hand. It's not too hot.

"Come on in. It feels great," Rose says sitting in the far corner. The steps are dry as I take them one at a time. Rose is looking into my eyes as I sink my body into the water. I sit in the molded seat across from her and rest my head back on the cushion. Our feet touch under the water. She starts to pull them away and then changes her mind as I feel her toes curl against the side of my foot. "It looks like there is plenty of room, until you stretch out your legs," she says. She continues to curl her toes.

"I don't mind. Do you?" I ask her. Her cheeks are flushed from the heat of the water, so I have no idea if she is blushing. I lift my foot and rub her ankle with my toes. I hear her small gasp, but she doesn't move her feet. I'm taking baby steps with her.

"Not with you," she says. Her eyes are golden brown as they bore into my soul. My heart is pounding, and not just from the heat of the water. "I'm glad we are getting some time alone. I love spending time with my brother and your sister, but I was counting the days until you got here," she says, dipping her head down. The steam surrounds her head when she puts her chin into the water.

"I was doing the same thing. Talking with you over the last few months made my days go faster. Several of my team could tell the days I was going to talk with you." They noticed I didn't have as many memory issues on those days, but I can't tell her that. I sit up and continue to stroke her ankle with my toes. "I realized we never talked about ourselves, outside of work and school. I told myself I would make the extra effort to get to know who Rose is." She sits up and pulls her legs back. I worry for a moment I overstepped.

"I realized the same thing when I drove down today," she says. She slides over so that she is in the corner next to me. The hot tub can comfortably seat eight people, so there is a space between us. "How about we start with I love the flowers you got me. Everyone thinks I love roses because of my name. I prefer wildflowers and tulips." She's looking at me now. Her cheeks are still flushed. "I like the color purple, but that doesn't make me a girly girl. My favorite color is blue. I love the cobalt blue of your eyes," she says. She shows me her beautiful white teeth with a shy smile. "Your turn!"

"I love all shades of blue. My home is decorated in blues and browns." I'm sure she will love my house with all the blues in each room. "I prefer wildflowers, if I buy flowers at all. Roses always remind me of Valentine's Day," I tell her. I lean towards her, letting my feet find hers under the water again.

"Me, too. I never understood why roses are the flower of Valentine's Day. I think because my name is Rose, I don't like them even more. No one puts a lot of thought into picking out flowers if they buy roses," she says. Her voice goes up in pitch and in volume. I can see how strongly she believes this. "Although, I wouldn't really know, today was the first time I got flowers from someone other than a family member."

"Really?" I ask her. I'm surprised. She's twenty-three and had to have boyfriends.

"I haven't dated since high school." She lowers her head, so I can't see her face at all. "I put all my efforts into finishing college early. I never had time to date with my schoolwork and internship," she says. Her head is still down and now her shoulders are curled forward. I know this has something to do what Brady mentioned earlier. I'm starting to think I know what happened, but she will tell me when she's ready. I'm not going to push her.

"I haven't dated much in the last few years myself," I tell her. She looks up and I can see the question in her eyes. She doesn't push the issue with me, probably because she doesn't want to talk about her issue right now.

"My favorite meal to make is macaroni and cheese." She changes the topic and I follow her lead. "Sometimes I put chunks of ham or hot dogs in it. I remember my mom would always put frozen peas and ham in hers. She said it guaranteed her kids getting vegetables in the meal." I see sadness flash in her eyes and then it's gone.

"I love making chili. I know there are a lot of different recipes, especially if you live in the south. I like it thick with a little tomato puree, black beans, and kidney beans. My brothers put hot peppers in theirs. I like mine milder," I tell her. Chili is one of those dishes people enter into competitions. There are so many ways to make it. Spicy or mild, soupy or thick, each part of the country makes it differently.

"I'm not fond of spicy, so I'd probably like your chili. Do you make cornbread with it or serve it with rice?" she asks. Again, there are so many ways to serve it depending on where you live.

"I do both. I'm told my chili is more of a chili con carne. I don't really know the difference. I just know what I like." I can see us sitting in front of a roaring fireplace with a hot bowl of chili while watching a game.

"I like mine with cheddar cheese sprinkled on top, so it can melt, and it gets gooey. It's one of those meals to have in the colder weather. My mom called it comfort food. Macaroni and cheese is that for me too," she says. She raises her arms to the surface of the bubbling water and starts making circles with her fingers. "I love grilled cheese sandwiches during cold weather months too."

"I have a recipe for stew I cook in my crockpot. That's my comfort food on a cold day. I bought a couple cookbooks when I left home. The one I use the most is the crockpot recipes book." I love walking into the house after a long day and know dinner is ready anytime I want to eat. The mouthwatering smell of stew or chili after it has cooked all day is amazing.

"My favorite food is Italian. Whenever Brady could take us out for dinner, we always picked Italian. I still need to learn how to make my favorite dishes. Your mom offered to teach me the basics while I was down there for Thanksgiving. Lily has also said she would teach me. I just haven't had the time." She sounded sad.

"I love Mom's Italian dishes. She tries to stay true to her heritage for special meals. Thanksgiving and Christmas, she made traditional dishes." I'm always happy when I get to eat traditional Italian food. I can't cook spaghetti sauce to save my life, so Mom always sends a container home with me when she makes a large pot.

"I was surprised by a lot of the dishes your mom served. I always thought all Italian food had tomato sauce and pasta of some sort. Your mom's risotto was incredible," Rose says, moaning in her remembrance of Mom's food. That small moan sends shock waves down under the water to my groin. I cleared my voice as she kept talking about the holiday menu. "I think the thing that surprised me the most was dessert. I'm around Lily's creations enough to know sugary desserts are a must after a meal. Your mom's simple tray of fresh fruit threw me." She's smiling, just enough, to show me a glimpse of her teeth. I'm looking at her lips, remembering each piece of fruit she bit into at Christmas. I watched the juice of the spiced pear sit on her red lips until her tongue licked it away. I so wanted to lick the juice myself.

"I think it is more of an American tradition to have sugary desserts after dinner. We have always had fresh fruit. It helps clear the palette, or so I've been told. Americans tend to eat a salad at the beginning of a meal. It helps your digestion if you eat it at the end of a meal. Again, it depends on where you live. When I was a kid, I thought giving us fruit at the end of the meal was Mom's way of never giving us too much sugar. Can you image six kids running around on a sugar high?" I ask her.

"I think your mom and dad could handle it, but I see what you're saying. Maybe it's the restaurant's way of making more money. I had my first cannoli when I went to an Italian restaurant, so I assumed that was a typical dessert." I think back to when Lily learned how to make cannoli and tiramisu. The cannoli sold out at the fund raiser first. Rose brings back my attention when she asks, "So why do people think of some desserts as being a traditional Italian thing?"

"I'm not sure. Maybe you can ask Mom when she's up for your graduation," I suggest to her. I look down at my wrinkled fingers and realized we have been in the hot tub awhile. I think we should be getting out soon, but I love talking with Rose and I don't want the night to end.

"Well, now we know favorite colors and foods. That's a start, but I think we should get out of the water. Look at my fingers." She places her hand in front of my chest. She must have read my mind. She leans closer and I can see her fingers are worse than mine. She really needs to get out of the heat. Her face is flushed a bright cherry red.

"Yeah. I think we need to get out too. We have a few more days to get to know each other." I stand up, my chest now out of the water as I extend my hand out for her to hold onto while she climbs out of the hot tub. She has been under the water this entire time, so I have no idea what I'm about to see. I am in shock when she stands up and I see a strapless bikini top in navy blue. She turns her head and looks in my eyes. I see the question in them. She is gorgeous and doesn't seem to know it. She steps on the seat and lifts her leg over to step down on the wooden steps next to hot tub. I stop breathing when I see the small gold hoop piercing lying flat against her flat abdomen. The striped blue bikini bottoms fit her hips perfectly, sitting just below her piercing. Her skin has a red tint from the hot water. I'm so busy staring at her body, I forget to let her go of her hand. When she is steady on the deck, she gently pulls her hand out of mine. My towel falls to the deck when she reaches for hers. After placing the towel around her body, she holds mine out for me. I quickly step out of the water, reaching for the towel. I'm not paying attention to the now wet steps and slip on the first step. I land, hard, on my back as my feet slide over the wet deck.

"Oh Michael, are you okay?" she asks. I open my eyes and see an angel leaning over me. Her eyes show concern. I can see the gold flecks sparkle in her hazel eyes. I place my hands on the lower step and sit up. Rose sits on the step next to me, our legs touching from hip to knee.

"I'm fine," I tell her, but I'm not. My body has jolts of electricity shooting through it. She asks me to lean forward and then I feel her hand running over my back. I hold in the moan I want to let out from her light touch.

"I don't feel anything out of place. Can you stand up?" She grabs onto my elbow to help me stand. "Go slowly." I don't need her assistance, but any excuse for her hands to touch me I'll take. She steps behind me and runs both hands up and down my back. I close my eyes and absorb her touch into my muscles. "I see a red mark across your back. You may have a bruise tomorrow. Are you sure you're okay?" she asks again. I turn around to face her. Her towel is covering her bikini, thank god. I don't need her to see an erection as she is looking me over.

"I'm fine Rose. A little embarrassed, but fine," I tell her. I take the towel she is still holding and wrap it around my waist. I hope this isn't going to be a habit between us. First, she takes care of my cut thumb at Christmas and now she has to look me over after a fall. Both times I was so busy looking at her, I didn't pay attention to what I was doing. We both laugh a little while we head back into the house.

"Next time I'll have you get out first then you can hold my hand as I get out. How about a cup of tea?" she asks. I tell her yes as she's heading over to the tea kettle on the stove. Her towel slips as she reaches for a couple cups. I get a flash of blue and olive skin. "Do you want to take a quick shower to wash off the chlorine while the tea is brewing?" she asks. She turns around when I don't answer. I was looking at her bare thighs. I can picture them wrapped around my hip as she moans my name.

"Oh yeah, that sounds like a good idea," I answer as she catches me ogling her body. I make a quick exit and head down the hall to the master bathroom. I turn on the water to get warm and strip out of my suit. I set it in the sink, so I don't get the floor all wet. I don't need another fall tonight. I test the water and then step under the spray. I reach for the soap to clean off the chlorine, and realize I need the water a lot colder if I'm going to be able to step back in the kitchen with her. I turn off the hot water completely and finish soaping up my body. Even with the cold water, I have a raging hard on. I rinse the soap off my body then soap up my hand one more time. I place one hand on the tile wall and the other around my erection. I know it won't take long to make the tea, so I don't let my mind go to my favorite fantasy. I grip myself roughly and jack myself off quickly. I can't stop the groan from leaving my mouth. I moan Rose's name as the last of the cum leaves my body. I hear a small gasp when I turn the water off. Did Rose just hear me masturbating? I hope not. I dry off and get dressed quickly. I decide on a pair of basketball shorts and a t-shirt. At home I wouldn't wear the t-shirt, but I want Rose to be completely comfortable around me.

I head back in the kitchen and see the steaming kettle on the stove and no Rose. I hear the other shower turn on. She must have waited for me then decided to take hers. I start to image her naked body under the shower spray with soap bubbles running down over her breasts and meeting in the juncture between her thighs. I have to stop thinking about her nakedness. I'm getting stiff again and I can't go take care of it again.

I pour hot water into the cups and start steeping the tea bag in each. The radio is still on. Scorpions are singing "Follow Your Heart."I know what my heart is telling me already. I hope I can be her light and her heart brings her to me. The song ends and I turn the radio off. I head into the family room to look through the movie collection on the shelves. These have to be Brady's. I see a few action, comedy, and horror, but most of the titles are military and law enforcement. I like the Harrison Ford titles he has, but I don't feel like watching a John Grisham book brought to film with Rose. I look over the comedy and decide on *Game Night.* I've seen the trailers for the movie, but never got around to seeing it. I'll suggest watching it after she is done with her shower. I don't hear the water running anymore, so I head back into the kitchen and finish up steeping the tea. I get a spoon out for the sugar. I learned a long time ago to drink coffee and tea without any sweetener, but I don't know if Rose puts sugar in her tea.

Rose's flowery scent floats into the room and reaches my nose before I turn to see her standing in the kitchen entry. I'm sure I would be dropping the teacups if I hadn't set them on the kitchen table before turning around to face her. She stays in the doorway as I look at her. Her cheeks are their beautiful soft pink. She has taken her hair out of its clip. It isn't wet, so she must have washed only her body in the shower. A few loose strands fall in front of her shoulders. She is in a loose blue night-shirt that stops at her knees. I can only assume she doesn't have a bra underneath. I can picture her not wearing underwear too. I continue looking at her from head to feet. Her fuzzy blue slippers make me laugh.

"Don't laugh. These were a gift from Anna when I left for college. She got them so that no one would mistake my shoes for theirs in the shower stalls. We had the bathrooms and shower area in the middle of the dorms. I was at the end of the hall and had to get a caddy to put all my bathroom supplies in. I went one time and all the stalls were full. I started taking my showers either at six in the morning or at ten at night. I can't tell you how happy I was when I got my own place. I had my own sink and shower I could leave my stuff on. I also loved that I could take a bath." Rose walks up and leans arounds me to get her cup of tea. "Thank you for finishing the tea," she says, taking a small sip.

"I picked out a movie, if you're up for it," I say, stumbling over the words. I should not be picturing her in the showers at school, I can't help myself. I remember Nick talking about hating the showers in the dorm. I guess it's a rite of passage to get through for all students.

"That sounds good. I'm not really tired yet," she says as she heads toward the family room. I follow her into the other room and can't stop myself from watching the fabric sway back and forth with each movement of her hips. I realize I've got it really bad as I stare at the back of her knees. Out of all the body parts people think are sexy, I would never have imagined the curve from her thighs to her calves as being sexy, but I do. I want to drop to the floor and kiss and lick the soft skin behind her knees. I clear my voice, set my cup on the coffee table, and go to put the movie in. "What movie did you pick?" she asks. She curls herself into the corner of the couch, placing her legs underneath her.

"*Game Night* with Jason Bateman and Rachel McAdams. Is that alright?" I sit on the other corner of the couch. I know I can sit here all night and talk if that's what she wants. I don't need to be entertained by a movie.

"I haven't seen it, so why not," she says. She leans forward to place her teacup on the table. I see the cotton material of her night-shirt stretch across her back. I'm right. She isn't wearing a bra.

Rose talks through most of the movie. She comments on how she couldn't do a kidnapping game. The game is similar to the game Clue, but with everyone having to find the clues to free the person who got kidnapped. I feel her body tense up during some of the scenes. I thought this would be a funny comedy for both of us to end our evenings and here Rose is getting nervous instead.

"Are you alright?" I ask her. We can turn off the movie if it's upsetting her. I don't care about finishing the movie now. I have a thought quickly cross my mind. Is Rose's secret worse than I imagined earlier?

"I'm fine. I didn't realize there would be this much violence." She stretches out her legs and tosses the blanket from the back of the couch over them. I reach out and squeeze her toes of one foot. I want to touch her skin but now isn't the time.

"Do you want to turn something else on?" I ask her. She is pulling the blanket up over her arms. I see the tension in her shoulders and her hands are shaking on top of the blanket. Again, I have to wonder what happened to her.

"It's almost over and I really want to know what happens to the brother," she says. We both look back to the television and watch in silence for a few minutes I keep rubbing her feet and squeezing her toes. I don't realize I'm doing it until Rose wiggles her toes.

"That feels really good Michael. I wish your hands could do that after all my shifts at the clinic. Some days my feet hurt so much I put an ice pack on them before bed. It helps a little," Rose tells me.

"If you take either job by me, I'd be happy to rub your feet every night," I tell her. Her feet slip out from under the blanket. I take her right foot into my hands and press the heel of my hand into the arch of her foot. She lays her head back on the couch and moans her appreciation.

"I would let you do that all day. That feels amazing." She moans again as I press my thumb into the ball of her foot. She scoots down on the couch cushion so that both of her feet are resting on my lap. After my accident, I went to physical therapy and massage therapy. Physical therapy worked on my large muscles. I suffered whiplash from how hard the horse's hooves hit my head. I agonized in constant pain in my neck and shoulders that physical therapy helped with. It was suggested to me to also have a massage therapist work on the rest of my back, chest, and arm muscles that were occasionally sore. Both therapists were great, but I have to admit when the massage therapist worked on my hands and feet, it made the rest of my body feel amazing. She called it reflexology. She explained that each section of our hands and feet match up with a section of our body. I now see her regularly to keep my body in balance.

We watch the movie to its conclusion. It wasn't as good as the commercials made it out to be, but that can be because of my concern for Rose. I have to move Rose's feet off my lap to take out the movie. She moans her disapproval of the interruption of the massage. While I was rubbing her feet, I heard the smallest of snores coming from the other side of the couch. I look back at her while placing the movie back in the slot I took it from. She looks so relaxed and at peace, I don't want to move her. It is late now and I'm sure she wouldn't want to sleep on the couch. I sit next to her and place my hand on her arm. She doesn't move. I don't want to startle her, so I whisper her name with no response.

"Rose sweetheart, it's time to go to bed," I whisper again, this time next to her ear. I hear a small moan and her hand glides up and over my shoulder. Her fingers tickle the hair at my collar.

"Can I have a kiss goodnight?" she asks. Her eyes are closed, and her fingers are curling around my hair. I don't know if she's asleep and dreaming or awake and not looking at me.

"Rose, open your eyes sweetie." I watch her eyes open. She pulls her hand back. I liked her fingers running through my hair, it felt wonderful. I don't move my head away. Instead I keep my face close to hers and my hand on her shoulder. I see the confusion in her eyes and then the gold flecks change to desire. "You fell asleep," I state the obvious. "The couch isn't the most comfortable to sleep on. I think we need to go to bed," I say and see panic take over her eyes and her entire body stiffens. I'm aware of her body clues and I pull away from her immediately. She must have thought I meant for us to go to bed together, which is not what I meant at all.

"I fell asleep?" she questions me. She takes the blanket, which is around her waist, and pulls it up to her chin. "I'm sorry, Michael. I was so relaxed while you were rubbing my feet, I must have dozed off." I get up and sit on the other end of the couch to give her the space she needs to feel comfortable again.

"That means I did a good job. I'll have to tell my massage therapist that I did such a good job, I put someone to sleep." I'm trying not to move too fast or startle her. She sits up, holding onto the blanket in front of her. I can see the moment she decides to give me a little bit of trust and folds the blanket up and tosses it on the back of the couch. Her back is straight, and her shoulders are thrown back as she stands up. I wait for her to walk into the kitchen to stand up and follow her. I'm giving her some space to figure out what just happened.

"Did his brother escape?" she asks as I follow her into the hallway. Her back has relaxed a little. I'm thrown by the question probably because I'm watching the night-shirt play around her knees. She turns around at her bedroom doorway. I've already lifted my eyes. After what happened, I don't want her to catch me drooling over her body.

"The neighbor was in on the game and set up his own portion of it. His brother went to jail for his crimes and then moved close to his brother after he served his time." I lean against the wall opposite of her room. There is confusion in her eyes again as I say good night and move down the hallway.

"Michael?" I turn to look at her. "Thank you for a nice evening," she says. She takes the two steps to stand in front of me. She lifts herself up onto her toes and rests both her hands on my chest. She gives me a light kiss on my lips. "Good night," she says and then turns around and goes into her room. She leaves the door open and I hear her get under the covers of her bed. I stay in the hallway for another moment then head to the bedroom down the hall. I close my eyes and can feel the tingle on my chest where her hands had rested. This will be a long night.

CHAPTER 6

I wake up to the smell of coffee and lemon. I put on my jeans and a t-shirt, leaving my boots in the room, and head for the kitchen. I freeze in my tracks the instant I enter the kitchen. Rose is bending over the oven door pulling out a cookie sheet. She is in her nightgown from last night still. The fabric slides up her thighs. I get a quick peak at her blue panties before she stands up to place the hot food on top of the stove. She has the radio on and starts to sway to the music. I continue to watch her body move around the kitchen. She reaches up to get dishes and cups down for breakfast and her thighs catch my attention each time she reaches up into the cabinet. She starts to sing the chorus lyrics of "What If" by Kane Brown and Lauren Alaina. I hope it reminds her of the kiss she gave me last night.

"Oh my! Michael, you startled me," she gasps when she turns and sees me standing at the entrance to the kitchen. She places her hand over her chest and drops one of the cups in the process. Her hand reaches out to try and catch it. I move forward, quickly, to reach for the cup but it shatters on the floor. Neither of us could grab it. I feel bad about scarring her and now I'm responsible for the broken cup that is now all around her slippers. Thankfully, she is wearing them, or I would worry about her feet getting cut up. "Oh no," she starts to cry. She places the dishes and the single cup on the table. We bend over to pick up the shattered pieces.

"I'm sorry Rose. I didn't mean to scare you," I say to her. I should have said something as she got the dishes down then this wouldn't have happened. "Let me get it. I don't want you cutting yourself." I realized coming from me that sounds funny. I have always injured myself around her. She is still crying as she picks up the largest piece of porcelain. Our fingers touch as we both go for the same piece. She looks up into my eyes. I can see the green tint taking over the gold flecks.

"It's not your fault. I should have held on to them better." Her tears are running down her cheeks and dripping onto the floor. I don't know what to do. I don't know why she is so upset, and I don't like seeing her cry.

"Rose, let me finish this. Do you have a broom and a dustpan?" I ask her to get her to stop picking up the smaller pieces. I know we would both get cuts on our fingers if we try to get the smaller pieces.

"Brady has one in the pantry," she tells me. She stands and sets the larger pieces on the counter. I watch her get the broom out of closet as I just stand there. I take the dustpan from her and let her sweep the cup into it. She has stopped crying, but she is still obviously upset. I throw the small pieces in the trash. Rose is standing next to the counter holding the large piece in her hands.

"What's the matter?" I ask her. I stand next to her and watch her hands shake. I want to reach out and comfort her, but I hesitate to touch her.

"This cup was my Mom's favorite," she says. Her fingers are running over the glaze. "I broke it, and I can't replace it." Rose walks over to the trash and hesitates to throw it out. She looks up at me and at that moment lets it fall from her hands.

"I'm sure we can get another one," I tell her, not really sure if we can find that exact pattern if the cup is that old. I will try my best though.

"No Michael. My Dad gave her a set of these for their anniversary. She loved tea and Dad found these on a trip they took. I don't know where, but it wouldn't be the same anyway." She is standing in the middle of the kitchen, hands shaking, and her tears are rolling down her cheeks again.

"I'm so sorry Rose." I step in front of her and she falls into my arms. I put my arms around her and pull her in close. Her body is shaking with each new wave of crying. I let her get it all out. My shirt has wet spots on each shoulder, but I don't care. Comforting Rose is the most important thing to do right now. I can always change my shirt later. The coffee pot beeps to let us know it is done brewing. I can smell the deep roasted scent mix with the lemon icing on the cinnamon rolls cooling on the stove top. I'm also smelling a fruit scent coming off of Rose. I'm not sure if it is her body wash or her shampoo, but it awakens something deep inside of me. She loosens her hold around my chest but continues to hold on to me. Her tears are tapering off.

I release her with one of my arms. I slowly move my hand and lift her chin with my index finger. "I will try and find another one for you," I tell her. The last of her tears are sliding down her cheeks. I move my hand to her right cheek and wipe the tears away. Her eyes are lowered as she leans her head into my hand. I tip my head towards her other cheek and kiss the tears away. I take my time kissing from her jawline up to her eye. "I promise," I whisper into her ear. Her body stiffens for a second. I lift my head and see her eyebrows scrunched up in uncertainty. I wrap my arm back around her and pull her into my chest. "Rose, I never want to see you cry. It breaks my heart to see you so upset. I am sorry about the cup, but there's nothing we can do about it right now," I tell her. I take a step back and reluctantly release her. "Are you better now?"

"I'm okay. I know it's stupid to get so upset over a cup, but I only have a few things of my parents and I cherish all of them," she says. She moves to the cabinet and gets out another cup. "How about I go get dressed while you get your coffee and then we can eat the cinnamon rolls?" she asks. Before I can answer her, she leaves the kitchen. I know she feels embarrassed right now, but she doesn't need to be, not around me. I get my coffee and place the tea bag she set on the counter into her cup to steep her tea.

I take the two dishes she set on the table over to the counter. I place a cinnamon roll on each plate and go to the table to wait for Rose to come back. I detect an aroma of lemon coming from the plate in front of me. I lick the icing and taste lemon. It's not strong, but it is clearly lemon. Now that she knows I love lemon I have a feeling Rose will surprise me with the flavor often.

"Do you like it?" she asks when she enters the room.

"I love it. I highly doubt you had lemon cinnamon rolls in the refrigerator. How did you make them lemon flavored?" I ask her. She brings her cup of tea over to the table and smiles at me as she sits next to me. She is in a pair of blue jeans and a solid royal blue t-shirt. The shirt has a modest round neckline and her jeans aren't tight, but after seeing her in the bikini last night, I can image all those curves under the fabric. Her eyes are still a little puffy and bloodshot. She put a little makeup on her eyes, I'm sure to try and hide the fact that she was crying. She looks beautiful to me, red eyes, and all.

"I mixed lemon flavoring in the icing before I iced them. I figured you would like it. I have never met anyone who likes lemon as much as you do." She takes a sip of her tea then lifts her cinnamon roll to her lips. I watch her open her lips to take a small bite. Icing sticks to her lips, like the meringue from the cupcake last night. My pants start to get a little tight. She takes another bite and the same thing happens. Icing is clinging to her bottom lip. I slowly lift my hand up to her lips. She startles and leans back to watch my hand. I wipe her lip with my thumb. When she realizes what I'm doing she leans forward into my hand. I wipe the first bit of icing off and bring it to my mouth. First, I lick my thumb and then I place it in my mouth. I suck all the sticky icing off and go back for another bit of icing. This time I wipe it off and offer my thumb to her mouth. I stare into her eyes as she opens her mouth and sticks her tongue out to lick my thumb. I feel a surge of energy from my thumb straight to my heart and the full erection that is making it uncomfortable to sit.

We continue sipping at our coffee and tea as we eat the cinnamon rolls in quiet. Each time the icing sticks to her lips I wipe it off and either offer it to her or bring my thumb to my own lips. I swear I can taste her in each bit of icing I take into my mouth. I take the last bite and see her looking at my lips. Is that desire I see in her eyes? Her hands are shaking as she lifts her fingers to my mouth. It is her turn to wipe the icing off of my lips. Her thumb slides over my bottom lip. She starts to pull her hand away and I place my hand around her wrist. I lean forward and open my mouth to lick the icing off. I taste her skin with each swipe of my tongue. Without realizing it, I pull her thumb into my mouth and continue to stare into her eyes. I run my tongue around her thumb and think about how I will, eventually, give her nipples the same treatment with the tip of my tongue. My jeans tighten a little more. I release her wrist and see that beautiful pink blush spread over her cheeks. She lowers her head as she pulls her hand back and gets up to take the dishes and her cup to the sink.

"Did you want another cup of coffee? I made a full pot because I don't know how much you drink." She has her back to me as she rinses the dishes off. I get up with my cup and head over to the sink without answering her. I stand behind her and reach my arm around her to place my cup on the counter next to the sink. She doesn't startle this time. Instead she rinses out my cup, dries her hands off with the towel next to her, and then turns around. I place both of my hands on the counter to each side of her. I'm hoping she doesn't feel crowded as she looks up at me. She places her hands on my chest and I think she's going to ask me to move. Her hands drop down to my waist and I can feel each finger move over every muscle she touches as her hands travel up my back.

"Michael, I'm not sure where to go from here. I like you a lot, but if I don't get either job in Oklahoma, I don't know how we could make this work.," she says. She rests her head on my chest and caresses my shoulder muscles with both her hands. I understand what she is saying, but I don't want to think about her not moving down by me. I run my hands around her waist and run them up her back, feeling all the muscles that are hidden by her shirt.

"We can figure that out in May. I know you will get an offer to work at one, if not both, of the jobs. You are an amazing, caring person and any office would be grateful to have you as an employee. I'm worried you won't be able to leave Colorado. I don't understand everything that got said last night, but I know it must be immense for you to consider not ever leaving Denver," I reply, hugging her tighter to my chest. I hear one of my favorite songs by Savage Garden start playing from the radio she has left on. "Listen to the words, Rose." I tell her. Her body starts to sway to the words of "Truly Madly Deeply". "I want to be all those things for you because you are already all those things for me. I don't know how to explain my emotions to you. My parents say all of us Corscos fall fast and hard in love. I have seen it with Brady and Lily, Nick and Anna, and Seth and Gabby." The song ends and we are still swaying back and forth in the kitchen.

"You are already in my fantasies Michael. I have never had fantasies before you. I know I have to talk to you about my past, but I'm not ready to tell you about that day yet. I'm not sure you will look at me the same way," she whispers the last sentence.

"Rose, I want you to know I love you and nothing will change that. I already have an idea of what it is, and you have to understand it wasn't your fault. No one should ever look at you differently for something that happened to you years ago without your permission." I squeeze her a little tighter. I'm thrilled to know she is fantasizing about me. That tells me she has been thinking about me while we've been talking on the phone these last few months. I curb my excitement, for now. "Why don't we go look at this horse and see where the day takes us. You can tell me in your own time Rose." I pull back and look at her. "The person in front of me is the strong, loving, patient woman I fell in love with, not the girl from your past. I have my own secrets that I want to talk to you about, but not today. Let's go see this horse. Okay?" I ask her. I feel her entire body relax as she pulls back, out of my arms. My body feels her absence right away.

"Sounds good to me! Where do we need to go for this horse?" she asks me. I'm hoping we can talk about each of our experiences before I leave. It would be nice to have it all behind us so we can move forward with each other as a couple. I don't know what I will do if she doesn't move down to Oklahoma.

"We need to go to Parker. I got directions from the owner this morning. I think it's only twenty minutes from here." We both leave the kitchen, grab our jackets, and then head out to my truck. I unhitch the horse trailer as Rose runs back into the house for a couple bottles of water. Rose isn't tiny, but she still needs to use the step to get up into my truck. I watch her as she climbs into the cab of my truck. Her jeans tighten over her backside and my jeans tighten in the opposite direction. I can't drive with a constant erection. I will have to keep a conversation going so that I don't think about how sexy she is. The weather is chilly so we both have our jackets on. I won't be able to see her perky breasts, which should help.

"Let's go get a horse," I say. I look over to see her buckle up. She looks up at me and I start the truck. I see her eyes light up when she smiles. She looks excited. I have done these enough times to know sometimes it doesn't work out to buy the horse. I'm hoping this time it works out. She looks like a child that got her favorite toy for Christmas.

I drive south on Parker Road, going through the town of Parker. It is a growing town with lots of new construction. We take a turn on Hill Top Road, heading to the eastern suburbs of Parker. We pass several ranches on both sides of the road. I feel like I'm at home with fenced in pastures and horses roaming the winter grasses. I have Rose check the address on GPS that we are going to. She sees the ranch sign up ahead and I drive over the cattle guard and drive down the dirt road until we see the large house. We park in front of the house and see someone walking up from the barn. I had called ahead and knew they are expecting me.

"Do you want me to stay in the truck?" Rose asks. I can see anxiety in her eyes and on her face. I tell her she can come see the horse with me. I want her opinion otherwise I wouldn't have invited her. I actually hoped this would give her another reason to move to Oklahoma. Rose stops at the front of the truck and waits for me to join her. I reach my hand out to hold hers and she doesn't hesitate to place her hand in mine.

"Did you have any problems finding the place Michael," the gentleman says as we meet up in front of the house. It's a brown two-story house with a wrap-around porch. I can see a wooden swing and several dark brown rocking chairs near the front door. Flower boxes, with multicolor pansies, and potted green plants that add a female touch to the outside of the house. I'm surprised the green plants are growing this early into the spring.

"No. Your directions were perfect." I let go of Rose's hand to shake his extended hand. "You have a nice place out here in the country," He reaches out to shake Rose's hand and I have to hold back a growl. I don't want anyone to touch her but me.

"Hi, I'm Alan," he says taking too long to shake Rose's hand. I see alarm in her eyes. "And you are?" he asks when Rose pulls her hand back. She reaches for my hand and I curl my fingers around hers. I feel a tremor in her hand, so I place her hand on my chest then I put my arm behind her back and pull her into my chest. I tell him her name is Rose when she doesn't answer him. Alan must have seen the alarm in her face because he steps back and looks back at me.

"You're here to see *Rosso,* so let's get you down to the stables and see her." Alan says. He turns around and heads back in the direction he had come from when we pulled up. I go back to holding Rose's hand because it's too hard walking side by side on the uneven ground. I look down and see Rose smiling up at me. I've only seen her around her family. I start to wonder if she has problems meeting new men or if she got a bad feeling from this man.

"Did you name her red for a reason?" I ask Alan. We all enter the stables. He looks over his shoulder and I see the surprised look on his face.

"My wife is Italian, and her favorite color is red. You'll understand when you see the horse." He passes several stalls and several horses stick their heads out to watch him. A few of them are very vocal. Rose says hello to all of them. I can see that she wants to pet them, but she stops herself.

"Here she is. *Rosso*, say 'hi' to the nice couple," he says. I feel Rose's fingers tighten in my hand. I have been thinking of us as a couple since we started talking on the phone the last few months. We talked on the phone and texted a few times in the last few months, but I don't think she thinks of us as a couple. I will change that by Monday.

Rosso sticks her head out of her stall and sniffs the air. She is a beautiful chestnut color with ruddy red hair in her mane. I didn't know Rose had carrots in her purse until she asks Alan if *Rosso* could have them. After Alan told her that she loves carrots, she walks up to the horse and lets her sniff her hands. Rose pats her soft mane then offers her one carrot at a time. Rose talks to the horse with a soft voice as I'm getting some information from Alan. The horse lets Rose pet her muzzle while she chops on the carrots. Rose reaches into the stall and runs her fingers through her mane, feeling each strand of hair.

"How is she around other horses?" I ask Alan again. We spoke on the phone about some of the same question, but I like to ask them again when we meet in person. "Does she startle easily?" I need to know how well she will do with the other therapy horses. If she startles easily, I will have to put some extra time into retraining her. I may not have that kind of time.

"She was my wife's barrel racing horse. She is used to the loud sound of a starting pistol and being around other horses. You are looking for another therapy horse. What will she need to do?" Alan asks.

"Like I said when I first spoke to you, the horses need to be patient around the autistic kids that have never been around a horse. Sometimes they can be very loud in their excitement. Our veterans need a mild-mannered horse, so they don't get re-traumatized by a skittish horse. The teens either have their own trauma to work through or have never been around a horse. They come from homes of drug abuse, alcoholism or physical abuse, so they need to trust the horse." I tell him. All my horses get fully evaluated before I decide which program fits them. I look over at Rose whispering in *Rosso's* ear. She looks like she has already made a connection with the horse.

"*Rosso* is eleven years old and has been in rodeos almost her entire life. My wife had such an attachment to her, even as a foal she brought her to each rodeo to school her around other horses, the racket that takes place almost twenty-four/seven and worked with the horse she had entered into the rodeo. I don't think you'll have any problems with her," Alan is saying as he hands me a file with all her awards, updated vaccinations report, and health records. "As you can see, she has no past health issues and the same veterinarian her entire life. She's never been bred either."

"Rose, what do you think?" I ask. Rose is still giving her small carrots and is quietly talking to *Rosso*. I want her to feel like I value her opinion in this sale. I can already see what her answer will be. She has fallen in love with *Rosso*.

"She's wonderful, Michael. I don't know if she will fit into your business. We haven't been talking about the horses for work." *Rosso* picks that second to push Rose's shoulder as she sniffs the air for more carrots.

"Alan, I think she will work well. Can I pick her up Monday morning since I'm in town for a long weekend?" I look over at Rose and see pure joy. She jumps up and down like a little kid. She turns to the horse and tells her she will be coming to Oklahoma. I see her eyes mist over. I don't worry about these tears.

"Sure. I'll be around all morning. Let me know when you're on your way and I'll make sure she gets a good brushing before you get here," he says. We had talked about how much he was asking for her when I first spoke with him. I thought it was a fair price when I spoke with him and I feel no further negotiations are needed now. We finalize the sale with a handshake. I practically have to physically pull Rose away from the horse.

"*Rosso*, I will see you soon. I'll even bring more carrots the next time I see you," she says over her shoulder as we leave the stalls. I like the thought of seeing her again at my home. Rose more so than *Rosso*.

"Nice doing business with you Michael and it was nice meeting you Rose," Alan says as we get into my truck. He keeps his distance and doesn't attempt to shake Rose's hand.

We drive the back road to get to Parker Road. Rose can't contain her excitement. She's talking a mile a minute about how gentle the horse was when taking a carrot out of her hand. Rose says it felt like the horse was kissing her palm. She explains how the hairs around her mouth tickled her fingers.

"Do you think the kids will like her?" I ask her. I'm drawing her into the thought process I have to be in when deciding on a new horse. I saw how gentle she was with Rose and how comfortable Rose was with her. She didn't startle when we came up to her stall or bolt when Rose reached for her. Granted, if a horse smells treats, they usually calm down and go towards the food. I think I will start her with the teens and then try her with the autistic kids. She may change a little when she gets to Oklahoma, but I think I'm fairly sure of her temperament.

"I think the kids will love her," she says, still on the energy high. "Thank you so much for including me today. Being around *Rosso* today, I found a release for my anxiety," he says looking at me quickly. "I'm not saying I was anxious around you."

"I have always found peace around the horses. I need to introduce you to each horse in the stables. You will find each one of them to be different, but they can all soothe a variety of emotions," I tell her. I wanted her to feel free to talk about her anxiety. I know she gets nervous around men and now I wonder if the horses will actually be the best thing for her. I still have the horse that sent me to the hospital. My family thought I would get rid of him, but he was my first horse and I love him dearly. The horse wasn't the only cause for my accident. If I had been paying attention, I wouldn't have the problems I have now.

"I would love that. I can see myself going to the horses after a hectic day and letting all my stress and worry go." She's looking out the window again. I can see the corner of her lips smile. When she looks over at me, I see her smile reaching all the way to her eyes. I love that she is thinking about being at my place at the end of a day. After she relaxes with the horses, she can come up to the house, eat dinner with me, watch a movie, or we can wash up in the large, Jacuzzi bath then make love in my king size bed.

"I'm sure *Rosso* and Chestnut would love that. Wait until you see the progress we have made with Chestnut! He is like a different horse all together," I say and hope she doesn't see the bulge that has started. I need to remember to keep my mind out of the bedroom when I'm driving. I have no way of adjusting my jeans with the small confines of the truck.

CHAPTER 7

"Any idea what you would like to do for dinner?" I ask her as we head north towards the house. I love my sister, but I'm hoping for alone time with Rose. I can always cook her something. I have a few meals that I cook for myself all the time. I know I won't burn those. She made breakfast so it's my turn. I don't care if we go out or order in as long as I'm with her.

"I think Lily is working a catering job today. She's usually exhausted if it's a large job. She would have baked everything yesterday but doing set up and break down today will get her tired. I think Brady is working a late shift today, too," she tells me. It sounds like it's just us for dinner.

"Do you want to go out for dinner?" I ask her. She hesitates rather than answer me right away.

"I'd rather stay home. I'm not much for going out to dinner if I don't have to." I see her tense up. Her hands go from flat on her lap to curled fists in five seconds. She's not afraid to be around people in general, but I can see there is an issue we need to talk about. As a nurse she will be around people every day. Granted, she will be helping them.

"I can grill up chicken or make it easy and do hamburgers or hot dogs," I suggest. I'd rather not be grilling at Lily's because then I would feel like I have to invite her for dinner. "Or if we want to make it easier, we can order in. I saw an Indian place around the corner from your place," I say trying to remember what other places I saw when I drove into town. I hear her saying yum, so I continue with my suggestions. "There is the Mexican place across the street from the Indian and I think I also saw an Anthony's pizza down the street." I give her a moment to think about what she wants to do.

"Let me call Lily then we can decide." She pulls out her phone from her purse, looks at me with a playful smile and dials. I have no idea what she's thinking, but that smile reminds me of her innocence. "Hi Lily. I was calling to see if we are doing dinner with you two tonight," she says, listening to whatever Lily is saying. "Okay. We can meet for brunch with you two tomorrow." She says goodbye to Lily and then tucks her phone back into her purse. She turns towards me with that same playful smile lighting up her face.

"I take it we are on our own tonight for dinner," I say with my own smile on my face. I don't let my mind wander right now. I have to keep my thoughts out of the bedroom so that I can get through the rest of the day. We haven't even had lunch yet and I'm trying not to jump forward to tonight.

"Yes. She has another two hours with the baby shower job. I never thought people would hire a catering company for a baby shower. Lily said there's over fifty people at the party. She has to keep replenishing the trays." I notice her hands are playing with the bottom of her top "I have orders not to even think about calling her or disturbing her tonight. She said she wants to get home, take a bubble bath and put her feet up for the rest of the night. Brady won't be home until after dinner. He's working security at the Rockies baseball game." We pull into her neighborhood and I realize we didn't pick up anything for lunch.

"I hope you have something for lunch in the refrigerator. I know I can't make it all the way to dinner without eating," I say as the thought of nibbling on her for a small treat races through my mind.

"Brady always keeps the place stocked with the basics. There is soup, peanut butter and jelly, and I think he picked up turkey and cheese for me. Any of those sound good to you?" she asks. I pull in front of my trailer and park my truck on the street. I'm sure I would eat asparagus, which I hate, if she put it in front of me right now. I can't think about anything but how I would love to kiss her pale pink lips and let my lips wander lower and enjoy her sweet taste for lunch. I watch her hips sway from side to side as we walk up to the house. I want to grab her hips and make them sway in a different way.

"Turkey and cheese sound great." She opens the door and we both head for the bathrooms to wash the horse smell and hair off our hands. Rose's shirt is covered in horsehair. I hear her yell back to me that she needs to change her shirt and then she'll meet me in the kitchen. I grab the first shirt I come across and then head down the hallway to the kitchen. I hear her moving around in her room as I pass by her door. I'm about to knock and tell her that I'll start on the sandwiches when I catch a glimpse of blue moving away from the bed. I stand in front of her door, with my hand up to knock, looking through the opening of her door. She didn't completely close the door and now I get to see the most beautiful vision I have ever seen. My eyes lock onto her blue lacy bra. She grabs a blue top, that matches my eyes, from the closet and looks up to sees me staring at her. She holds my eyes as she pulls the shirt over her head. I know I should move or at least look away, but I can't. I'm mesmerized by her eyes looking straight into mine. I'm still standing with my hand up like I'm about to knock when she opens the door. I'm totally shocked when she rests her hands on my chest and steps up on her toes to kiss my lips. It is a short whisper of a kiss, but it's a kiss. She moves past me fast and I don't even think to kiss her back. I tell myself that she is obviously getting more comfortable around me as I adjust my jeans. I walk through the living room and enter the kitchen. I think I have my body under control until I walk into the room and see Rose leaning into the refrigerator. Her jeans are stretching over her backside nicely. I'm staring at her hips when she turns around and catches me. She smiles up at me and brings all the sandwich makings to the counter. She turns on the radio then gets a knife out of the draw in front of her.

"Do you want a plate, or will a paper towel be okay?" she asks. I see her hips start to sway to the song on the radio.

"Paper towel works for me, less dishes to clean." I go to stand next to her. I rip off two paper towels for us and place them on the counter under the bread she is handing me. The mayonnaise, turkey, and cheese are between up, so I make my sandwich as she makes hers. We are both quiet and in our own minds, either listening to the song, or thinking about our day. The silence is refreshing. I don't feel like I have to keep up a conversation with her. We turn around at the same time to sit at the large table Brady left in the kitchen when he moved in with my sister. I'm over six feet and it still makes me feel small. I sit in the chair at the end of the table and Rose sits on the bench next to me. She gets back up and heads back to the refrigerator for drinks. The Cobalt blue of her shirt really brings out the gold in her eyes. She left her hair down today and I love how it swings across her back when she walks. It reminds me that her hips are swaying back and forth to have her hair do that.

"Is lemonade okay with you?" she asks. She already has the glass pitcher in her hands. I see the lemon slices floating at the top with the ice cubes. If I close my eyes, I can hear the ice clinking against the glass and smell the lemon mixing with the floral scent that I know is Rose's natural scent. I wonder if she intentionally made a new pitcher this morning. Now that she knows I love everything lemon, it makes sense to have lemonade for us to drink.

"That works." I respond. "Everything I Shouldn't be Thinking About" by Thompson Square is playing softly in the background. I'm listening to the lyrics as she raises on her toes to gets down glasses from the cabinet. "Do you need help with that?" I ask her as I enjoy a peek of skin when the t-shirt raises above her jeans. I'm not sure, but I think I see a tattoo when the shirt lowers back over the waist of her jeans. If it is a tattoo, I'm sure I only saw a small fraction of it. She brings the pitcher and glasses to the table without answering me. I reach for the pitcher and pour us each a full glass of the yellow liquid. In our silence I listen to the chorus lines of the song. I smile at some of the words. A lot of the song fits my exact thoughts.

"Thanks for lunch." I smile around the bite I take. I'm a simple guy and I'm enjoying a simple sandwich and lemonade with the woman I can see spending the rest of my life with. I need to tell her about my accident and the diagnosis of chronic short-term memory loss. In the little bit of time I have known her, I don't see her turning me away because of it. Rose is sweet, gentle, kindhearted, and compassionate. But like me, she has her own story to tell. I really want to talk about this while I'm here so that when she comes to Oklahoma, for her job interviews, it will be behind us and we can move forward.

"You don't have to thank me. You made your own sandwich. I'm sorry I didn't think about getting something from the store," she says while taking her last bite. "It's a good thing Brady stocked the refrigerator for me. I usually eat with them when I'm down here. He takes care of me by stocking the refrigerator with drinks and leftovers, if Lily has any." She starts playing with the paper towel in front of her. I'm taking my last bite when she rips the paper. I reach over and place my hand on top of hers.

"What do you want to do this afternoon?" I'm hoping she doesn't want to go back out. I want to enjoy the time with her, and only her. Without being obligated to spend dinner with our siblings, we have a lot of hours to fill prior to bedtime.

"I thought we could have a movie marathon. Brady left a lot of movies here. Lily said he has too many cop and military movies for her liking, so she made him keep them here," she tells me. "I grew up on them, so none of them bother me."

"That sounds good," I say as we throw away the paper towels and refill our glasses. Rose puts the pitcher back in the refrigerator as I head to the den to start looking for a movie. I remember looking through a lot of them last night. Brady has good taste with the John Wayne collection. He's a must watch for a true cowboy and I have my favorites of course. I even like a few of his military movies. I noticed a few of Clint Eastwood's better movies, too. "We can decide on dinner later." I raise my voice thinking she is still in the kitchen. I startle when I hear her answer me from right behind me.

"I'm sorry. I didn't mean to scare you," she says. "I was trying to look around you to see which movies you're looking at." I'm squatting down in front of the lower level of movies in the bookcase. She places her hand on my shoulders and my world stops. I can't breathe. I can't move. I'm consumed with her scent floating around my head and the lightning bolts shooting down from her hands straight to my heart. She leans into my back to pull out a movie above my head. The contact is pure pleasure and pain. "Instead of only John Wayne or Clint Eastwood, why don't we pick a couple movies that are all westerns?" she suggests as she's pulling out a few DVDs. She turns to set the DVDs down by the television. My back and shoulders feel cold without her warmth touching them. The flowery scent floats away with her.

"Which movies did you pick out?" I ask as I pull my large body back up. I step next to her and she lifts each movie for me to see. I have seen all of them. Her selection surprises me. She really did pick out a wide variety. *Butch Cassidy and the Sundance Kid, Rio Bravo, The Outlaw Josey Wales, Silverado,* and *Blazing Saddles.* She got all the big actors covered and I like that she threw in a couple of comedies. "Have you seen all of these?" I ask her. We'll watch any she hasn't seen first then move onto the ones she is familiar with. After dinner if we are watching one, we've both see, we can talk. Maybe I can massage her feet again, hopefully without her falling asleep.

It turns out we have both seen all five. We start with *The Outlaw Josey Wales.* We talk about what is going on in the movie, but nothing else. Rose voices her opinion on how the military treats Josey and his group of men poorly and how awful it is when the men get killed by their boss. We talk about how hard it would be to move forward after your family got killed and what a good man Josey turns into when he protects the family he gets attached to.

We go into the kitchen and refill our glasses and then put in Rio Bravo. Our afternoon flies by with each movie and our commentary on each. I notice how invested Rose gets to each movie. She talks about the good and bad things that happen. She always roots for the good guys and occasionally yells at the television when the bad guys seem to be winning the conflicts. I love seeing her face light up when the good guys win. Her face flushes a beautiful pink and the gold in her eyes take over the brown. I can see Rose in one of these movies yelling at the sheriff to do something or getting all the women and children to safety. However, I like seeing her in a snug pair of jeans and t-shirt rather than layers and layers of skirts and corsets under a dress. Although, now that I think about it, I wouldn't mind seeing her in a corset and panties with thigh high stockings. The gorgeous image going through my mind is starting to set off another reaction in my body. I have to tell myself to get back to watching the movie as my mind wandering will get me in trouble.

Between each movie we get up to stretch our legs and refill our glasses with more lemonade or water. I don't want to drink all the lemonade in one day. I still have tonight and tomorrow to get through. Dinner is approaching after the third movie. She is curled into her side of the couch under a throw blanket. No toes peeking out or foot massages this afternoon. I'm hoping to change that tonight as we watch the comedies. The final credits are scrolling on the screen when I get up and stretch my shoulders and neck. I'm not usually a sedentary person and I find being on the couch all afternoon is making my muscles stiff.

"Have you decided where you want to order from?" I ask her. She's still curled into the corner of couch when she looks up at me. I see her face light up and her smile reaches her eyes. I can look at this face every day of my life. She encourages me to look at life more positively and I can see my future I her eyes. I see a simple wedding with my family and few friends in the garden behind Mom and Dad's house. She's a simple person who would probably want to wear her mother's wedding gown, if her family kept it. I also see daughters with her hazel eyes and brown hair and sons with my dark hair and blue eyes. In that five seconds I see it all.

"I rarely have Indian up in Greeley. I would love to order Naan. There are several different flavors. I like the plain one, but I can do the garlic cheese Naan." She is rushing her words. "Being Italian, you would probably like that one," she says. Her hands are twisting the blanket still covering her legs.

"I like Indian food Rose. Order whatever you would like. I do like the plain Naan, so if that is what you want, go for it," I tell her. I don't know why I'm picking up nervousness from her right now, but I'll figure it out before we finish dinner.

"Okay. I usually order plain Naan, Chicken Tikka Masala or Chicken Korma, and Vegetable Korma. I love their mango and pistachio ice cream. If I'm at the restaurant and they have the buffet set up, I put one of the ice creams on top of their rice pudding. I can do without the dessert since we are ordering in," she says as she finally gets up. She pulls her phone from her back pocket and pulls up the number quickly. "I have it on speed dial for when I'm down here. I guess you could say I really like it," she says and gives me a relaxed smile.

"It's a good thing we have an Indian place about twenty minutes away from me then." She puts in our order and then looks at me. I see the confusion on her face. "Just because I live in Oklahoma doesn't mean we only have steak or BBQ places. Remember I'm within thirty minutes from Tulsa and Oklahoma City," I tell her. I get this reaction when I purchase horses outside of the southern United States. "We do have plays, operas, and musicals at the theater in Oklahoma City," I say.

"I'm sorry. I should know better than to judge where a person lives. I guess I picture Oklahoma as I see it in the movies and television shows. Lilla would tell me that was naïve of me. She's the sister that took me to see Wicked, The Nutcracker, and a few comedies in Denver," she says. Her fingers are twisting the bottom of her shirt. She stops tormenting her shirt and puts her hands in her back pockets. I see her breast push forward when she pushes her shoulders back and I concentrate on looking into her eyes and not down at her perky breasts. "Dinner should be here in fifteen minutes. What do you want to drink with dinner?" she asks over her shoulder as she heads into the kitchen. It was difficult not to look at her breasts and now that she has turned around in front of me, I can replace the lost image with her shapely cheeks. I want to reach out and grab ahold of them. I curl my fingers into the palm of my hands and remind myself to be patient. The time will come when she is ready. I honestly believe we will have a future together, which will include all the fantasies I dream of.

"My body is starting to think it is made out of lemons. How about some water?" Despite the sugar in the lemonade, my body is protesting the sourness of the drink. I feel like my mouth has turned into a lemon itself. I take my glass I have used all day and get ice and water from the dispenser on the outside of the refrigerator. The water hits one of the ice cubes the right way to spit water outside of the glass. I hear Rose giggling as I feel the cold-water soak through my t-shirt. I pull the glass back from where it is still shooting water over the ice cubes. "What are you giggling about?" I put my fingers in my water and flicking it at her. Her giggle turns into a full out laugh. She runs out of the kitchen, trying to get away from me, and I follow with my glass of water intent on putting an ice cube down her shirt. The doorbell rings and our foods here already. I dry my fingers on my jeans and head to the door. I wave her objection off and pay for dinner.

"Yum," Rose continues to say as she carries the bag into the kitchen. I follow her and see her placing each container on the counter buffet style. I place my ice water on the other side of the sink and reach above her head to pull down our plates. She rubs against the side of my chest with her shoulder when she reaches in the drawer for out forks and knives. I hear a small gasp when I continue the closeness and hand her a plate. She moves down the counter, taking something from each container. Her plate is full when she sits at the table. I follow right behind her placing my plate at the head of the table again. She has her eyes closed and I start to wonder is she is saying grace. I never thought to ask about her religion or customs she may have because of it. She takes a big breath in and opens her eyes.

"Were you saying grace?" I ask. I realize we still haven't learned enough about each other yet. I promised myself on the way here I would find out everything about her. So far, I have failed on that promise.

"No. I was taking in the scent of the food. I try and remember little things at big moments in my life. I'm not a religious person. I think of myself as spiritual," she says. I understand that. My parents came from deeply religious families, but they decided when they had us to teach us how to be honest, giving people. We do celebrate the holidays, but not in church. Mom always told us that we don't have to be in a church to have faith. I take in Rose's words and start to focus on what she said.

"What do you mean, a big moment?" I ask. I set my fork down and turn my body so that I'm fully facing her. She is curling the napkin with both hands. I notice this happens whenever she is nervous or anxious. I place my hand over her hers. She gives the napkin a reprieve and curls her fingers with mine. I give her time to answer. Her shoulders are tight and curling forward. She sits this way on the couch, curling into herself. Her eyes are closed again. I continue holding her hands, letting her fingers fidget with mine.

"Michael, I like you a lot. We have talked about me coming down to Oklahoma. I'm ready to move away from Brady if one of the interviews pan out," she is talking with her head down.

"Rose, I've already told you I like you a lot too. We can figure out everything when you move down." I think she is stressed about moving away from Brady and away from her home.

"I'm not worried about moving down. Your Mom and Dad said I could stay with them until I find my own place." She looks up and smiles, a tender look taking over her face. "Your Mom and Dad are great. They told me at Christmas I could stay with them anytime I came down."

"So, what's going on?" I ask. Our food is getting cold, but neither one of us seem to notice. I continue holding her hand and I sit patiently while waiting for her to tell me what she needs to say.

"Michael, I need to tell you what happened to me before I even think about taking a job in Oklahoma. I haven't always been the person you see in front of you today." She sits up straight and pushes her shoulders back.

"Rose, I know we both have things to tell the other but let's eat first. I think we should enjoy this wonderful food first." She starts to speak, and I tell her we have plenty of time to talk. I want to enjoy this meal. She releases my hand and picks up her fork. We do enjoy all of the food. It does remind me of the food I get down home, so she will be happy to know she can order Indian when she moves down. We discuss other foods we like, and she says how sorry she is she can't pick up *Rosso* on Monday and drive down with me.

"I'm sure she would love your attention and the treats she will now expect you to have every time you see her. You only have a few weeks left of school and then graduation. I'll be back in town a few days before everyone gets here." I lay my hand on the table, palm side up, and wait for her to take it. "I want you all to myself. The masses will take over your time when they get here." She takes my offered hand and squeezes it, giving me a small, sweet smile. I can feel the tension coming off of her still. We finish our dinner and clean up the kitchen. Rose suggests we sit in the hot tub again. I know she wants to talk, but is sitting half naked in the hot water the best place to have this discussion? I want to make her happy so if she wants to talk to me sitting in the bubbling water, then that's what we will do.

* * *

Rose is sitting on the same seat as the other night. Her naked shoulders are above the bubbling water. She must be in the same suit. My mind starts to recall the bikini that shows every sexy curve. She has her hair fastened on top of her head, little tendrils escaping the clasp and surrounding her face. I climb in after placing my towel on the hook. I have to remember to get out first this time. I don't want a repeat of last night. Has it only been a day since seeing her in that sexy bikini? It feels like I have been with her a lot longer. I take the same seat, I'm not sure if Rose will want me next to her while telling me her story. I'm sure I know a little bit about what she will reveal to me. I told myself, while getting changed, I will be patient, quiet, and not get angry as she talks. I know I will feel anger towards the person who hurt her, but she doesn't need to see that emotion on my face as she tells me her story. I don't want her to misinterpret my anger. I have no reason to be angry with her.

"I have only talked about this with my family and the therapist I have seen since it happened to me," Rose says as soon as I sit down. She lifts her face and looks into my eyes then lowers her face back down. I can see despair in the short glance she gives me. "Brady was in the police academy. Lilla was trying to finish high school early to get into a design school. Anna was starting vet school. We all had different interests, so we really didn't spend that much time together, outside of dinner. Even those we sometimes ate separately. I knew Charlie for years. I became friends with him when he moved in down the street in third grade. My parents knew his parents through school activities." Her shoulders rise and her chest expands as she takes a deep breath. I see her shoulders lower and then curl forward into her chest. "They never let me go over to his house. When I got older, they explained it was because his parents drank, and they didn't want me over there in case they were drunk. Charlie was allowed to play at my house anytime. Anna even played with us sometimes. After my parents died, he was around a lot. He asked Brady if he could take me to the winter formal at school. Of course, Brady said yes. He thought the dance would help get my spirits up again." Rose glances up at me. I see she needs to tell me her entire story, but all I want to do is reach over and pull her into my arms. I don't need to know the details. I want her to feel safe in my arms and know that I will never intentionally hurt her, ever. I lock my eyes onto hers.

"Anna took me shopping for a fancy dress. I knew we didn't have a lot of money, so I had her take me to several consignment stores. I found a beautiful ankle length, A-line teal dress, that made me feel like a princess when I tried it on. It fit perfectly. I already had a pair of shoes that would go perfectly with it and Lilla let me borrow her clutch that matched. Brady had me try it on for him when he got home that night. He told me I looked like Mom when she would get dressed up for the theater. Lilla did my hair the night of the dance." Her shoulders were curling further inward. She lifts her face up and peeks at me, then lowers it quickly. Even through the steam of the water I can see the tears escaping her eyes and rolling down her cheeks. If I could take away this pain for her, I would. I stay quiet as she continues.

"Brady had class the night of the dance, but Lilla and Anna were both home to take photos. Charlie was in a black suit with a teal tie to match my dress. He was being silly, lifting me in his arms for some of the photos or standing behind me with his arms around me. Lilla commented on how cute we were. He had borrowed his parent's car; I would have to lift the dress up to my knees to climb up into his truck otherwise. I should have known something was wrong on our way to the school. I noticed a sweet scent in the car, but I figured it was his cologne. He had never worn cologne around me. I thought he invited me to the dance as a friend, so I didn't understand when he started grabbing my thigh. We were never physical with each other, not even kissing. I told him he was wrinkling my dress and kept pushing his hand away. When we got to the dance, he went over to hang out with his friends, so I hung out with a few of my friends, too. He finally asked me to dance and apologized. I enjoyed our slow dances and when we danced to "You Are the Woman" he told me he thought of me all the time. He said he wanted to date me. I was surprised because I still thought of him as just a friend. I told him I didn't want to ruin our friendship. He seemed to take it well but asked if we could leave. I told my friends we were leaving and followed him back to the car. He opened my door for me, and as soon as I sat in the seat, he pulled the lever and the seat went flying back." She was looking at the bubbles in front of her. I can see the tears streaming down her face. She doesn't even try to wipe them away. They roll down her face and the hot water engulfs them as they drop off her skin. She can't see my fists under the bubbles. I'm biting my teeth so hard my jaw is starting to hurt. I notice she bounces back and forth from past and present while talking about him.

"He grabs the hem of my dress and pulls it up past my knees. I try and push him away, but he is pushing his other hand into my breast to hold me down. I yell at him to stop and he keeps pulling at my dress until it rips around my waist. I feel my cotton underwear dig into my thighs as he pulls at them." Her voice gets smaller and I really have to listen for her words. The jets are almost louder than her. "He pushes his fingers into me and I scream in pain. He's yelling that he has put up with all my whining about my parents for so long that I owed him. He tries to pull the top of my dress down, but it didn't rip. He pinches my breast threw the material, telling me that he knows I want it. I try yelling for help, but he put his hand over my mouth. I try and bite his hand, but he slaps me. I hit my head on the steering wheel when he flips me over the console. I feel the cold air hit my exposed skin when he throws the back of my dress up over my back. I hear his zipper and try to scream for help again. He pushes my face into the driver's seat and I feel him push into me. I yelled out in pain which only got me pushed into the seat further. I decided then to let him finish and be able to walk away afterwards without getting beaten more. The entire time he was in me, he talked about how much he loves me and how sexy I am. He tells me how this changes our relationship. He wants us to start dating. He finishes and pulls me back through the car. He puts the seat up, helps me sit back up in the seat, straightens my dress and gets behind the wheel and drives me home like nothing happened. Over and over he tells me how much he loves me." Rose's body is noticeably shaking, and her face is swollen and splotchy from crying. I'm not sure if I should reach out for her or not, so I sit there fuming inside. "When we pulled up to my house, I open the door as fast as I could and grab my destroyed dress so that I don't trip over it, then run to the door. He yelled that he would see me tomorrow and pulled away screeching his tires. I locked the door behind me after getting inside and then I collapsed in the hallway. Anna says I was screaming, holding my blood-stained skirt, and crying when she came upstairs to see how the dance was." I lift my arms above the water. I reach out to her, giving her the option to be touched. She leans towards me and I meet her in the middle of the hot tub. "Anna says she drove me to the hospital and called Brady to meet us there. I don't remember most of the hospital." I take a step over to the nearest seat and pull her down into my lap. She wraps her arms around my neck, resting her face against my chest. I feel her soft skin as my hands wrap around her body.

"I do remember waking up in the hospital the next day. Anna was in the room with me. I had stitches on my forehead from where I hit it on the steering wheel. One eye was bruised and swollen from where he hit me. I also had bruises on my breast and thighs." Rose takes a few shallow breaths before continuing. "The doctor came in and told me they did a rape kit in the emergency room. He wanted to know if I was on birth control. Then the nurse came in and gave me a pill. I later found out it was the Plan B pill. I think Brady and Anna made that decision since I was so traumatized." Rose is quiet for a few seconds. "I couldn't look at Brady when he got there. He kept yelling it was his fault. If he had been there this wouldn't have happened. My whole family trusted him, so it was no one fault but Charlie's. It turns out he was already a drunk, like his parents, and had a few drinks prior to picking me up. Brady made sure I saw a therapist right away and I got the help I needed," she says. I move my arm around her legs as she curls them up towards her chest. I image it's as close as she can get to the fetal position while sitting on my lap in the hot tub. Her crying has stopped, but her body is still tense in my arms. I turn my head and place a tender kiss on her forehead. We sit like this until our skin is completely pruned.

"How about I get you out of the hot tub, get us both some water, and we can finish talking inside?" I ask her. Her face tips upward and I can see her puffy, red eyes now.

"Michael, its' okay if you don't want to be with me anymore. I understand," she says as she uncurls herself from my lap.

"Rose, let's get out of this water and talk inside." I get out first and hold her hand as she climbs out of the hot water. We both wrap our towels around us and walk into the kitchen. She gets us both a bottle of water from the refrigerator as I sit down on the chair where not that long ago, I was enjoying a meal with her. When she goes to sit on the bench, I hold out my hand for her to come sit on my lap. Again, I give her the option and she grasp my hands and stands next to me. "Please, come sit," I say as I pat my lap with my other hand. She looks into my eyes and must see something that she didn't expect because she slowly lowers herself onto my lap. I wrap an arm around her back and rest the other over her thighs. We both have our towels on, so I'm not actually able to touch her skin, which is probably a good thing right now.

"I'm happy you had your family's support and it was good you got help right away. A lot of rape victims don't. Your brother mentioned that you had issues, and then told me he took care of it and you. I'm guessing that means Charlie got arrested." I look at her face as she nods her head up and down. "Did he go to jail?" I'm trying to get her to tell me the rest of it, but all she does is nod her head up and down again. "Rose, honey, look at me," I say and gently lift her chin with my finger. "I have to tell you about a conversation I have heard a lot, recently, in my parent's home. It seems that all the Corsco members fall in love very quickly, some even experience love at first sight. Lily had a wonderful marriage to Adrian, but it wasn't meant to be for life. She tells us how quickly she cared for your brother, but she felt like she was cheating on Adrian, so she didn't seek out a relationship with Brady. Your brother is stubborn and stuck it out until Lily realized she needed to get on with her life and be happy." I run my finger over her cheek, wiping away the tears that have started again. "Nick came up here to check up on Lily. Our family worries about each other and when she mentioned a man, we needed to know she would be safe. He tells us how Anna pushed every button for him. She was spirited and stubborn, just what he needed. He tells us brothers, after he had sex with her, he was completely blown away. He knew then he had to convince her to come home with him." Her tears slow as I tell the love stories of my family. "Seth saw Gabby at the clinic, while they were still getting it set up for Anna's practice, and told us that she was going to be the mother of his children. She had a lot of baggage and he helped her through it. There is nothing you could tell me about your past that will change my mind. I love you no matter what happened to you in the past. You are going to have to get that through your stubborn head." She gives me a small smile. "I want you to move down to Oklahoma because you want to. In time, I want you to move in with me, but we can take as much time as you need. I will never push you into anything, Rose. Believe me when I say this relationship goes as slow or as fast as you want," I say and kiss her forehead. Her arms tighten around me.

"I'm not afraid of you being like Charlie. My therapist tells me all the time I am who I want to be. My past does not define me, but it has taken me a long time to not feel like used goods. I'm still working on that, actually. If you give me time to see us as a couple, I think I will get there," she says lifting her eyes upward. I see the pain still in her eyes and I decide to work on bringing joy into each and every day for her.

"I can do that for you Rose. We still need to talk about my issues, but I think we need the night off from serious. Let's go wash off this chlorine and watch *Silverado*. We both need a good laugh," I say, knowing I will try not to think of Charlie but can't guarantee it. We take showers in our own showers and meet up in front of the television in our night clothes. I don't take the extra time under the water to take care of myself while fantasizing about Rose this time. Tonight, has been an eye opener on how the woman I love had her first sexual experience with violence and disgust. Rose said she doesn't date so I'm sure she hasn't had any other since then either.

The movie makes us smile and laugh. Rose is curled in the corner with the throw over her body. I'm sitting next to her this time, with her legs stretching over mine. I massage her feet and hear her breathing slow while sleep overtakes her body. The movie ends and I don't have the heart to move her. I know I will be in pain in the morning, but I lay my head on the other side of the couch and share the space with her to sleep. Our legs intertwine in the center of the couch with another throw covering us. We sleep like this all night.

CHAPTER 8

Sunday morning finds us complaining about our stiff muscles from sleeping on the couch. With brunch at Lily and Brady's not for a few hours away, we drink our coffee and tea while snacking on the lemon roll, she made the other day. We enjoy the morning hours in our comfortable pajamas.

"How are you today, Rose?" I ask her as I sit down next to her at the table. She is no longer red and splotchy. Instead, her skin is shining with a healthy olive glow. Her hair has a just got out of bed sexy look. Her eyes are more brown than green this morning. I haven't seen a tear since waking up. I don't want to remind her of sharing her story with me last night, but I want to know where her head is this morning. I still need to share my story with her.

"I'm doing okay. Thank you for listening last night. I know it was a lot to hear." Her voice dips into the volume of a whisper. She picks at her roll while talking to me. She hasn't looked at me since sitting down. I lay my hand down on the table and give her the choice to reach out or not. I will always give her the choice from now on. She glances over at my hand but does not take it. I leave it there.

"I will always be here for you Rose. I don't know if you caught it last night, but I said I love you and I meant it then and I mean it now. I love you Rose," I say. She reaches for my hand, slowly, and curls her fingers into mine. I see that she is a lot like

Chestnut. Working with a skittish horse is a lot like working with a skittish person who needs to find trust in another before letting themselves feel again. Loving this skittish woman will be my biggest challenge. A challenge I gladly accept.

"I heard you last night and I hear you now. I don't know what to say. I know I care for you a lot," she says. She stands up, letting go of my hand, and moves behind me. She places her hands on my shoulders and I reach up to cover both of them with mine. I am surprised when she leans forward and slides her hands down over my chest, connecting them over my sternum. I feel her breath on the back of my neck as she rests her chin on one shoulder. I can feel her breasts touching my shoulder blades. "I know I can trust you, Michael. I still need to see myself as you do. I have seen myself as a victim for years and only recently, through therapy, see myself as a survivor. Please be patient with me and I will try to get to that place where we can be a couple," she says quietly.

"Rose, I will give you all the time you need. When you move down, we can start by hanging out. Okay?" I ask her. I think the more time we spend together the more likely she will be able to move forward with me by her side.

"That sounds like a good plan. I can come over and see Chestnut and *Rosso* on my days off." She pulls her hands back up over my chest and off my shoulders. Instead of returning to her seat, she stands at my side. "I understand your family has a boat docked at the lake near your place. I would love to see it." I look up at her. She hasn't moved away.

"Yes, we do. The entire family uses it. Nick and Anna took it out for her to take pictures. I think she has some of them on the walls of the clinic and their house." I turn in my chair so that my body is facing hers. I part my legs so that she is standing between them. I lift my hands to hers and she takes both of them. She sits herself sideways on my leg with the table in front of her. I place an arm around her back and lay my hand over her hip. I place the other joined hand on her lap. "I'm sure both horses will love that. You haven't seen Chestnut in a long time, I'm sure he will remember you though." I watch her face as we talk about the horses and the boat. Her eyes sparkle with green slivers as we talk about the horses. I can see the trust she has given me, and I will never abuse it.

"We need to be at brunch in a couple hours. I would like to hear your story Michael. I want our last night together to be less stress and more fun. That is, if you're ready to tell me," she says.

"I have memory issues," I tell her as I adjust her on my legs. I don't want her to get up while I tell her my story. I like the fact that she is comfortable sitting there. "I was still getting my business together and buying horses. I had a vision of what my stables should look like. Before I could build all the stables I needed, I put a new horse in the row of stalls I had built." She squeezes my hands and looks into my eyes as I go on. "With horses you should try and have them with similar temperament horses in the neighboring stalls. I didn't have the space to do that yet, so I put the new horse I had picked up that day next to my horse. I have had Midnight from the beginning," I tell her. My thumb is rubbing circles on Rose's hand. I see concern in her eyes, and I haven't even gotten to the bad part yet. "Midnight has been around so many horses I never gave it a thought that there would be a problem with him. It turns out the female I put next to him was coming into heat. The owner I had bought her from didn't tell me and I never asked. I have learned from my early rookie mistakes. I was in Midnight's stall brushing him down for the night. I stepped behind him, like I've done a million times, and he reared up and then kicked me when he came back down." Rose lifts one hand to her mouth and gasps. "He got me on my forehead and left temple with his hoof," I say as I remember the pain. "I didn't have the staff I have now, so I wasn't found until Nick came by to check on the new horse the next morning. I was lucky that Midnight didn't hurt me more while I was lying there unconscious." Rose looks at my hair. I'm lucky my scars are covered by my hairline.

"Oh, goodness! Michael!" I see her need to touch my head, but she stops moving her hand halfway between her face and mine. I take her hand and pull it back to her lap. Her fingers tense up in mine. My left hand starts rubbing her hip. I need to do something with both my hands so that I don't reach up to the scar. Rubbing the scar became a bad habit when I was around people after the accident.

"Nick took me to the hospital. The doctor put a total of twenty-two stitches in my head and told me I had a severe concussion. Because I was out all night, I had to stay overnight for observation and have a neurologist run a whole bunch of tests" I tell her. I continue running my thumb over the one hand she has on her lap. I need the physical contact as I tell her the rest. "All the tests showed I would have permanent short-term memory loss. My employees are aware of my difficulties and work with me if I have any problems during the day." I look into her eyes and see concern for me. She doesn't say anything and I'm getting concerned she won't want to get involved with me now. "It gets worse at night or if I have a very stressful day." I'm waiting for her to say something. The longer she's quiet, the more nervous I get.

"How bad is your short-term memory loss? Is it every day?" she asks. I'm relieved she is finally saying something.

"I think I have a small amount every day. I'll remember what day of the week it is and what group is there that day, but I might forget a few of the people in the class until I see them. I remember all of their names, but my mind won't remember a specific person is scheduled in class that day." I adjust her on my leg and lower my head to avoid her eyes while I get my thoughts together.

"Do you lose blocks of time in your memory?" she asks. Being a nurse, I'm sure she has been taught about neurological issues. She lifts her arm and I feel her fingers running through my hair at my temple. I lean into her palm and close my eyes. It's so soothing.

"Not so much. Simple things like names of horses or staff names I sometimes have to search for. I get frustrated with myself when I can't come up with something I should know! My staff came up with the idea for them to always have an official Corsco Equine Therapy name tag. Also, each client has a simpler pin on name tag. It does help me not get so frustrated." I open my eyes and see sympathy in hers.

"Rose, I don't tell most people because they give me the look you are giving me." I sit straight up and pull her hand out of my hair. "I don't want your sympathy." I know my tone of voice has changed to one of irritation, but I can't help it. "I do fine and don't want or need anyone's sympathy." I see the hurt in her eyes as I start to slide her off my lap so that I can stand.

"Michael, you misinterpreted my look. I only mean to show empathy. I understand not wanting to get sympathy, believe it or not." She puts her hands around my neck and runs her fingers in the curls sitting on the collar of my shirt. "I didn't want people knowing what happened to me. No one knows what to say so they whisper behind your back about how awful it is that it happened to me, or they say something stupid like, 'You're a survivor you'll get past this.' I wanted to look at them and say 'Yes it was horrible and is for everyone who gets raped, not just me. You have no idea who I am or what I can or can't get through.' Or my favorite is 'I'm sorry.' Really are you or is that all you can say. Of all people, Michael, I understand not wanting sympathy!" she raises her voice at me.

"I'm sorry I got angry, it's a knee jerk reaction. I know you understand." I lift my hand off her lap and run it up her arm. I take a deep breath and relax my shoulders. I feel her fingers on my neck again. Rose leans her head forward until our foreheads are touching. I smell lemon on her breath and a fruity smell coming from her hair that has fallen forward and is surrounding our faces. She rubs her nose back and forth on mine. It reminds me of when my Mom put me to bed as a kid and gave me Eskimo kisses. The corners of my lips curve up as the past memory and the present action by Rose meet up.

"Thank you for sharing your story with me Michael. I can hardly wait to meet your staff; they must be remarkable people. I can only imagine the patience they have working with the kids and adults that come to you. They work with you every day and probably don't even think about your memory loss. I'm sure you get frustrated every day, but its' part of the job to the people working for you," she says. I'm looking into her beautiful green and gold eyes. I start thinking about having her in my daily life. I know Rose is a kindhearted, compassionate person who wouldn't see my issues as needing to be dealt with or tolerated. I just lost my head for a moment and bunched her in with others from my past. She is the perfect woman for me.

"How about we get dressed and go for a walk?" I ask her. I need to burn off my negative energy that spiked. I know how I would like to burn it off, but that isn't part of our relationship yet. We both took showers last night, so I know I don't need one. I hope she doesn't either. I can see my fantasies running through my mind now while she is under the spray of the shower.

"I have a suggestion," she says. She stands up and I feel the warmth of her body leave me. I liked having her on my lap. "How about I take you to where Lily works, and we can pick up some pastries to add to brunch?" Rose continues to talk over her shoulder as she leaves the kitchen area.

"That sounds great," I say, following her like a puppy. Nick and Anna told us about Mary's Café over our Sunday family dinner. It sounded like a place Lily fit into perfectly. I'd like to see it for myself though.

"I bet I can be ready before you," Rose squeals running through the living room. Her smile and laughter are contagious as I pass her in the hallway.

"You're on," I yell on my way past the door she is closing behind her. I slept in the t-shirt I had on yesterday, so I reach in my bag for a clean one and a clean pair of socks and boxer briefs. I pick up my jeans from the floor and take all the clothes in the bathroom with me. I drop my pajama pants as I grab my toothbrush. I wet it and put toothpaste on it as I step out of pants, kicking them to the side of the bathroom along with my shirt. I bend over and put my legs into my soft, black boxer briefs and pull them up with one hand as I start brushing my teeth. I reach down for my jeans and start pulling them up as I spit the toothpaste in the sink. I slosh water in my mouth as I pull on my grey Oklahoma Thunder t-shirt on. I spit the water out and reach for the brush to drag it through my hair. I sit on the toilet and pull on my socks then head into the other room to find my shoes. I'm walking out of the room fully dressed and ready in under five minutes. There is no way she's done. Woman always take longer than men. Her door opens as I'm about to pass and she runs right into me.

"Ow," she huffs out as she bounces off of my chest and falls into the wall behind her. I reach out with both of my hands to stabilize her as Rose grabs my arms for support. Her brown high-lighted hair is brushed away from her face in a high ponytail. She has a little glitter on her eyelids and a touch of pink gloss on her lips. She also opted for a pair of jeans and sneakers. Her top has my jeans getting tight. The dark blue peasant top dips low enough to show a hint of cleavage. The front lacing is taunting me to reach out and pull them free. We stand there, holding each other's arm, and stare at each other for a few moments. I actually shake my head to clear the wanton thoughts going through my mind.

"Are you okay?" I ask. We release each other and I instantly miss the contact.

"I'm fine," she says. She is looking at my lips before raising her eyes to mine. "I have to brush my teeth and I'm ready," she tells me.

"I won then," I let her know. I smile at her as she walks into the bathroom in the hallway. I follow her and stand in the doorway as she takes care of her teeth. I know some couples want privacy while they are in the bathroom. She doesn't seem to mind me watching her brush her teeth.

"Okay, you won," she says with a mouthful of toothpaste. "What did you win?" she asks, lowering her head to spit. She turns her head towards me expecting an answer.

"I don't know. We never said what the prize would be." I think maybe a simple kiss would be a great gift, but I don't want to step over the comfortable place we have found today.

"How about you get to pick the pastries today?" she asks as she wipes her mouth on the hand towel. I can see this is definitely her bathroom. The blue window curtain, dark blue hand towels, light blue washcloth, blue-grey body towels, and blue ocean scene for the shower curtain say blue is the design color of this room. I'm glad I like the color blue. Although, I would let her paint my house purple if that's what she likes.

"I was going to suggest a small kiss, but pastries work too." I walk down the hallway and into the living room behind her. I'm admiring her curvy shape. I don't even think about taking her car as we head to my truck. I get a quick peek of her lower back as she climbs into the cab. Again, I see a glimpse of the top of a tattoo.

* * *

The Sunday morning church crowd is forming a long line to the counter. I look around the small eating area of the Café. There is a waiting line for seating, so this must be an extremely popular place to eat. I smell bacon and bread as we go through the door.

"I guess this is the place to be on Sunday morning." I take a step to the left to see the display counter and a lot of the items are gone. "Is there going to be anything left for us to take to Lily's by the time we get up there?" I ask Rose. She doesn't answer my question; she gives me a knowing smile instead.

"Have any idea what you want to get?" she asks as we get closer to the counter. I see people order breakfast sandwiches, bagel with flavored cream cheese, pastries, and loaves of bread to take back home. There is a man cooking behind a small prep area along with two young ladies running the cash registers and getting everyone's orders.

"I can't see what is left, so how do I know what I want to get?" I ask her, still receiving the same smile. We are second in line and I see an elderly woman fill the display cabinets with fresh items. "You knew they would replace them, didn't you," I accuse her. I bump my shoulder into hers.

"Rose. You're back. Lily didn't tell me you were in town. Does this mean you are done with classes?" the elderly lady asks when she sees us standing in line.

"I have a couple more weeks then finally graduation." Rose is giving her a hug when she comes around the counter. "This is Michael, Lily's brother," she tells her. "Michael, this is Mary. She owns the Café."

"Nice to meet another one of Lily's family members," Mary says as she wraps her arms around my waist. This woman is tiny next to me, but her hug feels like a large bear is squeezing me. She steps back and looks at me from top to bottom. "Rose, you must snatch this one up," she says, winking at me. "Do they grow all men so sexy in Oklahoma, or is it only Lily's family?" She pats my arm and walks behind the counter laughing.

"Mary!" Rose shakes her head and I can see the color inching up her cheeks.

"I think it's the Oklahoma air. It makes us all big and strong." I tease back. Rose lifts her head up and sees me winking at her. "One day you'll have to come down and see." I start looking at the display cabinet and most of the items have been refilled.

"What'll you have," Mary asks us. I see Rose looking at the cheese Danish along with the cherry Danish next to them. I know I won the bet, but I ask her if she would like one of each. I move on to ordering several flavors of muffins. I see the cinnamon rolls, but after eating Rose's lemon-flavored ones, I don't think I will ever have a plain cinnamon roll again. Mary boxes our order up and tells us to say hi to Lily. She said the catering job yesterday was a complete success. One of the cashiers rings us up and we make our way through the waiting crowd.

We drive back to the house talking about Mary. She reminds me of my mom with her teasing. We knock on Lily's door and hear her yell to come in. I open the door and let Rose walk in front of me with the goodies. I love watching this woman walking. Her ponytail is swaying back and forth in time with her hips. As we pass the family photos on the wall, I stop Rose.

"This is Midnight," I point out the horse I told her about this morning. I see concern in her eyes as she looks at me. I take a step next her and put my arm around her waist. "It's okay Rose. This picture was taken the week prior to the accident." Rose rests her head on my shoulder as she looks at the photo. "I like that Lily put this one on her wall. She knows how much I have always loved that horse." I place a kiss on her forehead, and we head into the kitchen.

"Hey guys, I took Michael over to the Café. He met Mary," Rose says as I place the box of goodies on the counter. Lily is cutting up fruit at the sink, so Rose offers her a side hug. Brady comes in the room, apologizing for his tardiness. He heads straight to his sister and gives her a big hug then turns back to me and shakes my hand. "Is that bacon I smell?" he asks to no one in particular.

I see the dishes, silverware, and cups stacked on the table, so I walk over and start putting the place settings together at each seat. Brady follows me and asks how I'm doing. I hear the question he really wants to ask in his voice. I look over my shoulder and see Rose helping Lily plate the fruit.

"Rose told me what happened to her and also about you getting her the help she needed. She said she is still seeing the therapist sometimes. I asked her if the guy got jail time after testifying in court." I look up at Brady and see the anger he feels in his eyes.

"He got jail time, but not enough in my opinion." He takes a deep breath and slowly lets it out. "I'm glad she told you. My baby sister deserves a good guy in her life." He bumps into my shoulder then tells me if I hurt her, he will come after me, too.

"The same goes for you, but I'm pretty sure we have great ladies to share our lives with, we would never even think about it." I see his raised eyebrows as he looks back at his sister.

Rose brings the dish of fruit to the table as Lily gets the plate of pancakes and bacon out of the oven and sets them on the table. I bring the box of muffins and Danish over. Brady brings the coffee pot over and fills my cup along with his own then gets the teapot and serves Rose and Lily.

"Mary said the catering job was a success," I tell Lily. Lily fills us in on all the details from the other day. I guess the day was a trial run for a large hotel. Someone had rented out a conference room for a large baby shower. So many people came in from out of town, it made sense to have the party at the hotel. The hotel wants to contract someone for all their baking needs. We talk about the Café and if any of the items we bought today were made by her. It turns out all of them were. I tell her about what Mary said about her brothers. She laughs it off.

"She met Nick the last time, so I'm not surprised she said something. She is a big flirt even at her age." We finish our brunch and go to sit outside. The weather is beautiful. Brady and Rose talk about the years Denver received snow in April. I'm glad the weather has been good for my trip. I wouldn't want to load the horse tomorrow in snow. Driving I-70 east from Colorado to Kansas also gets windy and blowing snow is never a good thing.

"So, any plans for the rest of your trip? You're leaving tomorrow morning, right?" Lily asks. She seems a little off, but I assume it's from the busy day she had yesterday. Maybe Brady kept her up too late. I know what I would have been doing after the hot tub if Rose and I were further into our relationship, it wouldn't have been falling asleep watching Silverado.

"We haven't discussed it. Why? Do you want to do something?" I ask her. Her face is starting to look a little green and she runs back into the house. "What was that all about?" I ask Brady. Rose looks at both of us and smiles. I have no idea what she is smiling about. "What?" I ask her. Brady looks as lost as I do.

Brady stands to go after Lily, but Rose stops him. She tells him to give her a few moments. His patience runs out after a minute. He heads back into the kitchen, calling for her. They are gone for several minutes and Rose and I stay out on the deck, enjoying the warming sun.

Rose and I are talking about things we can do for my last afternoon and evening here. I remind her that I will be back in town the week before her graduation. I know we will all be busy picking up family from the airport and driving to Greely for the ceremony. We haven't finished nailing down everything for the graduation party, but I know Lily will have everything planned with Mom prior to her getting to town. I don't care what we do as long as I'm with her.

"Sorry about that," Lily says as her and Brady come back out to the deck. Lily doesn't look much better, but she and Brady are smiling. He pulls her to sit on his lap when they come over to the sitting area. He places his hand on her stomach and it hits me.

"Oh my god, you're pregnant, aren't you?" I ask.

"I think so. I had the bacon and it didn't sit well. You know how much I love honey hickory bacon. I'll run to the store and get a test so this big lug here," she hugs Brady head to her chest, "will stop freaking out." Brady lifts his head to kiss her. He has that stupid, funny look on his face. He hasn't realized yet what my father will say when Lily tells them. I'm sure the shot gun will come up with him from Oklahoma.

"Why don't Rose and I go pick one up? I want to get something for dinner anyway. You guys enjoy your evening in peace and quiet. We can spend more time together when I come up for the graduation," I tell them. I'm standing up, grabbing Rose's hand and heading out the side fence. We can both hear the happy, delighted crying as we make it out the gate.

We get into the truck, saying nothing. We are both smiling and beyond happy for them. I know Lily was planning on starting a family when Adrian got back from his last deployment. Those plans changed when he got killed while on a mission. Now she gets another chance at motherhood with Brady.

"I don't even know if they have talked about kids. I'm quite sure Brady planned on doing it in the correct order, engagement, marriage, and then kids. I'm sure your dad will have something to say," Rose says as we pull away from the house. "He's never talked to me about wanting kids. After raising all three of us, I kind of figured he'd want a break." She looks at me with a question in her eyes.

"I don't know if they discussed children or not, but I know Lily has always wanted a couple of kids." I reach across the seat and curl my fingers with hers. "Just so you know, I have always wanted children. How many will be up to you." There is no wavering in my comment. If she only wants one, that's fine. If she wants six that's fine, too. I am more than willing to add onto the house for more children. She's not looking at me. Her head is down, and she is playing with the laces on the front of her shirt with her free hand. "I don't mean to pressure you. I know you have a career to start and we need to move forward in our relationship before we even talk about children. I wanted you to know so there is no question moving forward," I tell her and finally receive a small smile. "Now let's go get something for dinner. I was thinking a salad, pasta with a Bolognese sauce, and Italian bread," I suggest it as we enter the store. I let her pick out everything she wants in the salad, since I picked them out the first night in town. Can that only be two days ago? She picks out Penne pasta and I tell her to never tell my mother I used a jarred Bolognese sauce as I place the jar in our basket.

"Do you want beer or wine tonight?" she asks me as we head to the cashier stand. I don't think alcohol is a wise decision if we sit in the hot tub again, so I tell her no. I'm placing our items on the belt when I hear a woman's voice saying something to me. I'm so wrapped up in my conversation with Rose. I hadn't noticed anyone else in the store.

"Is this the special lady you bought the flowers for?" It's the same cashier that checked me out two nights ago. She is smiling at Rose. The cashier raises her eyebrow while looking at the pregnancy test then up at me. I shake my head with a smile not giving anything away.

"It sure is," Rose tells the cashier with confidence. She tells Rose how lucky she is to have a man buy her flowers and cook for her. Rose smiles back and says, "I definitely am!" Rose seems to be more comfortable with the idea of us as a couple.

"Have a good day," the cashier tells us as we take our bags and head out of the store. I like that she remembered me. It tells me that she is observant, and her friendliness is a pleasant change from what has become the norm lately. People are so involved on their phones, iPad, or too wrapped up in their own lives, they forget to be nice to those around them.

* * *

We relax all afternoon, watching the last of our selection of movies. Blazing Saddles is a corny, but funny movie. It technically can be considered a western, but in my opinion, it is a slapstick comedy.

"Do you have a preference of where you want to work?" I ask Rose while watching the movie. I remember she told Mom she would be interviewing for two different jobs. Tulsa and Oklahoma City are within thirty minutes of my house.

"Either city offers me a job I see myself liking. I really want to work with women. I think I can help educate them on resources available to them and how to be healthier with proper care," she says. We are sitting on the couch with each of us at a corner and our feet meeting in the middle. She tickles my foot with one of hers and looks at me with happiness in her eyes.

"I understand why you want to work with women. At Christmas I didn't get it, but I do now." I move my foot up her ankle and find a tickle spot on the back of her leg. I push at her feet as she pushes back. We have totally forgotten about the movie. Her right foot slips off mine and comes down hard on my inner thigh. One more inch and I would be in excruciating pain. As it is, it did hurt quite a bit.

"Michael, I am so sorry," Rose says as she sits up quickly. "Do you need some ice?" she asks. She thinks she hit me in the groin. I can play this up, but I always want to be honest with her, never lie or fudge the truth. I sit up, with both legs hanging off the couch. She stretches out her hand towards my thigh but pulls it back before touching me.

"Rose, I'm fine. You hit my thigh muscle. I don't need any ice, thank you for the offer," I tell her. I would love to ask for a massage, but I don't think she needs to see the erection that would appear as soon as her hands touch my skin. I get up and walk around the room stretching out my legs. I will probably have a bruise, but I've had several in the past and I will probably have more in the future. No big deal.

"I really am sorry," she says to me after I sit back down. She isn't looking at me. Actually, her head is down, her fingers pulling at the laces of her shirt.

"Rose, really, I'm fine," I sit next to her and take her hands in mine. I feel the little tremor and slip my fingers between hers. Her cheeks are a crimson red, probably from the embarrassment she's feeling. She doesn't need to though. I suggest we go prepare dinner to calm her down. I walk into the kitchen still holding one of her hands. I want her to know I'm fine.

"I'll start the salad." Rose stops in front of the refrigerator and gently pulls her hand out of mine. I watch her lean into the refrigerator to get all the makings for the salad out. I watch the shirt ride up her back and I want to touch the skin she exposes. I'll need a cold shower tonight; my mind can't stop thinking about pulling her to my chest and ravishing her. I shake my head and get the pot out for the pasta. I'm browning the Italian ground sausage to put in the sauce while Rose cuts up the vegetables. I love that she adds so many things to her salad like me. I watch her make each cut with great precision. She slices the carrots julienne style and the celery diced small. She drains the can of sliced olives and then throws them in. She drains and washes the garbanzo beans to get the outer coating off the bean and puts them on top of the lettuce. The last item she puts on top of the salad is the parmesan crisps. The sausage is done browning, so I pour the sauce in the pan and start boiling the penne, making sure there is adequate salt in the water. She is tossing the salad and placing it on the table. I see a glimpse of red pepper when I look over my shoulder and watch her.

"Can you get the dishes and bowl down from the cabinet in front of you please?" she asks. I feel her at my side. Not just her body heat, but her energy. I think my body could feel her even if I have my eyes closed. I smell her shampoo and her own unique smell beyond that. My heartbeat increases and I feel the electricity go straight up my arm to my heart. I place the dishes on the counter in front of her and turn back to stirring the sauce.

"You won this morning and still let me pick out my favorite pastries and how do I pay you back? I kick you." I feel her hands on my lower back. My skin tingles as she slides her hands around my body and places them on top of my belt buckle. She leans her chest against my back and I stop breathing. Her breasts slide up my back as she stands on her toes and kisses the back of my neck. I could care less if the sauce burns at this point. I don't want her to move. She pulls on my shirt and turns me. Her hands are now resting on my chest. "I think I owe you a kiss," she says, licking her lips. I place my hands over hers. I know myself well enough to know if I place my hands anywhere else, I won't be gentle. I want everything that she has, but I have to wait for her to offer it to me. So, for now, I hold onto her hands and dip my head down to kiss her moist lips.

"Lily's muffins were great, but I'll choose one of your kisses over them anytime. But Rose, you didn't owe me anything." I let her know. The water spits out of the pot and the timer goes off telling me the pasta is done. Rose pulls her hands out of mine and I feel the warmth leave my chest.

"I know I don't, but I really feel bad about kicking you." She goes to set the table while I drain the pasta and mix it into the sauce. She gets us water for dinner and after a few minutes of simmering the dish, to mix in the flavors, I bring it to the table. I cut up the bread and we sit down to another home cooked meal. I love cooking for her. Granted last time was grilling and Brady manned the grill. I want to take care of Rose and if that means calling Mom for recipes, or buying more cookbooks, I will gladly do it.

"So back to the conversation we were having about your future work. Is there a specific field in women's health you want to tackle?" I ask her for two reasons. One to get her mind off kicking me and two, I really want to understand what she is passionate about. She goes over some of the topics in the last few classes she is taking to finish her degree. We talk about how important a patient's health history is. She has worked with adopted patients who don't have any of their information. "I can't imagine how difficult it would be when basic information is needed." I think of some friends I had in high school. Their parents adopted four of them, all biological brother and sisters. One of them became an alcoholic in high school. Another was diagnosed with juvenile diabetes. When the parents contacted the adoption agency to seek out a medical history from the birth parents, they were told the file was sealed on the request of the biological father.

"When a woman wants to have a baby and has a hard time conceiving, it can be due to medical issues. Something like endometriosis is genetic and can cause issues in a woman getting pregnant. It makes it easier for the doctor to come up with a treatment plan if they know the past medical history." She continues to talk while we eat. I'm amazed at the passion she has to help women. I know some of it comes from being assaulted, but I also know some of it comes from the early death of her mother. Having a mother and father, myself, I can't image what she missed. I know Brady and her sisters did the best they could, but a mother shares a piece of herself when raising a daughter. My mom once told me, raising a daughter is different than raising a son. I can understand a little. I saw how Mom and Dad raised Lily compared to raising five boys. Growing up on a ranch compared to growing up in the suburbs is a lot different, too. We finish our dinner and clear the dishes together. I wash the dishes while she dries and puts them away. We continue talking and I can see her eyes light up as we talk about her goals as a nurse. I'm sure I had the same look when I got Corsco Equine Therapy up and running.

* * *

"Do you want to catch the sunset?" I ask Rose. She's putting away the last pan and I want to do something other than watch a movie again. I'm used to movement all day and sitting around all day today has gotten my muscles all stiff.

"That would be great. I don't usually make the time when I'm at school." She heads for the backdoor and I follow. I have made it my mission to always follow her on this trip so I can see all her curves move in front of me. I can't help wanting to see her breast bounce with each step and the wiggle in her backside as they sway from side to side. We sit on the rocking chairs again. I place my hand on the small table between the chairs, palm up for her to take or not take. I turn my head towards her when she places her hand in mine. Her eyes are a golden green and her pearly white teeth are peeking out behind her lips as she gives me a beautiful smile. I can sit here all night watching her. The skies above the mountains have a beautiful array of colors, but I would rather watch her eyes as they change from brown to green to golden green. I haven't figured out what the color change means, but I will.

She turns her head towards the setting sun with a smile on her face. I decide, for tonight, I will watch the sunset. I will have the rest of our lives to watch her, but only a rare opportunity to watch the Colorado sunsets. There are a few clouds in the sky that hold a golden light around their borders while the sky around them is turning dark blue and purple. The colors hugging the mountains are a flame red and orange. The gold that takes over the sky when the sun finally dips behind the mountain range is beautiful.

"I think I will miss the sunsets when I go home. We don't have that many colors in the sky at one time. The sunrises and sunsets blend from one color into the next, but not three or four colors at the same time," I tell her. She is still holding my hand well past the sunset. I sit in quiet waiting for her to speak or get up to go inside. I know I will have to get a couple rockers or a swing for my house so that we can have these quiet times together at the end of our days.

"We need to bring the pregnancy test to Lily. I'm surprised Brady hasn't come over already." She holds my hand as she stands up. I continue to hold it while we go through the house and pick up the bag that is sitting on the counter. We walk out the front door and around the fence separating their houses. "Should we have called first?" I think she might have a point there, but we continue to the front door. We hear laughter as we knock on the door.

"We were wondering if you got lost," Brady says after he opens the door. His face is a little flushed. I look over at Lily on the couch and her face is a bit flushed too. They are both fully dressed, which I'm happy about. We didn't interrupt anything serious.

"We got back and watched a movie then ate dinner. I think we both forgot to bring it over until now," I tell him.

"What movie?" Brady asks. We walk into the living room in front of Brady. I'm again, behind Rose watching her hips sway from side to side. I can imagine her sway turning into a waddle when she is pregnant with our child. The image of her belly protruding out with my son or daughter makes me smile.

"Blazing Saddle," I say and hear Lily groan. "Rose and I picked out several westerns the night I got in and have watched them over the past few days." Again, I hear Lily give an unpleasant grunt. I look at Brady with confusion. I glance at Rose and she raises her shoulders and shakes her head confused, too.

"Your sister is not fond of my appreciation for westerns and military movies. I'm allowed to make her watch one movie from my collection at the house once a month and she's allowed to make me watch a musical once a month." He returns to Lily's side on the couch and Rose and I come into the room and sit in the remaining chairs. He gives her a kiss without any care that we are in the room with them. I see the love in each of their eyes when they look back at us. "So, is that the test?" Brady asks pointing at the bag in Rose's hand.

"Oh, yeah, sorry we didn't bring it sooner," Rose says. Brady gets up to take it from Rose and urges Lily to take the test now. They tell us to stay and wait. Lily yells over her shoulder to go into the kitchen and get dessert. I see Brady give my sister a small pat on her bottom and I have to laugh. I can see Lily is incredibly happy with Brady. My parents have nothing to worry about with their little girl being so far from home. He is taking good care of her.

"I hope she has some more of those lemon cupcakes," I say to Rose. She puts a pot on for tea as I search out the lemon desserts. I find the cookies on the counter and a couple of cupcakes in the refrigerator. I'm putting dessert dishes on the table and Rose is placing the teacups on the table when we hear a happy scream from the front of the house. "I'm guessing that means the test came out positive," I comment to Rose. We are still smiling when Brady and Lily come in the kitchen. They are giddy and the happiness spreads through the room.

"So, when are you telling Mom and Dad?" I ask the two. Lily knows Dad will insist on them getting married quickly. Mom and Dad like Brady but with her being pregnant, the circumstances have changed on planning a wedding for the future. Dad will insist it be now.

"I'll tell them when they come up for Rose's graduation. Please don't say anything," Lily pleads to me. We will all be back in town in four weeks, so I think that will give Lily enough time to find the courage to tell them she is pregnant out of wedlock. It also gives Brady time to arrange a small wedding while we are in town or get married before everyone arrives for the graduation party.

"Good luck. There is no way I would tell them. This is all on you two. Congratulations by the way." I hug Lily and shake Brady's hand and then Rose gives them both big hugs. I can hear the girls giggle with excitement.

"I don't want to take center stage Rose. This is going to ruin your graduation party," Lily says, obviously upset.

"Lily it is fine. I didn't really want a party, but when everyone started planning a BBQ, I went along with it." Rose reassures Lily that it won't be a problem with her. She would rather be attending a wedding if that's what Lily wants to do. Lily suggests we make it a mutual celebration. It will give them a chance to put together something small for the wedding and have the BBQ as a small reception and a graduation party altogether. Lily relaxes and holds Rose's hand for a second. "This should be fun," she says.

We all sit around the table and pick our choice of lemon heaven. Rose prepared tea for all of us and Brady and I drink it without a word. We both would have preferred coffee or milk. I get meringue on my nose and Rose is kind enough to wipe it off with her finger and puts it in her mouth. I can see a hint of desire in her eyes. I like where this is going. I would love to cuddle on the couch tonight and have a kissing session before we both have to get back to our lives. Our time apart will only be a few weeks. I know I can do this for her and knowing there will be a wedding in May is nice to think about too. I wanted Lily to be happy, and she is.

With Rose almost a registered nurse, she tells Lily to find an obstetrician soon and get on prenatal vitamins right away. She also offers to ask the doctors at the clinic if they can recommend anyone in the area. Rose only wants the best for her soon to be sister-in-law. Educating women on how to take care of themselves properly is starting with Lily.

We finish our tea and dessert, leaving nothing left of the lemon treats Lily made in my honor. I hug her goodbye and tell her how great the desserts were. I go to shake Brady's hand and he pulls me into a hug. With the wedding, just a few weeks away, I guess we are definitely family now. I stand at the door as Rose hugs both and squeals her excitement with Lily. We walk back to the house hand in hand.

* * *

We walk to the den quietly. Rose sits in the corner of the couch and pulls the throw over her legs. I sit at the other end of the couch enjoying the calm that surrounds us. I love that we don't need to have noise around us all the time. I don't know what she is thinking but sitting next to her at the end of the day is nice.

"Did you want to watch a movie or something on television?" she asks me. She is pulling at the laces of her peasant top, which makes me think of what I would really like to be doing.

"No. How about I start a fire and we can talk?" I suggest. With a small nod of her head I go to stack the wood for a blazing fire. Tomorrow is going to start early. Instead of heading back up to school tonight, Rose is staying with me. Her first class is at nine, so she will need to leave by six-thirty. She will have to stop by her apartment and pick up her class items. We talked about leaving at the same time. I can pick up *Rosso* and be on the way home by the time she is sitting in her class. We plan on talking every night until I come back up. I have the fire blazing red and orange flames in no time.

"When are you coming down for the interviews?" I ask. I thought she told my Mom sometime in June, but I want to confirm it with Rose.

"The middle of June for both. I'll take my NCLEX-RN test the Monday after graduation and then I'll have a month to feel like a normal person. I feel like I've been in school forever. I'm not sure I'll know what to do with myself when I no longer have to attend classes. I will miss my clinic time when I see patients, but I will not miss working for the doctors that run it." I have heard her say she doesn't particularly like them, but it sounds like there is more to the story.

"How bad is it working for them?" I ask, not sure if I want to hear the answer. I'm thinking about my girl fending off advances or something worse in the hands of these men. I will come up and take care of them if I have to. With her past, she can't be around people like that, even if she is required to work in the clinic for the nursing program hours.

"I'm tired of the doctors looking down their noses telling me I'm just a nurse. I worked awfully hard to get straight A's in college and the head nurse at the clinic tells me I'm the best student they have ever had. I know I might face that anywhere I go, but right now it pisses me off." She tosses the throw off and is sitting with her legs crossed Indian style facing me on the couch. Her face is flushed, and her voice volume has gone up with each sentence. She doesn't want me to meet these doctors that make my girl feel small. If you don't have a good nursing staff, it makes the doctor's job harder. They need to appreciate all the hard work she puts in for them. In a couple of weeks, when she is no longer there, they will realize what a treasure they had in her.

"You have worked extremely hard to get where you are. I'm sure your family and mine, are proud of you. Walk away from this experience with the knowledge you acquired. Being an intern is part of the course load so that you can learn how to work with the doctors and the patients. Remember, you'll bring all of that information with you on your next adventure in life," I tell her. I'm sitting sideways on the couch with my upper body facing her. I see the excitement in her face, and it flows over into her eyes. The woman in front of me has changed a lot while getting her degree. The baby sister who misses her mom is now a woman all grown and taking on the world. The victim is now a survivor bringing her knowledge to woman who can learn from her experiences and the nurse who will take care of her patients to the best of her ability. I'm hoping she will also be the woman who is willing to trust me with her heart, soul, and body. She reaches her hands out, giving me the choice to take them. I intertwine my fingers with hers quickly. Her eyes stare into mine. I see so many emotions pass over her eyes. I want to lean in and kiss her lips, but I know this is going to change my life and I have to wait for her to decide where to go from here. My eyes show her tenderness, desire, and patience. I will sit here all night looking into those golden green eyes and be perfectly happy. I have to admit when she raises up on her knees and moves to straddle my legs, a primal lust runs through my body.

"I feel incredibly lucky to have you in my life Michael. You always listen to my rants and never judge me. You accepted my past and still say you love me," she says. She rests her hands on my shoulders. I lay my hands on her hips and don't move them. "I hope I get one of the jobs by you. I want to love you completely." She runs her fingers threw my hair. Her words melt my insides. She is thinking about being physical with me. I so want to be able to touch every inch of her skin, taste everything she has to offer, and make love to her until she knows what being with someone should be. I want to love all of her.

"I'm the lucky one. I will always be there for you Rose. I'll be the ear to listen, the shoulder to cry on, and the arms to give you a hug. I want to be everything for you." I tip my head back, hoping for a kiss. I never lower my eyes from hers. I want her to know I hear everything she is saying. "I'm sure you will get an offer from both. You'll have to decide which one is the best fit for you." I have a feeling she will have a hard time picking one over the other. "Either job should be good for you, but you need to figure out which one will be great for you," I tell her. I start moving my thumb back and forth over her hip bone without realizing I'm doing it. When I do realize it, she doesn't seem to mind. I keep my touch soft and my motions smooth. "We all have pasts. Some are worse than others. You must know I would never hold your past against you. I love you right now, in this moment of time," I whisper the last part as she brings her face towards mine.

"I love you in this moment of time, too," Rose whispers. Our lips touch and I let her control where the kiss will go. Her lips are soft as they move against mine. Rose explores my lips slowly, without any urgency. She knows I will let her take what she wants when she wants it. Our breaths are uneven as she pulls away. I think I have figured out one of her eye colors as I see her gold eyes looking down at me. Her fingernails are massaging my scalp with each movement of her fingers. My jeans start getting tight. I can't help my body's response to her touch, especially when she is sitting on my thighs. I'm hoping she doesn't move forward for both our sakes. I don't want her feeling pressured to do something she isn't ready for and I don't think I can handle any more pressure behind my zipper. My fingers are still rubbing circles on her hips when she leans forward and kisses me again. I hear a small groan right before her tongue slips between her lips and touches the corner of my mouth. I was wrong. It doesn't take her hips moving forward to increase my erection. The sound of her moan tightens my jeans and then her tongue touching my lips stretches my jeans to an agonizing pain. For her, I'll deal with the pain. I hope it won't cause permanent damage. Her tongue slowly glides over my lips once. On the second pass she pushes her tongue in between my lips. I open them and give her full access. I have to remember she is inexperienced and let her find her way. She pulls her tongue back quickly after touching mine. I keep my lips slightly parted for her to touch me again, and she does. Her tongue dances with mine for a second and pulls out again. She leans back and stares at me.

"You're so patient with me. Thank you," she says, looking down. She pulls her fingers out of my hair and over my shoulders. They finally rest on my chest. Her body slides further onto my thighs. She looks up at me, quickly, with her cheeks turning red. "I'm sorry," she whispers. I can see the embarrassment take over her face.

"I'm not," I tell her. I place a finger under her chin and look into her eyes. "You don't need to be embarrassed because I'm physically attracted to you Rose. This will happen a lot when I'm around you," I say. Her cheeks are red, and her eyes are looking down at my chest. "Please look at me." I lift my other hand off her hip and place it on her cheek. "Just because I get an erection doesn't mean you need to do anything about it. I said we are taking this at your pace. I might need a few cold showers," I laugh.

"Is that what happened the first night?" she asks. She quickly realizes what she asked and covers her mouth, as if to pull the words back. I wondered if she had heard me, now I have the answer.

"You heard that, huh?" I ask. I lower my finger from her chin and place it on her shoulder. I keep my other hand on her cheek. I'm not embarrassed in front of her, but I don't want her thinking something negative because of it.

"I came in to tell you I would be in the den. I thought you would be done in the shower sooner. I figure I would yell through the door and that's when I heard my name." She leans her face into my palm. I run my thumb over her lips.

"We hadn't seen each other in four months and when I saw you run out to me, I almost lost it. I thought if I took care of myself in the shower, I could keep myself under control. I was wrong," I say. She tries to scoot back on my thighs. I lower both my hands onto her hips and still her movement.

"I don't want you to be in pain, Michael. I did learn it's not healthy for a man to have 'blue balls'." She makes the quote marks with her hands. "You must be in pain with your zipper," she says, trying to slide off my lap again.

"Let me worry about my pain. I don't want to let you go." I lean in for a small kiss and then let her off my lap with the agreement she would cuddle at my side for the rest of the night. We talk about her staying at my parents when she comes down for the interviews. My Mom is excited to have another woman in the house again. Rose tells me that Mom agreed to teach her a few dishes to make while she's down. Rose is excited to see the horses at the stables, too. I know she will want to see Chestnut and *Rosso* first. When Anna and Rose came out to see Chestnut at Thanksgiving, they only saw a couple stalls in the stables. I'm looking forward to showing Rose my home along with the entire stable area. I'm going to go through each room in the house and make sure there is a little blue in each before she heads down. I want her to feel comfortable there because one day it will be hers too.

CHAPTER 9

I have a cup of coffee while watching Rose make tea for her ride back up to Greeley. I already have my bag packed and sitting by the front door. We know we will see each other in a few weeks, but neither of us wants to say goodbye today.

"I should be home by five. I'll need to check in with everyone about the camp this week, so call me after seven," I say into her hair. She is hugging me so tight; I have to say the words softly because I can't catch a full breath. I will miss these quiet times with her.

"I have a class this morning and late afternoon and I'm working a couple hours today. I'll need to hear your voice, so you better be at your phone at seven," she says, jokingly. We pull our bodies away from each other and Rose rests her hands on my shoulders. I look into her eyes and see a tear suspended on her eyelashes. Before it trails down her cheek, I lean down and kiss it away and can taste the saltiness on my lips. I feel her fingers brush the back of my neck. I slide my lips from her eye to her lips. I let Rose take charge from there. I cup her face in my hands and glide my thumbs over her jawline as her tongue sneaks between my lips. I feel like heaven is stretching it's fingers down to us and giving us both a second chance to find happiness.

"I can do this all day, but then you would be late for class and I won't get home until after the sun goes down," I tell her. We open the front door and I give her a quick kiss on her cheek.

"I'm supposed to pick up *Rosso* at seven thirty, so we better get going." I walk her to her car and give her another hug and kiss before she gets into the driver's seat. "Please text me when you get home," I say. I know I'm being silly, but I want to know she made it there safely. I wait for her to start the car before turning towards my truck.

"Michael," she calls. I turn back and lean into the open window. "I love you in this moment," she says with a smile. I smile back, lean in and kiss her then tell her that I love her in this moment, too. She pulls away from the house as I pull myself into the cab of my truck. Those words will keep a smile on my face until I talk to her tonight.

I drive south on Parker Rd. The rush hour traffic around Denver is bad, but like Brady told me, traffic lightens up as soon as I'm past the Denver city limits. I'm enjoying the scenery as I head south. I can see the mountains west of me with their snow top peaks and the clear blue sky to the east.

I pick up *Rosso* without any problems and head back the way I came on Parker Rd and take the exit to I-225. I concentrate on the road when I see the sign for I-70 East. Rush hour traffic is still heavy. I stop at a truck stop to grab a quick breakfast already thinking about the long drive home. I check on the horse after I get my food and see she is doing fine. I wonder how close Rose is to Greeley as I climb back into my truck. My phone beeps with a text seconds later. I check my phone as I'm sitting at the light to get back onto the highway. Rose's message makes me smile again this morning.

"I'm here safe and sound but missing you already," she writes and ends the message with a smiley emoji and a red heart. I text her back before the light turns green. I try to never drive and text. I remember Nick's accident and his long recovery. It wasn't from texting, but any car accident is one to many. I'm hoping the kissing emoji puts a smile on her face.

I head east into the rising sun. I keep my speed steady all the way into Kansas. I stop along the way to stretch my legs and check on *Rosso*. The time seems to fly by. I'm heading south into

Oklahoma before I know it. I'm thinking of Rose the entire drive which is probably why the drive goes fast. The sun is over to the western horizon as I'm pulling into my drive.

* * *

I back into the parking area next to the stables and I see Jerry and Steph heading my way as I get out of my truck. It's nice to be home around the familiar smells and warmer air. Colorado had beautiful weather while I was there, but I missed the warm air that flows through the stables.

"I was wondering when you would get back into town," Jerry says. "I see you did get the horse. How much training will this one need?" He helps me open up the trailer and looks inside to see the red brown horse. *Rosso* is a little skittish after her long ride.

"I picked her up this morning and I made pretty good time on the highways," I say as Steph moves next to me to see *Rosso*. Instead of answering the questions, I ask one of my own. "So how was today?" I ask them. I'm usually around the first day of camp, even though my staff does a great job and I'm not really needed. I think this week is the trouble teens camp. I'm not sure if my memory is being difficult or if I'm so consumed with Rose and can't remember anything about camp.

"Carrie helped me out today. We have a whole new batch of teens. I can see us having a little trouble with two of the ten kids. Their parents made them come so emotions are running a little hot," Steph states. He moves back as Jerry and I are walking *Rosso* out of the trailer. She sniffs the air and neighs into the air. I think she is announcing herself to the other horses. We all hear a few of the stables horses respond. "I'm guessing she will be popular with the horses," Steph laughs.

All three of us work to settle her into her new home. I directed my staff to have a stall available without another horse on either side. I want her to get comfortable in the new surroundings before she gets introduced to her stable mates. Jerry gets the brush from the tact room and Steph stands at her head talking quietly. I get some grain and water, but not too much since her system needs to get used to the shock of moving today. We are also careful with the change in water the horse will now get. Between the three of us we get *Rosso* taken care of for the night in under an hour. I check my watch and I have plenty of time to talk with Steph about this week's camp.

"So, tell me about this new group of kids," I say to her. We head out of the stalls and sit down at the picnic tables I have next to the training corral. I talk with her about the two teen boys who are in the camp for acting out at school and at home. They feel a "horse camp" is stupid and won't do anything for them. One came from a recently divorced household and the other came from a home where the father is in the Army and is currently stationed overseas. I reassure Steph that I will help him this week. Maybe another male adult around will help these two. She mentions the others in the group. The trouble teens have a variety of abuse issues. They get sent to us either by the county judge or their parents desperately reaching out for anything that might work. I glance at my watch after we wrap up our conversation. I have enough time to wash up from the long drive and grab a sandwich to eat. The music is softly playing in the stables as I head up to the house. I'll check the security cameras before I go to bed, but I'm sure *Rosso* will settle in for the night fine.

I wash up and put on comfortable clothes then head into the kitchen to make my dinner. I'm heading into the living room when the phone rings, so I place my plate with my cold roast beef sandwich and chips on the coffee table in the living room. I'm counting rings, hoping she doesn't hang up. The water sloshes out of the glass as I search for my phone on the table. I don't want anything to pull my attention away from Rose's sweet voice, so I leave the television off.

I check the caller ID and see it's her. I have had the rare occasion of answering the phone with an endearment or a silly comment and it wasn't the person I thought it would be. It was awkward to then fall into a conversation without being embarrassed. The thought goes out of my head as I hit the talk button and place the phone to my ear. "Hi sweetheart," I say softly into the mouthpiece. It feels so good using an endearment with Rose. I have thought of her with endearments in my head for these past few long months. I'm waiting to hear her soft voice.

"Hi. How was your ride?" she asks. Her voice is exactly how I remember it. Soft, sexy, and musical.

"Good. *Rosso* handled the ride really well. She's all tucked in for the night," I tell her. I know she wants to hear about my day, but it was uneventful. I've picked up horses that fought being in the trailer or trying to get out when I stop to check on them. This trip went perfectly, which I can't say too often. "She announced herself to the stables right away," I tell her with laughter in my voice.

"I'm sure she will be popular. I'm glad it went so easy," she says then I hear her yawn. "With the early drive and classes today, I'm beat." I didn't think the early morning would have such an effect on her day. "Luckily, I only worked a couple of hours this afternoon. I really didn't want to be there."

"Do you want me to let you go and call you tomorrow?" I ask. I don't want her classes effected tomorrow by talking with me tonight. It is only seven o'clock in Colorado and eight o'clock in Oklahoma, but she does sound exhausted.

"No, no, no. I want to talk to you," she says. I can hear the hesitation in her voice. "Michael, can I call you back after I take a shower and get something to eat? I'm running on empty, but I didn't want to be late for our call. I thought you might worry," She's right, I would have worried that something was wrong.

"You go take a long shower and call me back while you're eating. I'm sitting here with my dinner in front of me. We can eat dinner together," I say with a light air to my words. I don't want our calls to stress her out or make her worry if she isn't keeping to a strict schedule. "If you were going to take a bath, I would have said to call me while you're resting under the steam and bubbles. It would definitely torture my imagination picturing you under the water," I groan with the thoughts now running through my mind. I hear a little moan through the phone.

"That sounds like something I should do in your tub. Do you have a tub in your bathroom?" she asks. Her words come out strained. She may be inexperienced, but her mind can fantasize like anyone else.

"I have two bathtubs. A standard tub in the main bathroom and a jetted two-person tub in the master bedroom," I say, starting to fantasize about her stepping into the steaming water and lowering herself next to me. I can see her breasts hiding under the bubbles. Her dark brown nipples peak out as she moves to get comfortable. My body is letting me know how ready I am for this fantasy to become reality.

"Let me call you back. I really need that shower now," she sighs. We talked about her hearing me masturbating a few days ago but we never talked about if she masturbates. It's a topic most people don't want to talk about. Rape, as her first experience with sex, would lead me to think she wouldn't. Maybe I'm wrong. "I'll call you when I'm putting together something for dinner." She doesn't wait for me to answer. She just hangs up. I can picture her cheeks a crimson red with embarrassment. This is one of those conversations we have to have in person, not over the phone.

I turn on the television and search the channels for something to watch while I wait to hear her voice again. I turn on the sports channel and get all the updates from the weekend games. I need to keep my mind off of Rose in the shower, but at the same time I don't want to get invested in a movie or show. I need to be able to turn off the television when she calls me back. My sandwich is sitting on the table, untouched. I meant it when I told her I'd eat my dinner with her. The ice in my water has caused the glass to sweat and leaves a ring around the glass. I forgot to put a coaster under it and now I know I will end up with a ring on my wooden table. I startle with the sound of the phone ringing thirty minutes later as I'm wiping the water up with my napkin. I place the blue stone coaster under the glass, thinking that I have something blue already for her. I turn the television off the sports channel and flip to the music station. I find the one

I have always played when we have talked in the past. I double check the caller ID and answer the phone when I'm sure it's her.

"Feel better?" I ask her.

"I feel human again. We had a few tough appointments today," she tells me and now her voice sounds more relaxed. She tells me about a mom and son who came in with bruises on their faces and the boy had a broken arm. "It is typical abuse symptoms and injuries, but they said he fell down the stairs. She wouldn't answer how she got the black eye or bruised cheek. I get so mad when patients won't let us help them." I hear the fury in her voice, and I know it isn't because of the injuries, but because they will go right back to the abuse after they get fixed up.

"Unfortunately, you can't help everyone. I know it is hard to understand that all people won't take the help. You've met Gabriella and talked with her over Christmas. She was in an abusive marriage and she wouldn't tell her parents and they lived in New York, too. Some patients are at different stages of abuse and they have to want the help and ask for it," I say, hoping she doesn't get mad at me.

"I know all about asking for help, Michael!" Damn, I didn't want her mad at me for my insensitive words. I know better than bringing up abuse, of any kind. "I want to reach out to these women and help them understand that they don't need to stay in relationships like the ones they are in." I hear her take a deep breath in and then let it out. "Her son was so scared to say anything. You could tell he was told what to say by the man who did this to him," she says. She takes a couple deeper breaths. I hear ice clinking in a glass.

"What did you make yourself for dinner," I say, deciding to change the topic. I agree with everything she's saying, but I can't help her feel better from the day she had. We both know she will have more days like today when she starts working full-time. Rose's heart is in the right place, but there is only so much she can do with the patients coming in to be seen. I know part of what she wants to do with all her patients besides treat them, is to educate them so they can make healthier decisions in their lives.

"I made myself a Waldorf chicken salad sandwich and a glass of lemonade. I forgot I had made lemonade before coming down to Denver," she says, again I hear the clinking. "You know me, I usually have water, but the lemonade was calling my name after today." I can picture the water trickling down her glass and around her slender fingers. We both like a lot of ice in our drinks, which of course, makes the glass sweat. "Did you wait to eat with me?" she asks, her voice more relaxed now.

"I did. I'm having a roast beef sandwich with chips. I didn't want anything hot. It was a long drive and the stables are warming up this time of year. I wanted something easy to make and I didn't want to still be cooking when you called." I reach over and place my plate on my lap. I grab a chip and crunch into the mouthpiece of the phone. I ask her what is in a Waldorf chicken salad.

"My mom would make the salad every week during the summer. I remember eating it over a bed of lettuce for dinner and she would always make enough for us to have it as a sandwich later in the week. There are several recipes out there. My mom always made the traditional recipe. She would cube the cooked chicken and put walnuts, grapes, celery, red onions, and fresh basil in a big bowl. She'd mix in mayonnaise and avocado oil then put it in the refrigerator and let the flavors mix and everything could get cold." I hear the crunch of her bite over the phone. It sounded amazing.

"I don't think my mom made anything like that for us, but then again, she had five boys who said they were starving at each meal. Maybe you can make it when you come down." I'm hoping she is imagining herself cooking in my kitchen because I can picture her in front of the stove with her hair all a mess and wearing one of my t-shirts. I take a bite of my sandwich and crunch a few chips.

"I can do that. Maybe I can make it at your mom's. It's the perfect dish for a light meal on a hot day. Cate told me how hot it gets during the summer months," she says. It sounds like Mom wants Rose to be prepared to make her decision, including the typical weather in our area. She is coming down in June, but July is the month she needs to be prepared for. We go to the lake to cool off most weekends.

"Colorado has to have its' hot months, right?" I ask her. I know they have the mountains that are colder than the rest of the state year-round, but the city has to have hot spells.

"We had an entire month of nineties last summer and even broke a few temperature records. Power went out throughout the state because of people running their air conditioning twenty-four hours a day. I think we had a few people die due to the heat and power outages." Once again, I hear a crunch over the phone line. She never speaks with her mouth full, so we have lulls in the conversation. I finish my sandwich and chips during one of these lulls. I get up and take my plate to the kitchen and run water over the plate. I put it in the dishwasher knowing I use so few dishes, I should probably wash it by hand, but I find running the dishwasher once a week works for me. I place the white plate in between the prongs, and I tell myself to run to Bed Bath and Beyond in Tulsa to buy blue dishes and glasses by the time Rose comes down. I'm sure they will have something I think she'd like. Mom gets the flyers, so I'll ask her to go with me and use the coupon. She'll give me her honest opinion and not tease me about changing my house to fit Rose. We don't even know if she will accept a job in Oklahoma, but I can keep praying that she will.

"Do I need to bring sundresses when I come down?" she asks. I can imagine her back bare of fabric and her calves looking sexy as she wears high heels. I don't think there is a man alive that doesn't love to see a woman in high heels. I don't answer and she asks, "I thought I would wear a skirt and blouse to the interviews."

"I wouldn't wear a sundress to the interviews. It may seem too casual for the office. You can bring a few to wear while you're here though. A skirt and blouse should be perfect for the interviews," I tell her. My mind wonders to running my hand down her bare back. I remember her straddling my lap the other day. I would love for her to be in a sundress and do that again. I clear my voice and shake my head. I don't need to get myself all worked up and have to take care of the problem myself tonight. "You might want to plan on bringing shorts and tops for most of the days. You will also need a pair of jeans if you plan on riding any of the horses while you're here." I torture myself some more when I picture her riding in front of me. Her snug jeans hugging her hips as she sways with the motion of the horse. I pick up my ice water and place the glass on my forehead to cool down my face. I should be putting the ice down my jeans to cool off another part of my body that has slowly been increasing in size along with my imagination.

"I'll bring a variety of things then. I have my test and interview the week after graduation. I was thinking about coming down right after that," she takes a breath and seems to be hesitating to say something.

"That sounds great. I'd love for you to come down so soon." I'm wondering if she is thinking again about moving away from Brady. She may want to spend some time with him this summer prior to her interviews in Oklahoma.

"I…" she stumbles, "I was wondering if your folks would mind me staying with them for the three weeks until my interviews. I don't want to overstay my welcome, especially if I take one of the jobs," she says, nervously.

"Are you kidding me? My mom would love having you around for the whole summer. She misses having another female in the house," I say. "I would love it even more. Are you really thinking about coming down so soon?" I ask her, hopefully.

"Brady and Lily will be working, and I won't have anything to do. Lilla might go to a show or two with me, but she will also be working. I'd rather be down there, seeing where you live and work. I want to spend time with Chestnut and *Rosso* before I go back to work. You also told me we would go out on the boat. I want to, finally, enjoy being out of school and enjoy life a bit." I hear the ice again and water running. She must be washing up her dish.

"Now I have something more to look forward to. I'm so happy right now," I tell her. My smile must be from one ear to the other. I hear a small giggle through the phone then she tells me how happy she is. We talk for another thirty minutes and I hear her yawn over and over again.

"Alright sleepy head, it's time for you to go to bed and get some sleep." We say good night and what is now our signature line with each other.

"I love you in this moment," I tell her. Rose repeats the words to me and then we hang up with the promise of another call tomorrow.

It's still early, but I head up to bed knowing I will be dreaming about Rose tonight.

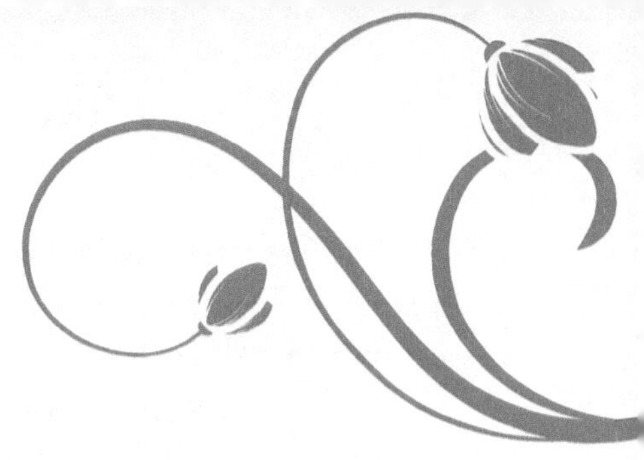

CHAPTER 10

The few weeks apart go by fast. We speak every night and talk about what we can do for the month she will be down in Oklahoma. We planned a few things, but I want to surprise her with a few things too.

I work with each group and the other employees most days but concentrate on training *Rosso* to be around the smaller kids. Her previous owner was right, little training needs to be done. None of the noises seem to bother her, including screaming children. All of the kids I have from the 4H club love her. Because she was a rodeo horse, I am comfortable with them all riding her in the training corral. Chestnut also likes *Rosso*. I think he likes her confidence, so I put them next to each other in the stables. Chestnut, it seems, does better in his training when she is in the corral with him. Rose will be so happy to see Chestnut doing so well.

The time to fly up to Denver comes very quickly. I'm heading up on the Tuesday before the graduation. Nick and Anna aren't coming up until Thursday and neither could get away from the vet practice to drive with me to the airport today. Seth couldn't leave the store and Gabby said she would help him since the clinic will be closed while Anna is gone. Joseph and Patrick aren't coming up because they need to take care of the ranch, so Joseph ended up taking me to the airport.

"You're very excited to get back to Denver bro," he says with a smile on his face. I hear the teasing tone and know he doesn't know the half of it.

"We got awfully close when I was up there getting *Rosso*. The De'Amedo family has found its way into the hearts of us Corscos." I hesitate for an instant then I decide to share my feelings. The guys in the family aren't the type to share their feelings often, but I have to tell someone. "I told her I love her. I now understand how Nick fell so fast for Anna," I say looking at him.

"Mom told us it could happen that fast for all of us. So, does that mean when we finally meet the last De'Amedo sister, Patrick or I will fall in love?" he asks with a chuckle.

"I doubt it. I've heard Anna, Rose, and Brady talk about how snobby she is. Rose once called her an ice queen." I shake my head trying to imagine anyone coming from that family so totally different from the rest. "Guess I'll know the answer to that on Sunday. I'll give you a heads up if she might be your type. Patrick isn't ready for a real relationship. He's still upset about having to come home and run his part of the ranch."

"I know. It hit him hard when he got hurt by that bull, but he should be grateful that he's still alive. He should also know we're all here for him." I nod my head yes in Joseph's direction. "Mom and Dad didn't have to give him a third of the ranch. They always thought he would come back and be happy to have the ranch to run," Joseph says, shaking his head from side to side. Our youngest brother got too used to the spotlight. Pretty boy always got what he wanted in life. He had all the girls after him as the quarterback of our high school. When he took the team to the championships and won, the whole school cheered his name. After graduation he moved into the rodeo circuit and did well for himself. Bull riding became his calling, until he got thrown and shattered his shoulder. Now his life is the ranch and he hasn't gotten over what he thinks he has lost.

We get to the airport in Oklahoma City and I jump out of Joseph's truck, throwing a quick thanks over my shoulder. I hear him laughing as he pulls away. I picture my reunion with Rose the entire flight and know I will be in her arms in under two hours.

* * *

I get off the plane with my carry on and head for the train that will take me to the pick-up area. She told me she would be at the top of the stairs from the train instead of the passenger pick up zone outside. My breathing is elevated with my excitement. I know I saw her a few weeks ago, but it feels like a lifetime since she's been in my arms.

I see the line of people behind the glass barrier waiting for their friends and family. Some are smiling as they see the people they are waiting for; others are screaming in excitement. I continue to scan the line of people and I see her beautiful face above a white sign with "in this moment" written on it with navy blue marker. She heads to the open area where I will come out and drops the sign when I take her in my arms. Her hands run up my back and her head tips back so I can place my lips on hers. The kiss is short but sweet. We are in a public place and I forgot to let her be in control of the kiss.

"I couldn't wait to kiss you." She is smiling up at me, not seeming to mind, with her cheeks turning a hint of pink. We turn towards the exit and I take her hand in mine. I miss the warmth on my back the instant she pulls away.

"I was hoping you would," she says, letting out a small giggle. "I'm parked in short term parking just outside the door." I follow her to the car without saying another word. She opens the trunk for me to throw my bag in, hands me the keys, and leans me against the car for another kiss. I'm leaning against the trunk as she places her feet between mine. Her hands scorch a trail up my chest. She places her palms on my shoulders and I stand still, giving her control of the eager kiss. I feel the tension in her body as the kiss deepens. Rose's tongue slides over my lips then pulls back, ending the kiss. I'm flustered when she smiles at me and heads to the passenger's side of the car.

"Rose, I don't know where I'm going. Why don't you drive?" I ask her.

"Lily lives here. You're going to have to get used to it sometime," she tells me and gets in the car. I get into the driver's seat and move it to fit my long legs. She has a big smile on her blushing face when I look over at her. I smile back at her. I lean towards her and whisper to her that we would get home faster if she drove. "We have a couple of days together before anyone else comes in," Rose states with a huge smile and a giggle. "This way you can help with airport pick-ups too." Her giggle is music to my ears as she looks forward.

"Okay, you're determined for me to drive so tell me how to get out of here," I say with a frustrated grumble. We head out of the airport and take Pena Blvd to the highway. It only takes twenty minutes for us to get to the house. We talk about what things Lily still needs help with for the celebration. Having the party for a wedding and a graduation turns out to be a lot of confusion for my sister. We stop at the store for a few items for the week. I plan on cooking Rose a few dinners and I need something besides lemonade and water to drink. We agree to go to Mary's Café for breakfast foods tomorrow. Rose grabs my bag from the trunk while I grab the bags of food from the backseat.

"Has Lily or Brady said anything about dinner with them tonight, or are we on our own?" I ask her, following her into the kitchen, after she tosses my bag onto the chair in the living room. I know what answer I want. I'm looking forward to making Marsala chicken with rice and vegetables. I confirmed the recipe with my mom. I've made it a few times but wanted to ask her a couple questions about a few changes I want to make to the dish.

"Lily hasn't been feeling all that great lately. I think the morning sickness has started. Most nights she's drinking ginger ale and eating crackers. I think we are on our own for mealtimes, except the day of the party." She's putting the food away in the cabinets as I put the food in the refrigerator. "She's lucky Mom and Dad are coming in on Saturday. I don't think she's going to be able to keep her pregnancy a secret until the wedding otherwise."

"Nick and Anna are coming in on Thursday. Do you still want me to put my stuff in the master until then?" I ask her as we both turn towards each other at the same time.

"Can we sit? I want to ask you a question," she says. I go to the table and sit in the same chair where we had my hard talk. She surprises me when she sits in my lap. I place my left hand around her back and rest my hand on her hip. She reaches for my right hand and holds it between her two hands, now resting on her lap. I don't know what else we have to talk about, but this feels serious.

"Are you okay?" I ask her when she doesn't say anything. My mind is spinning with what could be wrong.

"I'm fine Michael. I need to ask you a question and I want you to think about it before you answer. I want you to know it's alright to say no. I don't want to make things harder for you and I don't want anyone looking at us funny while they are here," she says, not looking up at me.

"You can ask me anything, you know that. And if anyone looks at us funny, they will have to answer to me," I tell her, not sure what she is talking about. I lift her hands to my mouth and place a soft kiss on our joined hands. She looks into my eyes then and I can see her cheeks turning from her natural olive tone to a Maraschino cherry red.

"I know Nick and Anna will need the room on Thursday and you planned on sleeping on the pull out in the living room then. I want to know if you would like to sleep in my room instead." She hesitates then rushes into an explanation. "I don't want you to have to sleep on the uncomfortable pull out and I would love to have you next to me in bed." Another hesitation and then she rushes into her next sentence before I have a chance to answer. "I don't mean for sex, Michael. I think we can cuddle and keep each other company without sex, but if you think that will be too uncomfortable for you, I understand," she says. I lift her up so that she can straddle her legs around the chair. She places her hands on my shoulders and lifts her face until she is looking into my eyes. I feel the small tremor in her body. It took a lot for her to ask me and I know this is a huge step for her.

"I understand we are taking baby steps, Rose. I would never presume sex because we are in the same bed together." I lift my hands to hold her jawline and make sure she is looking at me. I want her to hear what I'm saying and really see me when I say it. "I'd love to cuddle up to you each night. It'll be our next step in getting to know each other. I know you are concerned about me physically but know I can handle it." She knows that I will get an erection sleeping in the same bed with her, especially if I get to touch her. I will take the pain of not getting any relief just to be near her. She leans her face into the palm of my right hand and places her hands over mine. We both lean into each other and our lips meet in a tender kiss.

"Why don't you go put your bag in my room then while I get us something to drink," she says, getting off my lap after we share a few sweet kisses. "What do you want to drink?"

"How about we start off with water? I know I never drink enough water when I travel," I say as I head into the living room and grab my bag. I step into her room and look around. Her body distracted me the last time I looked in here. I can still see her looking straight at me while standing there in her bra. This time I am surrounded by her scent as I place my bag on the bed. It looks to be a queen size bed, which will be a tight fit for us. I have a king size bed at home to fit my long legs. All the Corsco men have king size beds because we are all six feet or taller. It will be interesting to see how we will make this work. I don't care if half my legs hang off the bed as long as Rose is in my arms.

"I'll be on the deck when you're done," she says loud enough for me to hear. I leave the scent of Rose's bedroom behind to go spend time with the person whose scent I can't get out of my head.

* * *

The two days alone with Rose fly by. We enjoy our time by talking about Chestnut and *Rosso*. I tell her about the summer groups we will have while she's in town and the staff I have along with the 4H kids. I think she will love the stables as much as I do. I have her tell me about the three clinics she's interviewing with. It sounds like any of them will work for her, but I'm really hoping on the Oklahoma locations. With the few details she gives me, the Tulsa clinic sounds like the best fit in my opinion.

Thursday afternoon we make the trip to the airport and pick up Nick and Anna. Rose has me drive so that I can come back and get my folks when they arrive on Saturday. We meet them at the top of the stairs by the train. Rose runs into Anna's arms and gives her a bear hug then turns to Nick and gives him a big hug, too.

"It feels like forever since I've seen you Anna," Rose says as we all walk to the car. We talk about their flight and the plans for this weekend. We promised Brady and Lily that the wedding would be a surprise, so we go over the location and food selection for the *graduation* party.

"We put you in the master bedroom, so you have the bigger bed," Rose tells them. She shows them down the hall to the room. I catch Nick's raised eyebrow as he turns and mouths the word '*we*' towards me. I send a small nod his way and he gives me a smile. He has known since Christmas how I feel and I'm sure he's happy for me.

"This will be a nice change from the small full-size bed at Lily's. My feet hung off the bed when I was up last time. Although, it didn't seem that bad when I had you next to me," Nick says, pulling Anna into his side.

"My little sister doesn't need to hear about that. I know she's an adult and all, but she's still my little sister," Anna says, giving Nick a little push to his chest and into the bedroom.

"Anna, it's okay. I am a nurse as well as an adult. I do know what happens between a man and a woman, especially when they are living together and sleeping in the same bed." Rose's giggle makes us all laugh.

"Well, we are on our own for dinner. Brady is working late, and Lily has an order to fill for the weekend. We thought about grilling and having a salad. How does that sound to you two?"

I ask. Brady picked up a small grill for the house, so we don't always have to head over to Lily's and use the one he took over there when he moved in with her.

"That sounds great. We haven't eaten since this morning, and that wasn't much. I was late getting in last night because we had another case of moldy hay. We really need to get someone in to figure out exactly what it is so the animals can be treated properly, and also find out who is selling it that way. I'm glad you haven't had any problems with your hay," Nick says as we all head into the kitchen.

"Didn't Luca's daughter go to school for some sort of biology?" I ask Nick. Luca is Joseph's foreman. He has worked on the ranch from the beginning, hired by my parents straight off the boat from Italy. His wife couldn't handle ranch life and took their daughter with her when she moved to California. I remember her coming for summers with her dad. She loved the ranch and was always hanging around the barn and the river whenever the weather got hot and we all decided to cool off.

"What was her name again? Sophia? No, Sophie. No. Luca always called her Soph," Nick was saying as the women pull everything out of the refrigerator. I get a platter out of the cabinet to put the steaks on and Nick raises his eyebrow at me again. Yes, I know my way around Rose's kitchen. "Luca was strutting around, all proud when she graduated with her bachelors in biology. I know she didn't make it back to the ranch the last two summers because she's been working on her masters. I don't know the exact field though." We head out to the grill to get it heated up as Rose and Anna make up the salad. We hear Rose ask about Chestnut when we close the screen door.

"When we get back, we should have Joseph ask Luca if she could help. I remember the huge crush she had on him when she was a teenager. We used to tease him so bad about it, too." We take care of the steaks and yell into the house when the steaks are ready.

"We went over to Mary's Café and bought a few things for dessert and breakfast. Of course, some of them are lemon flavored for Michael," Rose teases me. I don't mind, its all-in good fun. We all enjoy the steak and the big salad while we talk about the vet practice. The entire family is happy with the expansion of Nick's practice to fit Anna into his life. Who would have known Nick would bring home a partner in life and business when he came up to Denver to see how Lily was doing in her new life? Everything seems to be going well for all the Corsco family. Now if Rose accepts a job in Tulsa or Oklahoma City, my life will be going well, too.

We end the day by watching TAG. I wanted to make sure this movie didn't bring out any bad memories for Rose, so I watched it at home and brought it up with me. We laugh all the way through the movie. Nick and I talk about the games we played when we were young. Having an entire ranch to play on made for a lot of fun as kids. Anna and Rose join in regaling us with tails of Brady having tea parties with them and letting them put nail polish on and hair clips in. He drew the line at make-up though.

Anna starts yawning and Rose realizes she's on Oklahoma time and must be tired. Traveling is always hard when crossing time zones. I get up to use the bathroom. As I'm walking back toward the family room, I see all three of them coming towards me.

"Everyone is tired, I suggested we all hit the sack," Rose says to me.

"Oh, okay. I'm done in the bathroom, it's all yours," I tell her. Nick and Anna are closing the door to the master bedroom as I head into Rose's room. I'll get into my basketball shorts while Rose is in the bathroom. It's been nice having the house to ourselves for a few nights. I love holding Rose while she falls asleep. Even when she rolls onto her side in the night, I spoon her so that I'm always in contact with her body. I have to keep reassuring her that I'm fine when the morning arrives, and she feels my erection up against her backside. We both laughed about it being a 'morning thing'. She enters the room, shuts the door, and climbs into bed next to me.

"I know there will be questions tomorrow morning, but I don't care. I love sleeping in the same bed with you. This cuddle time means so much to me, Michael. You have no idea how much," Rose says, climbing into bed and curling into my chest. I am laying on my back. I have one arm behind her shoulders, pulling her in as close as I can get her. She places her hand on my chest and puts one leg over mine. I rub my left hand up and down her arm as I place my right over her hand on my chest. This is what I want for the rest of my life, Rose right next to me in bed and in my life. Then, of course, some kids climbing in bed with us in the mornings and maybe a dog or two. As I'm imaging what our future might look like Rose falls asleep. I hear her soft breathing and feel her soft breaths across my chest.

CHAPTER 11

Rose doesn't have any difficulty talking to Anna about me sleeping in bed with her. She tells Anna that we aren't having sex yet, but that she is working up to an intimate relationship with me and that I respect her decision and fully understand why. At breakfast that morning, Anna comes up and gives me a big hug and whispers in my ear that the Corsco men are amazing.

I head to the airport Saturday to pick up my parents. I'm glad they are staying with Lily instead of with us. I don't know if my parents would understand the living arrangements Rose and I have at the moment. All their kids, who have partners, are living with them out of wedlock and I know their traditional Italian ways frown on that. Rose came across as very delicate when she was at Mom and Dad's during the holidays. I don't want either of them thinking I'm taking advantage of her in any way. Rose's past isn't my story to tell for my parents to understand what is happening.

I'm standing at the top of the stairs once again. I see Dad's tall figure before I see Mom. All of us men got his height. We say a quick hello and head to the car. They haven't seen Lily since Thanksgiving and I know they are anxious to see her. I know Dad is chomping at the bit to find out when the wedding is going to be. He is not happy even though they are engaged. This party will be a big surprise for the whole family.

Pulling up to the house, I park Rose's car in front of the house and explain which house is Lily's. I grab the bags from the trunk as everyone comes out to say hi. Lily is looking a little green and Brady is holding her arm, keeping her upright. Rose runs over and gives them both a hug as Anna and Nick say hi.

"Brady, are you not taking care of my baby girl? She looks sick. Are you working too hard?" Mom asks. She pulls Lily in for a motherly hug. I see Dad raise his eyebrows at Brady as I walk past them with the bags. I want out of this conversation quickly.

"Mom, Brady is taking care of me fine. I don't feel well right now. He has gotten me everything I have asked for, Ginger Ale, tea, crackers, soup, and anything else he can think I need," Lily tells her. "Come in and let me show you my house." Lily turns around slowly and starts the tour of the garden, the swing on her porch she's always wanted and then into the house. "Leave Brady alone, Daddy. I'm fine. Come inside now." Dad is walking up to the front door as I slap Brady on the back, wishing him luck and head over to Rose. We roll our eyes and laugh, walking next door.

We have a surprise for Rose tonight. I'm hoping Lily can make it to dinner. The doctor told her not to eat spicy food and take an antacid if she has problems. Italian probably isn't the best food for her to eat, but we really want to surprise Rose with Maggiano's. Brady says that was the place he would take her for her birthdays and special occasions. It was her favorite restaurant growing up.

"Your father looked like he was ready to kill Brady. He should be really happy after tomorrow," Rose says as we walk into the house. "Did you talk to your folks about what they want to do for dinner tonight? I don't think we have enough of anything to feed all of us." Rose is looking in the refrigerator and looks above the door at me, waiting for an answer.

"We talked about going out. Mom wants it to be easy on everyone since we are cooking tomorrow night. I agreed with her," I say shutting the door next to her. I need to call Brady and see what time he made the reservations for. "Can you wear the teal sundress you told me about on the phone? I would love to see you in it." I don't want her to guess where we are going so, I'm trying to be very casual about asking her to dress up.

"It's supposed to be warm tonight, so why not." She walks into my arms and tips her face up to mine. "I don't think I've worn a dress around you, have I?" she asks. I shake my head no because I've lost the ability to talk while looking into her gold flecked hazel eyes. "I guess it will be one more new experience for us then," she whispers. I can guarantee I would remember if she had. I look forward to seeing her back exposed. I plan on placing my hand on her soft skin several times during the night. She places her lips on mine and we continue holding each other in the kitchen, kissing and nibbling on each other's lips until we hear someone clear their voice. I'm not sure how long we were kissing in the kitchen, but I hope whoever is behind me hasn't been there long. I don't want Rose to be embarrassed. As I pull back from her lips her cheeks are a soft pink.

"Didn't mean to interrupt, but Brady said dinner is at seven. Anna wants to take a shower before we head out," Nick says while looking at the wall in front of him. "Is it okay if we drive with you? Mom and Dad are going with Brady and Lily and Lilla is meeting us there," he says. I hear Rose's quiet gasp and Nick and I both look at her.

"Are you okay, Rose?" I ask her.

"I'm surprised Lilla is coming. I expected to see her tomorrow so why's she coming tonight?" she asks with weariness in her voice. She almost sounds upset. None of us have met her so Nick and I are both confused by her reaction.

"Brady thought it would be a good idea for her to meet the family prior to tomorrow." I give her a simple and believable explanation. It is surprising to all the Corsco's that we haven't met her yet. It has been almost a year that our families have been joined and no one has met her. Lily hasn't even met her yet. She's always working on a project and not able to get away. If we were different people, we would start thinking she didn't like us even though she hasn't met us.

"I guess that makes sense." I'm glad that went so easily. "Tell Anna the shower is all hers. I took mine this morning." She didn't tell him that I took mine right after her. We stayed in the bathroom while the other was in the shower talking. I handed her towel to her around the shower curtain. She still isn't ready to share her body with me. I also put my towel on in the shower so that I wouldn't make her uncomfortable. I have no issue showing her my body, when she is ready. We talked about how she doesn't like being in large groups. She knows no one will purposely touch her as they are sitting in the chairs or walking up for their diplomas, but she has anxiety about it. We worked on breathing exercises for her to do while walking in the group.

"We'll be ready at six-thirty," Nick says to us. He nods his head at me, silently asking me to come talk to him.

"Honey, can you get me a glass of water? I'll be right back," I tell her over my shoulder. I take a few steps into the living room and stop. Nick looks a little embarrassed, rubbing the back of his neck. I ask him what's up and am surprised my older brother's cheeks are blushing.

"I want to take a shower with Anna. Can you make sure Rose doesn't hear us? I don't want to embarrass her. We have been quiet at night, but I'm not sure how quiet we will be in the shower." He continues to rub the back of his neck.

"We'll go in the family room and watch something on television. I can't guarantee she won't hear you though. She understands you have sex with her sister. It's okay Nick." I laugh and head back into the kitchen. Rose is biting her lips and trying hard not to laugh. She heard the entire conversation.

"Michael let's go outside. It's beautiful out," she says loud enough for Nick to hear as he walks back towards the bedroom. We both hear the swear word as he shuts the door. "I can get changed right before we leave." We sit in the rocking chairs facing the mountains. The sun is high above the mountains and beautiful to look at, even without the multi-colors of a sunset.

* * *

We all meet up at the restaurant at six-thirty. Rose has tears coming down her cheeks as we pull up to her favorite restaurant. Lilla is running late and calls Brady to tell him she'll be there in twenty minutes. We all laugh when Anna and Rose roll their eyes. I guess this is a normal occurrence with her. We are ordering our entrees when a gorgeous woman walks up to the table and stands next to the server. She has beautiful dark hair with highlights around her face. Her eyes are the same hazel as Rose's with the gold flecks sparking through the librarian glasses she has perched on her nose. She is in a deep red dress, the sweetheart neckline hinting at a cleavage and the hemline sitting above her knee. The matching red shoes are so high that I wonder how she can stand on them.

"I would like a whiskey neat," she tells the server, interrupting him taking our orders. She looks down at Brady and flips her hair behind her shoulder. "I have had the worst day. The Italian brute I have to deal with for tiles is simply impossible." We all stop talking and look at her as she takes the only seat left at our table. I'm glad it is between Brady and Anna because I don't want any of that negative energy rubbing off on me.

"Hello, Lilla. It's nice seeing you too," Brady states with irritation in his voice directed at her. He then starts the conversation with the acceptance of a brother used to Lilla's unique personality. My parents are sitting at the table with their mouths open. The table continues to order their food and Lilla catches up and she orders last.

"I'm sorry everyone," Lilla says to everyone at the table after getting a stern look from Brady. "I'm trying to finish up a project and my tile supplier has sent me the wrong tiles twice." She glances back at Brady and he smiles and nods his head.

"Everyone, this is our sister Lilla. She is the interior decorator of the family and is always hip deep with some sort of decorating emergency," Brady says after standing up at the head of the table. "Lilla, this is my fiancée Lily." He places his hand on Lily's shoulder. She is nibbling on bread and sipping a Sprite when she looks up to say hello. "Next to her is Cate, her mom and her dad, Sal." They say hello in Italian, and she answers back in Italian. "Next to Anna is her boyfriend and business partner, Nick. He is Lily's brother and then sitting next to Rose is her new boyfriend, and Lily and Nick's brother, Michael." We all hear Cate and Sal gasp and look down the table at us. Rose and I both smile at the group and say nothing. Rose's cheeks are turning a deep crimson and I reach my hand behind her and rub the bare skin of her back. Brady sits back down and raises his glass for a toast to family, *famiglia*.

"I'm so glad all of Rose's family can be here for this momentous occasion. Rose worked extremely hard to get her master's degree in nursing and now it's time to raise our glasses to her accomplishments and wish her well in her future career," I say after standing up next. The server brought Lilla her drink just in time to toast her sister. "I know how hard you had to work to get to where you are now and I love you in this moment and in the future, so let's hope you get offered a job in Oklahoma. I don't think I can run my therapy center from Colorado," I say, and everyone laughs and offers up their congratulations.

We talk through the meal and Lilla discovers how the rest of the De'Amedo family is now connected to the Corsco family. Lilla knew Brady moved in with Lily a few months ago but didn't realize Anna is now living with Nick, another Corsco, in Oklahoma. She's not impressed. She has taken off her glasses and still looks uptight. We now understand why the sisters have called her the ice queen. I don't see her coming down to Oklahoma and enjoying the holidays with us. She is, if nothing else, high maintenance.

We all enjoy our food, except Lily. She makes sure not to order anything with red sauce but still turns a little green when her angel hair with garlic wine sauce gets placed in front of her. When the server brings us the dessert menu, Lily surprises the entire table when she shouts out "cheesecake for me". The table gets a selection of desserts and we all try a spoonful or forkful from the person next to them, except Lilla who ate her dessert in silence. I fall in love with the lemon cookies and enjoy the

Spumoni Rose is sharing with me. The entire table watches Lily devour her cheesecake and half of Brady's Spumoni. Rose and I both catch Cate's eyebrows go up. I think the secret is out.

We all say our goodbyes to Lilla and tell her that we will see her tomorrow. The rest of us climb into our vehicles and head home. Rose and I can't say anything about Lily in front of the Nick and Anna, so we remain quiet on the short ride home. It's still early so we all decide to climb into the hot tub and relax the rest of the night.

Rose is a little nervous when we go to bed. I know she doesn't want to be around all those people tomorrow. She could have opted to get her degree in the mail and not do the ceremony, but she wants to do ceremony for her family. According to her, they're the reason she has come as far as she has. I feel she doesn't give herself enough credit in becoming the strong, independent woman who can do anything she sets her mind to do.

She cuddles up to me and places her hand on my chest. She puts her leg over mine and I can't help but place my hand on her thigh. "You know how I feel about tomorrow, but with you there and both families supporting me I'm sure I'll be fine." I think she's trying to talk herself into it. A couple of hours tomorrow and then the rest of her life will begin.

"I wouldn't be anywhere else, sweetheart," I say to her. She lifts her head off my shoulder and places her lips over mine. We have been good about not getting physical while in her bed, including kissing. She says she doesn't want to tease me, so I am more than surprised by the kiss. Her fingers inch up from my chest into my hair and I feel the tip of her tongue run over my bottom lip. I go to take a much-needed breath and her tongue slips into my mouth. Her curvy body climbs over mine and I place my hands on her cotton covered hips. She wears a large t-shirt and boxer shorts to bed each night. On her it might as well be the most expensive lingerie because she's sexy in anything she wears. Her kisses are more demanding now and both her hands are in my hair. I can't help but become hard with her on top of me.

"Rose, sweetheart, what are you doing?" I ask as I run my hands up her back. I know she's not teasing me on purpose. She's not that type of person. I know my control is good, but this is pushing me over the edge.

"I need to think of something else, Michael. I love you and don't want to keep us apart anymore. I know what I went through and I know you are not him. You would never hurt me," she says. Her hips start to grind down on me. I know she can feel my erection as she shifts her hips.

"Rose." I say her name to get her attention. She continues on kissing me, running her hands through my hair and grinding her hips. I hear a few low moans coming from her throat and I have to put my hands on her shoulders and push her gently away. I end up saying her name in a firmer voice for her to hear me. Her eyes are glazed over with passion as she looks at me. "I would love to make love to you, but not like this. Your first time shouldn't be to get your mind off of how nervous or anxious you are. I want our first time to be romantic, tender, and perfect in our bed at our house."

"What are you talking about? Our bed and our house?" she asks. I see confusion take over the desire in her eyes. She has the little V between her eyebrows.

"I want you to know you are mine and I am yours. Trust that I will always protect you. I want you to live with me as my wife and know that what I have is yours. My house will be our house. My bed will be ours," I tell her. When she looks at me, I see a steady stream of tears escaping her eyes. I wipe the tears falling down her cheeks with my thumbs. "Don't cry, sweetheart. I love you so much and want to do this right." I sit up with her in my lap, my erection pushing against her cotton bottoms. I lean against the headboard and pull her into my chest for a hug. Her tears slowly stop. I look into her eyes as she leans back on my thighs and looks at me.

"I'm sorry. I don't want to cheapen the experience. I want it to be perfect, too. My mind jumped to sex when I tried to figure out what I could do to settle my nerves. I've heard other women talk about how relaxed they are after sex. I heard this joke, in one of my earlier classes, an orgasm a day keeps the doctor away," she says. Her face is directly in front of mine, but her eyes are looking down.

"We are moving at your speed, Rose, but not like this." I'm sure she understands. "I can offer you a little release without us making love," I tell her. Her eyes raise and look straight into mine. "It's up to you." I can't make this decision for her, but I'm willing to help out. I am a man after all.

"What are you talking about?" Rose asks, sliding further back onto my thighs. She feels my erection on her thigh and looks down at the spot on my jockeys. My pre-cum leaks out onto the fabric and confirms how turned on I am. I lower my hands to rest on her hip bones. I see her hard nipples pushing against the cotton of her top.

"Do you trust me?" I ask her. My fingers are rubbing circles on her hips. The fabric is still between our skin but if she allows me to do what I want it will be gone soon.

"You know I do," she says, still looking confused. I have to remember she hasn't had any experience with sex. She has all the book knowledge. She has taken classes containing information about sex but has no real-life experience except the rape. I want to show her how tender and loving any experience with sex can be.

"Then take your shorts off," I tell her and see desire glaze over her eyes again. She climbs off of my legs and stands at the side of the bed. The shirt covers her hips as she wiggles out of the boxer shorts. They drop to the floor and she stands next to the bed with her hands squeezing the end of her shirt. I can tell she is fighting with herself over something. Before I know it, Rose pulls the t-shirt over her head and looks into my eyes with a confidence I haven't seen since I caught her, months ago, getting changed. I move to the center of the bed and offer her my hand to get back into bed. She takes it without saying a word. "Lay on your back, beautiful," I whisper to her. I'm so overwhelmed by her beauty; I can't catch my breath. Her olive skin is only interrupted by tan lines from her bikini. Her breasts are firm mounds with brown erect nipples. I can't wait to taste them. She has a small patch of trimmed brown hair at the junction of her legs. My plan had been to touch her a little and maybe enter her with my finger to help her have her first orgasm, but now I have to hold back my thoughts and needs because all I want to do is devour her and bury myself deep into her.

"You are the most beautiful woman I have ever seen, Rose." I'm lying next to her, leaning on one arm to keep my head up. I want to be able to see all of her. I use my free hand to run my index finger down her arm closest to me. She's not nervous or filled with anxiety now. "Thank you for trusting me. I won't hurt you. I promise never to hurt you, sweetheart," I tell her as I glide my finger over her bellybutton and play with the gold ring piercing the skin above the indent.

"I know you won't Michael," she responds and lifts her hands, one going to my hair and the other covering mine over her abdomen. She lifts my hand and places it over her breast. "Show me what real love feels like." I watch her eyes as I squeeze lightly. The gold flecks have taken over the brown in her eyes. My erection tries breaking through the fabric of my shorts when she lets out a small moan. I knew her breasts would be a perfect fit for my hands and mouth. I lean over her and take the nipple of the other breast into my mouth. I run my tongue over the hard point as I lightly pinch the other nipple between my fingers. "That feels wonderful," Rose says, her breaths shallow. I kiss my way up to her neck and whisper softly into her ear how it will only get better. She turns her head and I treat her lips to a tender kiss. I kiss my way back down her body. I hear a small giggle when I kiss her collar bone. Her breasts keep my attention for several minutes. Their firmness fits in my hands perfect and the soft skin covers with goosebumps when I breathe over them. Her moans, each time I pinch or nibble on her erect nipples, encourages me to move down her body. I inch my hand over her hip bone, which makes her giggle, on my way down to her thighs. I move my body down the bed and run both hands over her thighs, knees, calves, and end at her feet. I massage the arch in her feet for a minute. I know she enjoys this attention from our time on the couch. When I look up at her face, she is watching me. I keep eye contact as I run my hands back up her calves and alternate kissing each leg until I reach her knees, leaving a moist trail behind.

"Are you okay?" She nods her head up and down. "I will stop at any time. Just tell me, okay?" I want her to understand this is still on her terms. She nods her head again. "Rose, sweetheart, I need to hear you say it." I rub circles on top of her knees as I wait for her response. Her skin feels like silk.

"I'm better than fine. Keep going, Michael. Keep loving me!" she whispers the last part as she relaxes her legs and they fall open a few more inches. I run my hands up and down the outside of her thighs, slowly inch by inch before gliding over to the center of her thighs. I'm working my way inward with each excited noise she makes. Rose opens her legs completely and rests her knees outward when I edge my hands up the inside of her thighs. I see the moisture clinging to her outer lips and breathe in the scent of her excitement. Her fruity soap and shampoo smell, mixing with her natural scent, drive me crazy. I keep reminding myself to slow down and stay in control. I want to make love to her so bad, but not tonight. I place myself in between her thighs and lean over to kiss each hip bone, nibbling the outline of her lighter skin. Her whimper, along with her hands in my hair, emboldens me to move the two inches lower to the heaven that awaits me. I never imagined I would be touching or tasting Rose on this trip. I thought I wouldn't get to touch her like this for a while. I'm making this as special as I can for her.

"Stop teasing me, Michael. Please," she groans, lifting her hips up to my face. "I need more." I circle my arms around her thighs and hold her hips down. I lower my lips and kiss my way down her slit. I swipe my tongue back up and her hips try and move. Her moaning is getting louder and I tell her to turn on the radio. I don't want Anna embarrassing her in the morning talking about how they heard us. Of course, the song that fills the room makes me smile. *H.O.L.Y.* by Florida Georgia Line is playing. Yes, she did save me. I hope I can give her enjoyment with this first experience and in turn, save her. I let the love from the song fill me and tenderly swipe my tongue back down. Her fingers are clenching my hair now.

"Rose, I need you to relax baby. Don't pull my hair out," I tell her. I hear her say sorry as her fingers relax but remain in my hair. I push my tongue against the bundle of nerves waiting for me. She arches her back and sighs out my name. I love my name on her lips. I pull my right arm back from under her thigh and let my fingers slide up and down her dampness. With each moan and sigh she is getting wetter. I alternate pushing my tongue against her clit and circling it. "Sweetheart, are you doing okay?" I need to know before my fingers enter her body.

"Yes." I wait for her to catch her breath. "Do it Michael. I'm only thinking about us." With that statement I move forward and place one finger at her opening and slowly insert it. She is so tight; I know if she wasn't already wet, I would have a hard time putting my finger in her and moving it in and out. I curl my finger so that I hit the inside bundle of nerves right away. I take my time, enjoying her moans and sighs. Her natural lubricant increases with each swipe of my tongue. Her body is jerking with need and I know exactly what she needs even though she doesn't. Flicking my finger, quickly, back and forth and pushing down hard on her clit with my tongue, she comes quickly. Her inner muscles squeeze so hard, my finger starts tingling in numbness. She screams out my name and I'm sure the music did nothing to help cover her voice. As I hear my name coming from her lips, my body decides that's all it needs to ejaculate my own pleasure into my boxers and into the sheets below me. Now there is definitely more than a wet spot on my boxers. I raise myself from in between her legs and wipe my mouth of her sweet juices with my hand. I watch her chest rise up and down quickly and know her first experience was good. I want to climb over her and give her an after-sex cuddle, but I need a moment to clean up.

"I need to go get a washcloth. I'll be right back." I stand next to the bed and look at the pink blush on her cheeks and chest. Her eyes are half closed and the smile on her face makes me puff my chest out a little. I open the door quietly and clean myself up in the bathroom and change into a clean pair of boxers. I wring out a washcloth with warm water to take into the bedroom. I close the bedroom door quietly behind me and walk over to Rose. I sit next to her on the bed and ask her to open her legs. She blushes and does what I ask. I gentle clean her sensitive muscles. I hand her the t-shirt and take the same washcloth to wipe down the wet spot on the sheets where I came in my shorts. I feel like a teenager creaming my own shorts, but I have to admit hearing her scream my name was heaven.

"What are you doing?" Rose asks me. She sits up and looks down the bed.

"Your moans were so sexy and hearing you scream my name was so hot, it sent me over the edge, sweetheart. Now you don't have to worry about my physical need causing injury," I joke. She's looking at me shocked. Maybe I shouldn't have said that. Before I know it, she is laughing, loud. I laugh with her as she cuddles up to my side, naked, and whispers an orgasm like that will definitely keep the doctors away

CHAPTER 12

The next morning, we all grab quick showers and a pastry from the kitchen and head up to Greeley. Mom and Dad are driving with Brady and Lily. I'm hoping she made it through the night without giving away her pregnancy. After the surprise wedding today, they will be ecstatic about being grandparents. Lilla said she will meet us up there so that she has her own car. Nick and Anna sit in the backseat of Rose's car and Nick is complaining about the space not being made for tall people.

"I have to go line up. I'll see you after the ceremony," Rose says, still a little nervous sounding. I hug her and remind her how we solved that last night. She giggles and walks off with a smile. I hope that gets her through the line up at least. Anna smiled at me this morning but said nothing to either of us. Nick gave me a 'thumbs up' as we were leaving the house. I gave them both smiles and said nothing.

We all find seats, after tracking down Lilla, for the ceremony and I notice Mom fussing over Lily. Brady switches seats with Lily as the ceremony starts. I'm sure Lily asked him to so Mom would stop it. Dad is giving him a stern look and I'm sure the cat is out of the bag. We all clap in appropriate places as the graduates accept their degrees and pose for a picture with the president of the university. When Rose comes to the stage, we all stand and cheer. Nick and Lily give out ear piercing whistles. I'm sure Rose is blushing, but we are so proud of her and want her to know it.

The ceremony takes a couple hours and then Rose comes to find us in the confusion of families and friends waiting for their graduate. I walk up to her as soon as I see her coming our way. I pick her up, spin her around, and give her a big kiss. "I'm so proud of you. You didn't seem nervous at all." I give her a sly smile.

"We are so proud of you Rose," Brady says, giving her a hug. Anna hugs her right after him and then Lilla takes her turn. Even today Lilla seems a little stand offish. Maybe she is still having work issues with the Italian. I'm hoping she is more pleasant at the party/wedding. I know if Lilla ever comes down to Oklahoma, I don't want her staying with us.

"I've spent five years of my life here. I say it's time to get out of here and get the party started," Rose says, walking back into my arms.

"Now that sounds like a smart college graduate. Let's go get our party on," Anna says and Nick seconds it. We all head to our vehicles saying that we will all meet back at the house.

"We have to stop and pick up drinks for the party. We'll be right behind you though," I tell my folks. Mom, of course, made several of the dishes last night and Brady is going to go by Mary's Café to pick up the BBQ meats and the cake right before the party. Lily made the wedding/graduation cake days ago and stored it in the large refrigerator at work. No one wanted Mom and Dad seeing it. The car ride is happy and loud on the drive back down to Denver. Anna tells stories of Rose going through school and the help she needed with some of her first year of classes. Nick and Anna talk about the classes they took that were hard for them. I reach over and take Rose's hand in mine as we continue down the highway. Now that the ceremony is over, Rose can't seem to stop smiling. She has one more test to take, but she doesn't seem to be worried about that one.

"Where are we going?" Anna asks when Rose turns off the highway.

"I thought we could go to Wallaby's. They have a bigger selection than the liquor store down the street," Rose tells her. I know we need to pick up non-alcoholic drinks for Lily and the bigger store will carry both.

"I didn't even think about Wallaby's. That's a great idea," Anna says, turning to Nick and asking if he wanted a non-alcoholic beer for the party. Nick doesn't drink, except a shot of Grappa during the holidays.

Wallaby's is busy as we walk in. Colorado law changed and the liquor stores are allowed to be open on Sunday if they choose to be. A lot of graduations are happening around the state, so I'm sure there are a lot of parties in progress. Rose and I head to the non-alcoholic drinks first then meet Nick and Anna at the register with a basket filled with a couple cases of different beers and several choices of wine. We pick up white, red, and sparkling wine to give everyone a choice along with a variety of sodas. Nick is pushing a basket filled with bags of ice to put in the coolers at the house. Anna has a couple bottles of Prosecco for Cate. We load up the trunk and head to the house.

Setting up for the party was easy. We took down a section of fence between the two houses and set up both decks for entertaining. Each house has CD player for music and chairs for guests to sit. Mom is busy making the last of the food and Dad is helping bring the folding chairs from Brady's garage to the deck in back of Lily's house. Rose and I set up the other deck with the arch where Lily and Brady will share their vows. Rose twists flowers around the metal as I set up folding chairs, leaving a row for Lily to come up. We put ribbons on the end of each row and roll out the white runner with rose petals for her to walk up with Dad. Brady heads out to Mary's Café to pick up the last of the food and I go over to get Lily.

"Lily, Rose needs your help with her hair. She said you would French braid it for her." We planned ahead on how to get Lily over to the other house to get her wedding dress on and surprise our folks. She looks around the kitchen and catches Mom's eyes.

"Go ahead dear. I've got this." Mom is laying out the food on the large table Brady rented for the day. Everyone is still in their clothes from the graduation, so the only ones who need to get changed are Lily and Rose. Brady had worn a suit this morning and only needs to put back on his jacket for the ceremony. Lily said she would help Rose into her bridesmaid dress then she can help Lily get into her dress and veil. By helping each other with their dresses, no one else needs to know about the wedding. I head out front to get the cake from Brady as he pulls up. We are going to set up the cake on the large table at Brady's house to keep the surprise intact.

"I'll see you over there," I say to Brady and head up to the house with the cake in hand. Rose is waiting at the door to open it for me. She is wearing an off the shoulder, royal blue satin dress that hugs her shape down past her hips. The small flare at the bottom of the dress ends at her knees. Her hair is braided with white baby's breath tucked in here and there, ending with a royal blue ribbon. She has a sprinkling of gold eye shadow on and her standard lip gloss. She is so beautiful; I have to stop to take it all in. She smiles and tells me to get the cake out of the sun.

"I don't know if I will be able to keep my hands off of you in that dress. You are gorgeous." I place the cake on the table and turn to take her in my arms. My hands go to her hips and I feel the smallest bit of fabric under the satin. "No boy shorts?" I tease her.

"Lily and I stopped at Victoria Secrets when we bought the dresses," Rose tells me. I don't want to think about my sister in sexy panties or lingerie, but Rose is another story. She raises herself onto her toes and whispers in my ear, "I had to wear something, so I found a blue thong." I can't breathe as she lowers herself back down and pulls out of my arms. She gives me a teasing smile as she leaves the kitchen. Dad and Brady walk in a moment later and I'm still standing, speechless, in the kitchen.

"Brady said you needed my help with something son," Dad says. He walks over to the cake and then looks back at Brady. "What's this?" he asks, looking at both of us.

"We didn't want to wait to get married. Most of the family is here now, so we decided to surprise everyone with a wedding today. It was Rose's idea," Brady tells my dad. Rose comes into the room and walks over to me. She tells Brady it is time for him to go outside. He can't see Lily in her wedding dress until she is walking down the aisle. Dad turns around and sees Lily in her dress for the first time. This is her second wedding and she chooses to wear a halter style, cream satin, form fitting, full length dress. Her back is bare except for the ribbons hanging down from her multi-color floral ring for a veil. Her hair is hanging down her back and has big, bouncy curls. If you knew to look for it, you could see the small baby bump.

"Lily, you are breathtaking," Dad tells her as she walks into his arms. Rose holds the blue Delphinium bouquet for her. Of course, my sister uses one of the ten naturally blue flowers in nature. "Has your mother seen you yet?" he asks her when she pulls back and dabs the tears from her eyes.

"No one has seen me yet. Everyone should be outside by now, including Mom." Rose hands her the bouquet back and I look out the screen door to see if everyone is ready for Dad and Lily to come out. Brady gives me the thumbs up. I give my little sister a hug and tell Rose I'll see her out there. I walk out and go to sit next to my Mom. She is crying already, finally knowing what is going on.

* * *

Everyone is surprised by the wedding and happy for both Brady and Lily. Those that don't know Lily and are here for Rose's graduation go with the flow. Brady has a lot of his co-workers here and a long-time friend is standing up with him. They say their vows, which they wrote themselves, get pronounced husband and wife and everyone claps and shouts. The song *Baby I Love Your Way* by Peter Frampton, starts playing from the CD player at the back of the deck.

Brady and Lily walk down the aisle and head into the house. I'm sure they want a moment. Questions will start as soon as they come back out. We all stand around and talk until they come back out. Instead of following her brother and new sister-in-law back down the aisle, Rose finds me and joins the conversation my mom and dad are having with me.

"How long have you known about this?" Mom is asking me, pointing her finger in my face. I know she isn't really mad, just surprised. She thinks she is kept in the loop with all of her kids. Wait until she hears the next announcement!

"Rose didn't want a big graduation party, so she suggested a wedding at the same time. Like I told Dad, everyone was already here." Rose puts her arm behind my back and shrugs her shoulders looking at my mom.

"I hate big parties. For that matter, I hate large crowds. When I suggested it, Lily and Brady said they didn't want to take away my big day. I had to reassure them that I would have been happy with the dinner last night. I hate big parties, especially when they are for me!" Rose says the last sentence so emphatically, no one pushed the subject after that. I give her a reassuring squeeze and whisper in her ear the next announcement will get her out of the spotlight.

Brady and Lily come out the screen door and everyone turns their attention to the happy couple. Brady has removed his jacket and rolled up his sleeves and Lily has left the bouquet in the house.

"We want to say thank you to everyone who came. We know you came for a graduation party, which it still is. Sharing our vows in front of our family and friends, in a small ceremony is exactly what we wanted. We do have one more announcement. Everyone can go between the houses and enjoy the food and games we have set up in a moment," Brady says. He looks down at Lily and shakes his head. "We are pregnant and due around the holidays," they say at the same time. Brady places his hand on Lily's stomach. They are looking at each other with so much love, no one here can miss it.

Mom and Dad run up to them. Mom is screaming and Dad is shaking Brady's hand telling him, in a stern voice, it's about time they got married. Rose and I stand back as everyone offer their congratulations and slowly moves off the deck.

"You knew about this since coming home with the horse?" Nick asks.

"We were sworn to secrecy Nick." I reach for his hand that is squeezing the back of my neck. "I promised her I wouldn't say anything to anyone." Nick releases me with a smile.

"I wouldn't have said anything Michael. You know me, I still have a few of your secrets tucked away for when I need a favor." He walks away to congratulate the happy couple just as Rose looks up at me with raised eyebrows.

"Don't ask, sweetheart. It's stupid kid stuff." I see the laughter in her eyes and when I hear the musical sound slip out between her lips, I tip my head down and touch my lips to hers. God. I love this woman. "Let's go get some food before my brother gets there." I guide Rose towards the opening in the fence.

Rose and I sneak over to get changed while the rest of the guests are getting their BBQ. I suggest she may need my help with the zipper. Everyone is at Lily's house eating dinner, but we shut the bedroom door just in case. We both pull out a pair of jeans and t-shirts. I lay my clothes on the bed and look towards Rose. She is standing next to the bed with her back to me. She pulls her braid over her shoulder and looks at me with a shyness I don't expect.

"Will you unzip me, please?" she asks. I step behind her and slide my hands up her sides, feeling the satin hug her curves. I tell her that I will help with anything she needs. I lean forward and place a kiss on her shoulder while I reach for the zipper. I watch her zipper descend and her olive skin appear. The blue thong, at the bottom of the zipper, teases me. Her tattoo is fully visible now. It looks like a flower, but in a Celtic design with the words *In spite of what you took, I am whole* written below it. Black and grey cover the area between the dimples of her cheeks with a tricolor blue for the flower. She takes her arms out of the sleeves and lets the dress fall to the floor. I take her hand and hold her steady as she steps over the fabric. She sits on the bed to take off her heels as I stand there and look at her beauty. She looks up at me and I drop to my knees. This woman will always have this effect on me. "Michael?" she questions me, not sure what she is asking, but the desire in her eyes is obvious.

"I'll take care of you sweetheart," I whisper in her ear as I reach around her to take off her strapless blue bra that matches her thong. As the fabric falls to her lap, I lean in and kiss each erect nipple. I place each of my hands on a breast and lift my head to kiss her. The kiss starts off tender and sweet and ends demanding and hungry when her fingers curl into my hair and she pulls me in. Her moans sound desperate. I run my hands down to her hips and place my fingers under the side of her thong. "Lay back," I whisper into her ear. She leans back and props herself of her elbows. She watches as I place kisses on her breasts, her hipbones, her belly button, and then she lifts her hips so I can take the thong off. I open her knees and slide my shoulders in between them. I kiss one calf and then the other. I push myself up her legs and kiss one thigh and then the other. I reach the soft curls at the junction of her thighs. The moisture is clinging to her curls and I smell the scent of her natural aroma. I glance up at her face, she's still on her elbows, and I kiss the top of her slit while watching her give over to desire. Her head tips back as a she releases a slow moan. I stick out the tip of my tongue and find the bundle of nerves. I learned what she liked last night so I swirl my tongue around the bud. I sweep my tongue down and then back up her slit. I find her bud again.

"That feels amazing Michael. Why did I wait so long for something that feels this good?" she asks between breaths.

"I'm glad you did sweetheart. I want the honor to be the one you have all your firsts with," I realize after I say the words, I'm not the first for everything. She tenses for a second.

"Michael, you are my first for everything that matters." She is looking down at me, staring into my eyes. I see no memories of the past, only love and desire. I lean forward and tease the bud until I hear another moan. I run my finger down her wet, pink lips and place the tip at her entrance. I hesitate for a second and slide it into the moist, tight muscles. I remind her to try and be quiet. We don't know if anyone has come over to this side of the fence. With a curled finger I find her G spot and brush back and forth. Her thighs tighten around my shoulders and I can tell she is almost there. She screams my name when her body explodes around my finger. Like last night, my finger starts going numb. I can only image her squeezing around my erection.

"You didn't finish this time, did you?" Rose asks with a giggle. She sees the obvious bulge in my slacks when I stand up. I don't care that I didn't finish. The next time I come, I want it to be in her. "I'm sorry Michael. I didn't think about what this would do to you." She lowers her face and looks at her legs.

"Sweetheart, I'm not. I will always give you what you want and need. It wasn't a hardship on me to give you pleasure. I love hearing your moans and you screaming my name," I say after lifting her face up so I can look into her eyes. "How about we get changed and head back to the party? I'm sure someone is wondering where we are." She stands and starts getting dressed. I see her constantly looking at my erection. "As long as you keep looking at me like that, I'll never get rid of this." I point to the bulge now covered by my jeans. We leave the bedroom and I excuse myself to the bathroom. I get myself under control, take Rose's hand and walk outside to head over to Lily's.

Lilla shows up in time for the cake cutting and is confused at what she missed. She explained to Brady how the contractor called her on the way back to town and she needed to stop by the site for several emergencies that had come up today. Brady had to explain what she had missed but wasn't happy that her career took priority over her family again. I heard him tell her that they would have a talk this week and Rose commented on how Lilla knew she was in trouble just by the face she made at Brady's back when he went back to his wife.

The party goes on for hours and luckily Lily is feeling better today to enjoy herself. We find her sitting a lot, but always having food in her hands. Brady is very attentive to her and I am so happy for her. Like predicted, Mom and Dad are so over the moon happy to be grandparents they forget to be upset about her being pregnant before getting married.

CHAPTER 13

The next few days go by quickly. Rose takes her test and feels confident that she got a high score. All of us think she probably aced it.

After the party goers left on Sunday, Mom had suggested that Rose use one of the ranch vehicles during her visit to the ranch, so she doesn't need to drive down by herself. Instead she flies to Oklahoma with me. We talk about spending time together and a schedule for her to come visit Chestnut. Her interviews aren't for a few weeks, so we have plenty of time to see each other before she goes back to Colorado. My hope is she takes one of the jobs and only goes back to get the rest of her things to move down here permanently.

"Thanks for picking us up at the airport," Rose says to Joseph as we pull up to Mom and Dad's place. Joseph tells her no problem before he drives away. Mom is already on the porch waiting for Rose. I know how inappropriate it would look for Rose to stay with me, but I still wish she would. Mom insisted she come stay with her since the house has so many empty bedrooms. Rose wants to learn how to cook, so this works out for Mom to have her there. I have to look at it this way, she's going to come out and visit me and I will get the benefit of Rose knowing how to cook when she does move in with me.

I carry her suitcase up the front steps and hug my mom. She tells me to put it in my old room. Mom hugs Rose hello and

I see Rose's cheeks have turned a rosy pink. I wonder if she is thinking about sleeping in my old bed every night.

"I have your cooking lesson ready for dinner tonight," Mom tells Rose as she puts her hand on her lower back and guides her into the house. I come back down the stairs and find them in the kitchen. Mom is explaining what all needs to be prepped prior to cooking the meal.

"Mom, we just got off the plane. She has been going nonstop for days. Can't cooking lessons start tomorrow? Maybe let her settle in for a day." I'm really surprised by Mom jumping right to it. She's usually tuned into her kids better and knows when to give us our space.

"Rose, I'm sorry. I've been a little off since our trip. We haven't left the ranch in a long time and I worried while we were gone." She places her hands on her shoulders and turns her towards me. "Go check on that horses you two talked about constantly during the party." She looks straight at me, points her finger in my face and says, "Have her back for dinner at six sharp! You're welcome to stay for dinner, too." She hugs me and gives both of us a shove out the door after handing over a set of keys.

We find the truck around the back of the house and I show her which keys are for the house and the truck. Dad is heading back up towards the house as we pass him in front of the barn. I stop to tell him I was ordered to have Rose back at six for dinner. Dad laughs and tells us he will see us both then. He had a worried look on his face after we pull away. I wonder if it's the hay again. Mom also said she had been worried. I'll have to find out at dinner what is going on at the ranch.

"How long does it take to get to your place?" Rose asks. She looks and sounds excited. She wore comfortable yoga pants and a loose T-shirt on the plane. I can't see all her curves in her outfit, but I remember them all. She looks beautiful with no makeup on. Instead of answering her, I continue to stare at her. "What are you looking at?"

"I'm looking at the most gorgeous woman I know." She giggles and shakes her head. "You don't believe me?" I ask. Her cheeks are turning from a soft pink to a sunburn red.

"Michael, I have my old comfy clothes on, no makeup, and my hair is in a messy bun. How can I look beautiful like this?" She continues to shake her head.

"Rose," I reach for her seatbelt and unhook it while we are still on the ranch road. I pull her to my side, and she latches the middle seatbelt on. "When will you understand? You can be sitting next to me in a potato sac covered in mud and I will still think you are the most beautiful and stunning woman I know. I love you just the way you are," I tell her as I rest my arm behind her head on top of the seat. She places her hand on my thigh, looks up into my face and I can see love in her eyes.

"I feel beautiful and loved when I'm with you, Michael." Rose rests her head on my shoulder as we leave the ranch. We drive south on highway forty-eight in quiet. The radio is on 99.7 FM playing oldies. They play two Bryan Adams songs back to back and I see her mouthing the words. "Run for You" is the first song. She knows every word and looks at me while mouthing the chorus. "I don't need to run, do I Michael?" she asks me. Her hand starts running up and down my thigh. The zipper of my jeans gets tight. My voice is stuck in my throat, so I shake my head no. The second song "Heaven" comes on and she starts singing the words to me. "You have shown me heaven already. It's my turn to show you," she is saying as I turn onto County Road thirty-three. I look at her in surprise, my eyebrows high up onto my forehead.

"Rose, we don't have to rush. I understand why you want to go slow. You may not even be staying in Oklahoma. I don't want you to regret what will be the most precious gift you could give me." What am I doing trying to talk her out of making love? My body is telling me I must be crazy. We continue to talk about not rushing it as we get closer to Sapulpa. Her hand runs up my thigh and continues up to my chest. She lays her hand over my heart and she leans her head onto my shoulder.

"Michael, I cancelled my interview in Denver," she whispers in my ear. I had forgotten all about it when she said she was going to fly down with me. "I want to be here with you." Her fingers are running over the muscles of my abdomen. "I told Brady I would be back for my stuff in July. Anna also knows." I don't know what to say. I place my hand behind her head to pull her in for a quick kiss.

"You have no idea how happy that makes me," I say with the biggest smile on my face. At that moment Scorpion starts singing "When You Came into My Life". We both look at each other and start singing the song. She came into my life months ago, but it feels like years since falling in love with her. When the song is over, I tip my head down and give her a kiss and tell her I love her at this moment.

We pull up to the house and I see the afternoon class wrapping up with Steph in the corral. Rose and I see the teen walking towards the stable at the same time. She is holding her arm, so I change directions and drive us down to park next to the stables. Rose jumps out her side of the truck and runs up to the teenager. As I walk up to Steph to see what happened, I see the blood on the girl's sleeve.

"Hey Michael. Nat's horse spooked and threw her. She landed on a bush. I think one of the branches scrapped up her arm fairly good." Steph is looking at Rose tending to Nat's arm. "Who's the lady?" he asks me while we head over towards them.

"That," I say patting his shoulder, "is the woman I'm going to marry." He smiles and laughs asking me if the lady knows that. "We started a long-distance thing after Christmas. She's getting a job down here and staying with Mom and Dad until I can talk her into moving in with me."

"Nat are you alright?" I ask the teenager. She puts her head down and doesn't answer me. I step behind Rose and stay out of her way while she is looking at the wounds.

"Michael, I need a first aid kit with tweezers," Rose says, without looking up at me. Steph goes to get the fully stocked box from the stables. Since my injury in the stables, I have a fully stocked first aid box with bandages, gauze, sports tape, smelling salts, liquid glue, alcohol wipes, shoulder slings, antibiotic ointment, hydrocortisone cream, plastic gloves, hand sanitizer, scissors, and tweezers at all times. I'm looking over Rose's shoulder and I can see wooden splinters in her arm and bloody scratches.

"Rose, is she going to be alright?" Rose, again, doesn't look at me as she tells me yes. "Do you think it's broken?" The girl is still holding her forearm, keeping her elbow at a ninety-degree angle. I get a quick shake of the head no. Rose is gentle and calm while talking to Nat. The girl's response to Rose is better than I expect. Nat's psychiatrist recommended the program to be around other teens in similar situations. Nat can be a handful, but Steph has been working close with her.

Steph comes back with the box and Rose gets to work quickly fixing Nat up. She has a few splinters from the bush and lots of scrapes, but nothing more serious. Rose put bandages on the bigger cuts and talks with Nat about what happened on the ride. The story she gets is not what Steph got told by the teens that were around her. Nat tells Rose about one of the other teenagers, a boy, who kept making kissing noises at her and she was trying to get further ahead to get away from him. I look at Steph and he tells me he will take care of it. The group is in the stables taking care of their horses. Nat keeps glancing at me with a scared look on her face. I tell Rose I'm going to take the first aid box back into the stables to give her more time to talk with Rose. They seem to have developed a good rapport already. I put the box in the tack room and head down to the other side of the stables. Conor is yelling at Steph. He sees me walking his way and drops his volume, but I can still catch what he is saying. I know I need to talk to Conor's father again. Conor has made passes at every girl in each of the groups he has been in. His father said he would speak with him, but obviously it hasn't stuck. He is here for petty theft, but it's his third strike. The judge gave him this last chance and I don't think it is working. Unfortunately, I think he will have to go to juvie to learn his lesson. Conor doesn't understand some of the girls here are from abusive homes and don't see his advances as cute or wanted. Nat happens to be one of those girls. We don't make any of our clients tell their group why they are here. It's up to them to share their story. We usually try and keep Nat with a group of mostly females, but this was the only group Conor fit into this month.

I see Nat's mom pulling into the pickup area after I finish talking to Steph. I have to decide how to handle this situation and quickly. I walk around the stable and meet her walking up to the table her daughter is sitting at with Rose.

"Hi Alice. Nat took a small fall and scratched up her arm. Rose doesn't think it is broken, but you might want to get an x-ray just in case," I tell her quickly. I can see the instant concern on Alice's face as she quickens her pace towards her daughter.

"Who is Rose?" she asks, looking at me for the first time. I understand her concern. She knows all of the staff and all the kids that help out with the horses. Alice is incredibly careful who is around her daughter now. She divorced her husband after she found out what he did to her. It had been going on for years and Nat never told her. Nat couldn't keep her secret after she ended up in the hospital with a miscarriage. Her mom called the police from the hospital to pick up her husband and charged him with rape and divorced him soon after. After the divorce, Nat took pills to kill herself. After she came to the horse therapy program, she stopped threatening to kill herself and saying she wanted to die. She has a great connection with the horse she always rides. Diamond is a yellow palomino with a stark white diamond on her forehead. She is calm, sweet and loves her treats.

"Rose is my girlfriend. She just graduated last week with her Masters in nursing and will be moving down from Denver for a job." I felt like I had to tell her Rose is a nurse for her to be comfortable with Nat getting first aid here.

"Oh Michael, that's wonderful. I'm so happy for you." Alice goes up to Nat's side and calmly asks her daughter what happened. Nat answers her quietly. She tells her mom about Conor and I see the anger in Alice's eyes as she looks up at me.

"I'm speaking with his father when he gets picked up today. He will be out of the program and Nat will never have to see him again," I assure Alice quickly. Rose looks at me with an understanding glance. "Alice, this is my girlfriend Rose." I come to stand next to Rose. "Rose, this is Nat's mom, Alice" They shake hands and share pleasantries. Nat tells her mom that Rose took care of her and that she is fine.

"Alice, I don't think it's broken. Nat has some pain in her elbow, which is probably just a bruise from where she landed on it, but I think she should get an x-ray just in case," she tells Alice the same thing that I had, but I think Alice will listen better to the nurse than the horse trainer.

"Rose, thank you for taking care of my girl here," she says as she places her arm around Nat's shoulder and pulls her in tight. "I don't know what I would do if something happened to her." Nat pulls out of her grasp and thanks Rose. She heads to her mom's car with her head down.

"It was my pleasure. You have a special girl there. We've been having a good conversation." Nat talking to Rose as much as she did surprises me. Nat is usually very quiet around people and only opens up with her horse. "If you ever need to talk, Michael knows how to get in touch with me. I've been in her place and had great counseling to get me to the survivor I am today." Now Rose completely surprises me. I thought she might connect with some of the kids, but not so fast, and not so completely.

Alice looks at Rose then to me. I think both of us are in shock but what Rose just revealed about herself so casually. Neither of us knew what to say. I put my arm around Rose's shoulder and smile down at her. I don't see pain or grief in Rose's eyes. Instead, I see understanding and kindness toward Alice.

"Thank you. I might just do that," Alice says then heads to the car that is blasting a Keith Urban and Carrie Underwood song that fits the situation. Rose hears the song and chuckles next to me. "Fighter" is a song about being there for the other one.

I see Alice pass the incoming car near the house. I'm not looking forward to this conversation. I know I've given Conor several chances to follow the rules, but I still feel bad sending any kid to juvie. "I'll be back in a moment," I tell Rose as I walk towards Richard. I explain what happened today and tell him that Conor can't stay in the program any longer. I will notify the courts tomorrow and I recommend Conor get some type of therapy while he is incarcerated. Richard understands and shakes my hand goodbye after he collects his son. Conor is yelling at his dad saying that the bitch was flirting with him. I feel sorry for Richard, but the program has rules in place for this exact reason. Clients can't feel threatened, abused, or frightened while here for therapy.

"Ready to head up to the house? You can see Chestnut and meet everyone later," I tell her. I want her back in my arms and we only have two hours before we have to be back at Mom and Dad's. She lifts her head towards me, smiles and nods her head yes.

* * *

"Thank you for helping Nat." We walk hand in hand up to the house. "She hasn't talked to anyone but Diamond. I'm surprised how easily she talked with you," I say as we head up the deck stairs. We are entering from the back of the house. I built the deck onto the house as an afterthought. I wanted a place for the family to gather for a BBQ and a place I could sit with my wife and kids to look up at the stars one day. I purchased a set of rocking chairs after coming back from Denver in April. I can see Rose and I sitting out here like we did at Brady's.

"Oh Michael, you have rocking chairs!" Rose squeals. I pull her past the chairs and into the kitchen. I don't want to spend time out in the hot sun when I can have her in my arms in the air-conditioned house. I stop in the open area of the kitchen and living room to let her take a moment to look around. I accomplished putting blue in every room the same time I purchased the rockers. The kitchen now has blue dishes and glasses. The living room has several shades of blue throw pillows on the furniture and I had to search for a blue shower curtain I liked for the guest bath. I also put a blue ceramic soap dispenser and toothbrush holder in the master bath.

"What do you think?" I really want her to like it, but at the same time, I will let her change anything she wants when she comes to live with me. I want her to be happy. She releases my hand and walks around the lower level of the house. She touches the pictures on the walls, I explain Lily took a few of them and I have several Anna took on the lake as well. She walks up to the mantel and picks up one of the frames. Her eyes are brimming with tears when she looks at me.

"When did you take this?" she asks. I have a couple pictures of her in my house. I snapped a quick photo of her and Anna when they were singing to Chestnut. Anna was at the end of the horse, so she wasn't in the photo. The one I have at the side of my bed will surprise her even more.

"At Christmas when you met Chestnut. You were singing to him while Anna was checking him over." I knew back then that this would be the only woman for me. "Do you like it?"

"I do. I felt nervous that day. Chestnut was so calm after we started singing to him. He settled my nerves that day." She places the frame back on the mantel and walks towards the steps at the front of the house. "I think that was the day I knew I really liked you," she says after taking the first step up.

"I was sure I liked you at Thanksgiving. By Christmas I was sure I was falling in love with you," I tell her taking each step one at a time behind her. I'm watching her hips sway from left to right as she continues to look at all the photos going up the stairwell. "Each text, email, and call after made me fall further and deeper in love with you."

"When you told me 'we could love each in that moment in time' is when I knew for sure. I had a lot of thinking to do while you were gone. I knew graduation would come quickly and I had to make a big decision for myself and for our relationship. I knew graduation day that I was going to call and cancel my Denver interview." Rose is standing on the upper landing looking into my eyes. She places her hands around my waist and leans her head over my heart. "I knew in April I always wanted to be with you. You will never intentionally hurt me, Michael. I'm ready to move on with my life." She takes a deep breath and I feel her hard nipples push against my chest. "My life with you," she says. I place my finger under her chin and lift her face up to mine.

"Do you know how happy I am to hear that?" I place my lips over hers. She is still in charge and we will always move at her pace, but all I want to do right now is to carry her to my bed and devour every inch of her skin.

"Rose, we have the rest of our lives together and I'm willing to take this at whatever speed you need," I tell her while I pull her down the hallway and into the master bedroom. She pulls me to a stop when she sees the bed.

"Did you do this for me?" she asks. She lets go of my hand and walks up to bed to run her hand over the navy-blue lace duvet over the light blue quilt. I have dark blue sheets and several different blues for throw pillows. When I put the bed together, I thought it looked a little feminine for my taste, but I knew she would love it. Before I have a chance to answer her, she sees the silver picture frame with a photo of her laughing with her sister.

"I put blue in every room after you told me it's your favor color. The towels in the bathroom are blue also," I tell her as I come up behind her. I touch the picture frame with her and whisper over her shoulder, "That was the first time I heard you laugh. I snuck the photo with my phone." I take my hand off the frame and place it on her hip. I reach up with my other hand and sweep the hair that has escaped the messy bun away from her neck. I place several small kisses where her shoulder and neck meet. I hear her small gasp as I nibble behind her ear. She puts the photo down and places her hand over mine. She turns in my arms to face me.

"The bedding is beautiful. You remember the little details that make me feel special." Rose places her hands on my shoulders and lifts her face up and I see desire in her eyes. "I love you Michael, in this moment in time and forever," she tells me then runs her fingers into my hair and pulls my head down. Her lips are sweet and demanding. I wrap my arms around her waist and return the needy kiss. Her tongue sweeps across my bottom lip and I feel her nibble at the corner of my mouth. I open my lips for her to show me where she wants this kiss to go. I'm surprised when her tongue pushes against mine. This is an aggressive side of Rose I've never seen. I'm trying to keep up with her when she turns our bodies and guides me backwards until my knees hit the mattress. Her fingers find my belt buckle and unfastens it. I want to rush through stripping, but I keep telling myself to let her be in charge. Her fingers run behind my jean's button, sending a shiver over my body. With the button undone, Rose tugs my t-shirt up and runs her hands under the soft cotton. Both hands push up until my shoulders get in the way. She pulls away from my lips and lifts the shirt over my head. I look into her eyes to make sure I don't see any hesitation. All I see is desire. Her hand goes to my zipper and lowers it. I try to stop her.

"Rose, honey, I need to take my boots off first." I hold her hand to make sure she understands I'm not rejecting her. "I'd like to take this slow for you," I say, trying not to moan.

"Michael, I appreciate you wanting to go slow. You have told me this will be at my pace. My pace is faster." Rose pulls her hand out of mine and reaches for the bottom of her shirt. I stop her hands from lifting the material. I hear her frustrated exhale. I'm sure she thinks I'm trying to slow things down still.

"Rose, that's my job," I laugh out. The smile reaches her eyes when she realizes what I'm saying. "I want to uncover every inch while running my fingers over your silky skin. I need to see every inch again." She releases the shirt as I start to pull the soft material over her hips. I lean my head over and kiss her as my hands glide the material over her breasts. My fingers linger over her lacy bra for a moment. Her nipples are hard and need my attention. "I want to taste every inch of this beautiful olive skin." We pull apart to pull the shirt over her head and I throw it to the floor. I kick my boots off, and she slips off her blue sneakers. "I can smell your excitement Rose." My scenes are soaring, and I don't think

I can stop. "I want to hear you moan my name again." I'll give her one more chance to say she's not ready. "Rose, are you sure?"

Rose drags her fingernails, gently, down my chest and over to my hips. She's staring into my eyes as she pushes my jeans down. They drop to the floor on their own and then her fingers are under the waistband of my briefs, shoving them down too. I'm standing there with socks over my calves and a pile of clothes around my ankles. She says "I'm sure" before I feel a delicate, soft-skinned hand wrap around my stiff erection.

"Please don't squeeze any harder unless you want me to embarrass myself. When I come, I don't want it to be in your hand." I see the nervous look shoot through her eyes and think about what I just said. "Rose, what I meant is I want to be making love to you. I'm sorry if it sounded like I want oral sex. I didn't mean it that way." I'm feeling lousy for my slip. I know I need to be more careful in what I say.

"Michael, it's okay. I didn't mean to pull away for that second. We already talked about this." We did talk about how I never expect anything specific from her, especially oral sex. I don't know if she will ever be ready to experience me in her mouth. Her hand is running up and down, softly touching my stomach. "Can you take off my yoga pants? I'd like to get on that bed with you," she says releasing me and pointing to the bed I'm still leaning against. If it weren't for the mattress behind me, I think I would have fallen over when she touched me. I step out of the pile of clothes at my feet, toe my socks off, and then reach behind me to throw the quilt down on the bed. I see the throw pillows go flying all around the bed in my peripheral vision because I'm focusing my eyes on her the entire time. Her cheeks blush a soft pink and my hands reach out to touch her again. I lay my hands on her hips and we take one step away from the bed.

"I will make this good for you, sweetheart." I bend my knees and kiss my way down the curve of her bra. When I reach for the clasp behind her, she points out the hook is in the front. I flick it open and kiss each nipple. I promise her I will give them more attention when I have her lying on her back on the cool sheets. My fingers slip under the stretchy material as I kiss down to her belly button. Her hips are next on my list for kissing and I give her a love bite on each hip bone. I hear her breath escalate when my hands drag the material down over her knees. I ask her to hold onto my shoulders as she steps out of the legs of her pants and her lace panties. Today she has a matching teal bra and panty set. I give the small curls between her legs a small kiss then I stand and guide her up onto the bed.

We lay on our sides, facing each other. I run my fingers through her hair and remove the clasp holding the velvety silk away from her face. I pull a few strands forward and lower it over her breast. The ends of her hair tickle her nipple and she giggles a sweet sound. I remember wanting to push her hair away from her breast so I could gawk at them more at Christmas. Now I can feel the silky softness of her hair next to her skin. Her skin is warm and flushed, but just as soft.

"You're so soft all over. My fingertips need to touch you everywhere." I place the palm over her perfect sized breast. Rose rests her forehead against mine while watching my hand squeeze and fondle her. Her nipple stiffens with every swipe of my roughened skin. I pinch both nipples between my thumb and finger and then slide my hand down over her curvy side. I rest my hand on the soft flesh of her backside.

"Michael, I need to touch you everywhere, too," she whispers. Her hand runs up and down over my chest. The feeling is pure heaven. I tell her to take what she wants and roll onto my back. I know she's nervous, so I don't move. I leave my hand on her hip and let her explore. She distracts me from her hands when she kisses my ear. "I love you," she murmurs then kisses a path down my jaw to my chin. She places a quick, hard kiss on my lips. I don't have time to return the kiss before she continues down my neck and over to a nipple. She kisses then nibbles each nipple, alternating until both are rigid and sensitive. I continue to relax my fingers on her skin. I don't want to leave any bruises on her hip. My other hand curls around the pillowcase below my head. I can't stop the groan from slipping out of my throat when her lips leave my chest and head south to the dark path running from my abdomen to my thighs. She moves my hand off her hip while peeking through her eyelashes up into my eyes. I place it next to my hip so I can touch her as soon as she moves her body back up. I'm still staring into her eyes when I see her tongue poke out of her lips and slide over my hip bone. My entire body stiffens. I try to brace myself for what comes next. Her tongue runs from one hip bone, into my belly button, and over the other hip bone. Rose moans out a sound that has me a second away from shooting cum all over her chest.

"Rose, I'm about to lose it. Please give me a moment." I hate to ask her to stop, but I wasn't joking when I said the next time I come, it will be inside her.

"I'm doing it again. I'm sorry." She pulls away and I roll on my side and grab her hip to keep her next to me. Her eyes are showing confusion when I lean my head next to hers.

"I love what you're doing to me, sweetheart. I didn't want to come all over you. You can do whatever you like in a moment," I tell her, lifting her chin up so she has to look into my eyes. I smile my best smile at her and hear her laugh. I see the laughter take over her eyes. "And what is so funny?" I huff.

"Your smile, I've learned that smile." She leans forward and kisses my cheek. This is not going the way I thought it would. No man wants his woman laughing when they are naked in bed. It can hit the ego in a bad way.

"What about my smile?" I'm trying to comfort her and make her not feel rejected and she's laughing at me. I'm not taking it personally or getting offended because I'm naked next to the woman I love, so we are heading in the right direction.

"That smile is the one you give me when you are trying to calm me down." She stops laughing but I can still see the humor in her eyes. I guess I do change my smile with her.

"I want you to know I still want you and am not rejecting you. You pulled away from me." I always want her skin to skin with me in our bed, not pulling away.

"I understand what happened. I realize this has been one sided and wanted to show you the love you have shown me." She runs her fingers down my chest. "Can I continue now?" she asks me with a big smile.

"Rose, it hasn't been one sided in my eyes. I assure you I have enjoyed every moment of it, sweetheart. By all means continue," I tell her, rolling us both over. Rose is now across my chest and pulls her knees up next to my hips. She feels how hard I am between her hips. "Can I touch you while you continue?" I ask her. I need the feel of her skin under my rough hands. She nods her head yes and then presses her lips over mine. Her tongue runs over my lips and dances with my tongue when I part my lips. I slide my hands up over her arms and into her hair. She's devouring me like someone who has been starving for affection her whole life. I tip my hips upward when her hips push down. Her fingers are grasping my shoulders and I feel her nails poke into my skin. I'm enjoying the slight pain when I realize one hand is lining me up to enter her. Her soft wet folds are enveloping me in their warmth.

"Are you..." I start to say, and she places a finger over my mouth.

"Don't say a word. I'm doing exactly what I want." Her eyes show me she's anxious. I lay still with my fingers running through her hair. I lean up and kiss her lips. The only word that comes out of my mouth is 'relax'. Her shoulders lower after she inhales a deep breath. I let my hands run slowly down her spine and feel the muscles loosen. When I place my hands on her hips, I am a few inches inside her tight, wet walls. She is tighter than I thought she would be, and I have to move slowly and only when she is ready. Basically, she is a virgin. I slip one hand down between her legs and run my thumb in circles over her swollen clit. She sits up, places her hands on my chest and tips her head back moaning in pleasure. I'm holding my breath until she has completely lowered herself on to me. I take a deep breath and place my other hand on her swollen breast. She opens her eyes and looks back down at me. "You feel wonderful!" Rose tells me with words and the look in her eyes. She raises and lowers her hips until I slide easily in her. Her nails dig into my skin again. I'm sure I will have crescent shaped marks on my shoulders and chest tomorrow. "This feels amazing!" she gasps. I smile at her words and start to enjoy the sounds our bodies are making.

"Do you trust me?" I ask her although I know the answer.

"You know I do." She raises her eyebrows as she tells me she does.

"If you want control, you can stay on top." I give her a moment to answer. When she doesn't, I add, "I would like to make love to you and that means rolling over with me on top. Which would make you more comfortable?" I didn't want to push her, but I don't know if she will be able to have an orgasm while on top.

"I trust you Michael. Can we roll over and then give me a minute to center myself?" she asks. No shyness from my girl this time, instead she lets me know what she wants and needs. I feel Rose's firm muscles move around until she is laying on top of me. I circle her body with my arms and bend my knees then roll with her to the center of the bed. I'm happy I splurged on a king size bed right now. She places her feet next to my knees and opens her legs wide. I stay inside her warmth during the roll and I push in a little to let her know I'm there.

"Look into my eyes Rose. I want you to see me making love to you the entire time. I want you to see the love I feel for you and I want to see your love for me," I tell her, drawing her hair to the side. I place my hands next to her body and lift myself off of her. I pull almost all the way out and then glide forward into the heaven I have found with her. Her eyes hold mine and I see love, desire, and raw need in her eyes that are now almost completely gold, the green and brown have slipped away. I speed up my thrusts until I hear her moans.

"Oh Michael," she whimpers. Our bodies are sweating, and I can feel her walls clamping down on me. "Yes! Faster, Michael! Yes!" Rose closes her eyes only for me to tell her to look at me. Her fingers are running up and down my back, scratching now and then. I speed up and I can feel my balls tighten, wanting to release soon.

"Rose, are you close baby?" I need her to enjoy her first time, then I can take my pleasure from her body. She is moaning and sighing noises now. Her eyelids close halfway as she continues to look at me. She nods yes and I pick up my pace. I don't want to be rough with her and pound into her, but my body takes over and thrusts her hard into the mattress. I feel her muscles spasm around me, her body shaking as her fluids surround me. She screams my name over and over, digging her nails further into my skin, as I fill her with my release. I feel every muscle tense before my final release of cum. I have never felt so powerful in my life. This woman has reduced me to a shaking mess before I fall on top of her. It takes me a moment before I can lift my body up and rest on my arms.

"How are you feeling?" I keep an eye on her reaction verbally and physically. Her body is starting to relax, and I slip out of her. There is a flow of liquid coming out of her and that is when I realize I forgot a condom. I hope she isn't mad about the oversight. Then again, she didn't remember either.

"I'm wonderful! That was amazing Michael. Thank you for making it special," she sighs as she curls around me, still breathing hard. I roll onto my side and place her head on my shoulder. She places her hand on my heaving chest as I glance at the clock and see we still have an hour. I don't feel like I made it special, but I definitely made sure she enjoyed it.

"When we catch our breath, how about we take a shower?" I feel her body relax and hear the steady breathing. She has fallen asleep in my arms. My ego is telling me I did a good job, my heart is exploding with love, and my mind is telling me to let her sleep for twenty minutes then get in a quick shower. I wouldn't mind smelling like her for the night, but I think after our travels and sex, we both need a shower to feel fresh around my folks.

CHAPTER 14

We are a couple minutes late for dinner. Mom shakes her finger at me as we enter the kitchen. My damp hair gets a small tug when Mom hugs me hello. Her eyebrows rise when she pulls away, but she doesn't comment on it.

Our shower took a little longer than I had planned. Rose was shy washing my body and even more shy as I washed her body. After making love and taking a nap, naked and wrapped in my arms, I thought Rose's shyness was adorable. When I asked if she wanted to take a shower by herself, she told me how silly that would be at that point. I should have let her have some space. I will make her as comfortable as possible with each new step.

"I'm sorry we are late. It is my fault," Rose tells my mom after giving her a hug. "Michael let me take a nap and I didn't want to wake up." Rose's cheeks turn a crimson red and we are both sure my folks don't believe a word of it. "We also had a problem with some of the kids from the group when we pulled in." Rose, I'm sure, doesn't realize she said we. I'm smiling at her for the slip up.

"Oh, what happened?" Dad asks us. We sit at the smaller table in the kitchen for dinner. We discuss the trouble with Conor and Nat. I usually don't discuss the problems I have with any of the groups. I try and talk about all the positive things that come out of each program. After the accident, Mom and Dad were so proud I turned my difficulty into something positive and took it upon myself to reach out to others with my programs. Mom, Dad, and

Nick understood my need to do something trauma based. I had to explain what Trauma Focused Equine Assisted Psychotherapy, TF-EAP, was to the whole family. When I explained I would also be doing Equine Facilitated Learning, EFL, for autism and emotional and mental disorders, they were concerned I would be stretching myself too thin.

"I didn't understand how intense each program can be for the individual. I thought the clients got away from their life problems for a little while and got some quality time with a horse." Rose reaches over and takes my hand in hers. I see tenderness and love in her eyes. "I found out how wrong I was today. I've always wanted to volunteer somewhere I thought I could make a difference. Corsco Equestrian Healing may be just that place." I squeeze her hand and tell her how happy that makes me. My folks continue eating and give each other that knowing look. I think Mom has added me to the wedding planning group she has going with my brothers.

We finish dinner and I volunteer to do the dishes with Rose again. She chuckles that I put away the food this time and let her handle the knives. Before Mom leaves the kitchen with Dad, Rose and I thank her for a wonderful dinner. The marinated flank steak, potato salad, and watermelon salad tasted great on a long, warm day. Rose asks Mom to teach her the potato salad recipe while tasting it at dinner.

The dishes get finished without incident. Rose and I listen to the oldies station Mom left on the radio while in the kitchen. She closes the dishwasher and wipes her hands dry. I'm standing behind her, ready to take her in my arms and dance around the kitchen to Frank Sinatra. "The Way You Look Tonight" fills the kitchen as I place my right hand in Rose's and my left hand on her waist. We glide over the wooden floor. Rose laughs as I tip her at the end of the song. We both hear my Mom whisper to my day Dad from the door. I look up from the dip and see Mom giving me the thumbs up before closing the door.

"I have to say, I'm starting to like this station. It brings out the romantic in you, Michael." Rose places her arms around my neck and gives me an *Old Blue Eyes* worthy kiss. I leave the kitchen a little frustrated. We sit in the family room with my folks and surprise them with Rose's decision to stay in Oklahoma and not interview in Denver. Mom screams her joy and Dad just shakes his head at his wife's reaction.

I stay with Rose after Mom and Dad go to bed. She asks me a lot of questions about each program. She lets me know she was serious about volunteering. I tell her it isn't volunteering after she marries me. It will be part her business too. I see the surprise in her eyes and want to make sure it isn't from what I said.

"I know we will get there when you're ready. I'm not rushing you to move in with me. I'm saying I know eventually we will be married and sometime after that we will have kids." She smiles at me and sits across my lap to cuddle closer. "I know you want a career. You didn't go to school for so long not to have one. I will support whatever you want to do. If you want to keep working after we have kids, I'm fine with that. I'm sure Mom will offer to babysit all the time when the time comes." I run my hand down her hair and skim over her shirt until my hand rests on her hip. She feels so relaxed, I start to wonder if she fell asleep on me again.

"I appreciate you being so understanding. I don't know how I will feel about working when I have kids. I do know I want to have kids with you in the future though." Rose lifts her head off my shoulder and leans in for kiss. I keep it short and sweet. I need to head home soon, without my jeans being tight. "When will I see you next?" she asks.

"I was just thinking I needed to head out. Let me call you at lunch tomorrow. I need to talk to my staff and get back into the swing of things at work. I owe them all a raise after all the time I've been gone these last few months." I feel like they have picked up more than the normal slack because of me. I know Mom will keep Rose busy and Anna asked her to visit at the clinic this week. She will have more to do than spend time with me.

"I don't want to interfere with your work, but I do want to get to know the staff and your clients. And of course, I need to come spend time with Chestnut and *Rosso*." Rose gets off my lap and leads me to the front door. "I'll be cooking or baking with your mom all day tomorrow, so call me whenever you get a chance," Rose says. No pressure, no expectations, and no anxiety. God, I love this woman.

"I will. Get a good night sleep. My Mom's cooking lessons can be intense." I wrap her in my arms and enjoy her scent. This time I smell my cedar body wash and shampoo on her, but I can still detect her wonderful smell underneath the woodsy scent. "I love you, sweetheart." I give her one last kiss and open the door.

"I love you too. I want you to know how much I will enjoy spending time in the room you grew up in," Rose says. I see the laughter in her eyes and head out the door.

"Don't think about all the years I was a horny teenager in that bed. You'll never get to sleep. Oh, I think there may be a few magazines under the mattress you won't want to see. Don't tell my Mom though." I walk down the stairs when I hear her yell at me.

"How do you expect me to sleep now?" She shuts the door to my laughter. I want her to think about me as much as I'm going to think about her. My sheets are going to smell like her from earlier, so I know I won't be sleeping tonight. I need to remember Rose is down in Oklahoma for good and eventually, she will be living in the house and sleeping next to me in the bed always.

* * *

Rose invites me over for dinner when I call her today. I catch up with all the employees and 4H kids during the day. I get time to check in on Chestnut and *Rosso* before I leave for the ranch. Chestnut is ready for a rider and I'm going to surprise Rose with a ride when she comes over Saturday for the day. *Rosso*, I'm glad to see, is settling in nicely. I put her in a stall next to Chestnut and they greet each other over the open stall doors. I'm looking forward to getting her into one of the programs. I'm thinking about which program would best fit her personality while driving to my folk's. She is so easy going I think she will fit into any of them. I need to have a meeting with my staff and get their input before making a final decision.

I see Rose in one of the rocking chairs on the front porch when I pull up to the house. Her Tiffany blue sundress flows around her calves as she runs down the steps and into my arms. I can get used to this! Although, I think she may work longer hours than me some days. I might be the one meeting her at the door.

"I missed you," Rose tells me. She puts her arms around my neck and leans into me for a quick kiss.

"I missed you, too." I spin her in a circle to feel her dress move again. "You look beautiful. Is there a reason why you're all dressed up?" I remember this sundress from Colorado. It hugs her curves nicely. I'm sure I will have a difficult time saying good night later without running my hands to places they shouldn't go to at my folk's house.

"I wanted to look nice for you," she whispers in my ear. I set her down and take her hand in mine. We walk up to the house with smiles on our faces.

"Sweetheart, you always look nice. I like that you made the effort to look extra nice for me but know you don't ever have to." We walk into the house and I breathe in the wonderful aromas of the kitchen. "Whatever you made smells amazing! What did you and Mom do in the kitchen today?" I ask her. Mom is taking a dish out of the oven and Dad is sitting at the table, which is already set for dinner.

"Your mom promised me she would teach me how to make spaghetti sauce another time. She had sauce in the freezer so for tonight we used it and I made stuffed shells with salad and garlic bread," she tells me. She's so excited and happy as she pulls my hand and jumps up and down. Mom places the dish on the table, and it looks delicious.

"Wow! You're learning Italian right away. I have to say, my mom's sauce has been a family secret so you should feel honored." I give Mom a hug after she sets the hot dish down. "You're willing to share the recipe with Rose, huh?" I smile at her. I know she only offers to share the family recipes after a ring gets put on a hand. Mom and Dad both smile at me and I know the wedding planner is in full gear.

"Technically, Rose is family now that Lily and Brady are married," Mom says. She turns her head away from me when she says it. I know her and I know she has color schemes in mind along with floral arrangements for each season planned in her mind.

"That's enough talking. I'm starving. Let's eat." Dad is cutting the garlic bread and offering a piece to everyone. "Unlike you, I have smelled this great dinner every time I came inside the house today." Mom passes him the salad and then serves him several shells so he can start eating. When Dad gets hungry, he gets irritable. Mom always makes sure he gets served right away.

"The entire meal tastes wonderful. Who do I thank for dinner?" I look at Rose then Mom. I'm figuring Mom told her what to do but Rose did all the work. I reach for Rose's hand and pull it to my lips. "I'm looking forward to future meals if this is any example."

"Thank you, but it's your mom's sauce that makes it taste so good," Rose says not taking any credit for the dish. Mom corrects her right away by telling her that food is only as good as the person making it. Rose's cheeks blush to a soft pink.

Rose asks how everything went for me today and we start talking about the next program starting next week. Mom and Dad ask about *Rosso* and then I talk about how great Chestnut has been doing with his training. I get so wrapped up in talking about the horses, I don't notice when my folks leave the kitchen. Rose and I get the dishes loaded in the dishwasher and the leftovers put away while we listen to the oldies station that is still on the radio. This time when Rose turns away from the sink, she leans into me for a quick dance around the kitchen. Frank Sinatra is once again singing as we glide across the floor. This time "My Way" fills the air around us.

"I don't regret anything with you," I whisper into her ear. I smile next to her hair when she tells me the same. "I will always be happy you took a chance on me, sweetheart." The song finishes as I dip her on the last note.

"I feel like you are the one that took a chance on me. Thank you for sticking with me for these months. I don't know what I would be doing, besides working all the time, if it weren't for you." She stands from the dip and kisses me. "I'm so thankful Lily moved next door to my brother. I'll have to thank her one of these days." Rose slides us to the refrigerator and opens the door to show me the lemon meringue pie she made. "I had to make sure you got your lemon fix in." She sticks her finger in the meringue and dabs my nose with the fluffy white sugary goodness. We are laughing when Mom comes in to see if we are ready for dessert. When she sees my arms around her and the meringue on my nose, she laughs and excuses herself from the room. I hear her tell Dad the meringue might be all gone before he gets any of it. Their laughter reaches us while we continue covering our noses in the white sugary fluff.

* * *

Saturday arrives with loud thunder rattling the walls of the stables and bright lightning shooting across the sky. I have the music playing over the stereo system to help calm the horses. I told Rose to meet me at the stables because of the storm when she called to tell me she was on her way. We had dinner with my folks every night and Rose prepared every meal. She may not have learned to cook from her mom or sisters, but she is a natural.

"Michael, where are you?" Rose yells over the thunder as she enters the stables. I'm surprised I can hear her over the loud claps of thunder.

"Down with Chestnut," I yell back. I've had most of the horses here for years. They don't startle easily, and thunder never seems to bother them. Chestnut, on the other hand, is making quite the fuss. *Rosso* seems to be trying to calm him down by neighing to him. I think the storm is upsetting him so much because of his own trauma with his previous owners. Rose walks down the aisle until she finds me cooing to the horse. *Rosso* sticks his head out of his stall and neighs to her. I see the smile Rose gives her before she walks up to give her attention. The horse responds

186

to her gentle touch and soft voice similar to how I do. I place a blanket over Chestnut and try patting his muzzle, but he tries to nip me. I leave the stall before he picks up on my nerves. Chestnut is so nervous; it's making me nervous which only makes the whole situation worse.

"Don't you take all her attention," I tell *Rosso*. Rose is running her hand over her crest and the horse is loving all the extra care. I can see her leaning into Rose's touch. "I think Chestnut might need that De'Amedo touch. This storm is scaring him more than I expected." I come up behind Rose and pull her back into my arms. I see the horse change her stance and I think she is actually jealous.

"I can hum that tune to him like last time," Rose says over her shoulder. I release her for a moment. She stands at Chestnut's stall door and starts humming. Chestnut sticks his head out of the stall and calms immediately. Rose runs her hand over his muzzle, and he pushes back against her hand. She really does have a great touch with horses. I wrap my arms around her again and whisper in her ear how her touch soothes me, too.

"I was going to surprise you with a ride today. It will have to wait for a day when the summer storms aren't in the area. I wouldn't want YOUR horse to throw you." She doesn't catch my use of words. Subtlety obviously isn't going to work. "I want Chestnut to be your horse. He seems to respond to you better than anyone else and you are the only one who has been able to calm him like that." I see the surprise in her eyes the moment my words sink in, then she is in my arms and Chestnut is neighing loudly. I look over Rose's shoulder at the horse and say, "It's my time with her now Chestnut! You'll have plenty of time with her now that you're her horse."

"You mean it? Chestnut is mine?" Rose asks quickly. I nod my head yes. I will give Rose everything she wants if she keeps holding me like this. She releases me and I see the look in Chestnut's eyes as Rose runs her hands over his mane and rubs on his muzzle. "Did you hear that Chestnut? Your mine," she tells the horse. She continues to talk with Chestnut as I check on the other horses. We drive her car up to the house after the thunder rolls eastward. "Thank you for my gift. I can't tell you how excited I am to know I have my own horse to ride." We jump over the puddles and make our way into the house.

"I decided on my way back home in April to train him for you." I step into the kitchen and put water in the kettle for tea. We are both wet and cold. I have several ideas on how we can warm each other up. I think a hot cup of tea and sitting in front of a fire is a good start. "Why don't you find something to watch and I'll start a fire after the tea is ready?" I ask her over my shoulder. I'm surprised when I feel her lean wet body against my wet back. She puts her arms around my waist and kisses me on the back of my neck.

"I'm cold down to my bones Michael. I have a better idea to warm up," she tells me. I set the kettle down on the stove without turning the burner on. "I saw an exceptionally large tub in that bathroom of yours, and I have always loved bubble baths. How about you join me for a bath?" I feel a tug on my belt loop and Rose pulls me out of the kitchen towards the stairs. I like her idea a lot.

"I think I may have bubble bath under my sink from when Lily was visiting. Mom and Dad don't have a large tub at their place." I didn't think about it at the time, but I guess I should keep female comforts at my place now. I followed Rose up the stairs. Her swaying hips leave me in a trance. She's still holding my hand as we enter the bedroom. My mind goes fuzzy and all I see is the gold in her hazel eyes and the gloss on her lips. I sit on the bed and try to pull her with me. She shakes her head and walks towards the bathroom. Her shirt hits me in the face as she throws it over her head and behind her.

"Where is the bubble bath?" Rose asks. I get up from the bed and see a trail of shoes, socks, and jeans. She is leaning over the tub running the hot water.

"What bubble bath?" I ask her. She looks at me and I see her brows scrunch inward. She doesn't answer me, instead, she removes her aqua bra and panties. I stand inside the bathroom door confused. "What are you talking about?" I ask, fully dressed.

"You said Lily left some bubble bath here. We are going to take a bath together, aren't we?" Rose walks up to me confident in her nudity. I look at her eyes and I feel fuzzy again. "Are you alright Michael?" I see the concern on her face. "Are you having one of your forgetful moments?" Her concern turns to worry. I see her anxiety level go up.

"I'm okay, I think. What did we talk about downstairs?" I feel myself sink into confusion. This is the first episode in a long time. I had started to think my body was healing more and the memory loss was getting better. I guess I was wrong.

"You were going to make tea and start a fire. You asked me to pick something to watch on TV." Rose walks me over to the tub and I sit on the side. "I suggested we take a bubble bath to warm up instead." I don't remember talking about a bath at all. "You told me Lily left a bottle under the sink in your bathroom because she wanted to take a bath in the big tub." Rose sits next to me and rubs my back with her hand. I look at her and forget she is naked. All I see is the gold in her eyes. I shake my head and finally see her naked beauty.

"Well, you finally get to see what I was talking about. I'm embarrassed right now." I place my hand on her knee and rub the soft skin under my rough palm.

"Michael you shouldn't feel embarrassed by something you can't control. I understand that trauma to the brain can be life long and you don't know when things like this will happen." She takes my hand off her knee and places it over her heart. "I also know that I love you. We will work through this like your staff does, one day at a time." She checks my pulse on my wrist and feels it going down. "Tell me, did you experience anything different when this happened?" The nurse in her is taking over when all I really want is the naked, sexy, confident woman I love to fill the tub and forget this ever happened.

"My mind felt fuzzy like I hadn't been asleep in days and I saw the gold in your eyes and pink of your lips but nothing else. I don't know how else to explain it," I tell her. I pull my hand away and remove my boots. I just want to get into the bath with her.

"Were you intentionally focusing in on my eyes and mouth or was that where your mind took you?" she asks. I have to think how to answer her. I remember walking up the stairs with her and then sitting on the bed. My head felt like it did the last time I had a head cold. When I looked at her, the only things I saw were the gold and pink colors on her face. I didn't see her facial features or hair. My mind zoomed in on gold and pink. I try and explain it to her, but I'm not sure she understands any better than I do. Usually I forget details about a group or time someone is due. Sometimes even names, but never have I been so focused in on colors.

"My eyes only saw the gold and pink on your face. I wasn't intentionally focusing on them." I try and start taking my pants off to move forward on the bath, but she stops me. "Can we just forget about this and take a bath? I want to feel you next to me." I unbuckle my belt and stand up to push my jeans down.

"Are you dizzy at all?" She stands with me and holds my hands on my hips before I can push my briefs down.

"No, I'm not dizzy. Can we relax in the bubble bath? Please." I'm almost begging at this point for her to let it go.

"Humor the nurse in me. Follow my finger," she says. Her index finger goes from one side to the other in front of my eyes. I tell her I'm fine again, but she continues moving her finger up and down asking me questions. I pass the tests and she tells me how concerned she is.

"Rose, I appreciate the concern. It has passed and I'm fine." I pull my t-shirt over my head, push my briefs down, and take my socks off. The water is hot, and I put the stopper in and adjust the temperature. I walk around her and get the bubble bath. I hand it to her so she can put in as much as she wants. She says nothing until the tub is full of bubbles and we both get in and sit down.

"I understand you didn't want me to see this happen to you, but you will have to get used to my concern. I plan on being with you for the rest of our lives. This will happen again while I'm with you." I'm sitting behind Rose with her leaning back against my chest. My arms surround her waist and my legs rest against the outside of hers. "Get over the embarrassment now." She sits up and twists her upper body until she can see me. "You don't think I was embarrassed telling you how stupid I felt after being raped? Even after therapy I told myself I should have known he was drinking. I should have seen it coming. I should have been able to stop him. Embarrassment is not a luxury you and I can have with each other." Her face is turning red and I'm not sure if it's from the heat of the water or from the temper I have rarely seen but know she has.

"It hasn't happened in a long time and I was hoping you would never have to see it firsthand." I lower my head and she puts her finger under my chin, lifting my face back up. I see the love and tenderness in her eyes even though her voice is nothing but firm with me.

"Get it in your head now," she says and pokes me in my chest. "I love everything about you. That includes the broken pieces. You helped me put together the broken pieces that still remained. Now it is my turn to help you." Rose turns back around and rests her back against my chest. She takes my hands and rests them on her breasts. "Now if our first argument is over, I would like to know what it feels like to make love to you in this huge tub," she says and then runs her fingernails over my thighs.

I kiss the side of her neck and realize just how much I love this woman. "Yes ma'am," I tell her. I used to think she was like a skittish colt. She needed time and experience to move forward in her life. Now I see she is the elegant mare, strutting herself around for all to see her confidence. My fingers find her nipples and pinch the erect points. She shifts her hips back only to find how turned on I am by her. My erection rests between the cheeks of her backside. I let my finger glide down over her stomach and dip into the curls between her thighs. I get better access to her neck when she tilts her head back and moans. I'm leaving love marks on her neck as my fingers dip between her swollen lower lips. I tease her entrance with a short in and out motion.

"Please," I hear her whisper the word and it makes me harder. Surprise sets in when I feel her hand on top of mine. Rose places her legs over mine, opening herself up more for my pleasure. When her fingers push mine inside her I can feel my precum leak out of my rock-hard erection. Her moans almost make me come in the water.

"Rose, honey, please turn around. Sit on top of me." She does exactly what I ask her. When she lowers herself and takes every inch of me inside her tight, wet walls I have to take a deep breath and think of anything else but what we are doing. She places her hands on my shoulders, digs in her nails, and proceeds to thrust up and down. The bubbles and water spill over the side of the tub. I don't care. All I care about at this moment is feeling Rose's tight walls shudder around me with an orgasm and to hear her shout out my name. I can tell she is almost there. I've gotten to learn her body very quickly.

"Michael! I am so close," she yells, splashing more water over the side. I feel the tremors start and enjoy the tightness around me. "Oh…Michael…Now!" she screams, and I go over the edge with her. All it takes for me is hearing my name on her lips.

* * *

I build a fire and turn on the country video channel on the TV. We enjoy watching the music videos and Rose comments on the artists she knows and songs she has heard. I comment on the songs that remind me of her. Lyrics that fit how I feel and artists I would love to take her to see. "Unforgettable" by Thomas Rhett comes on as I return with the hot tea, I had started hours ago.

"When we would talk on the phone after your shifts I would listen to this channel. I love Mom's oldies station, but I'm a country boy at heart. I actually started a list of songs I wanted you to listen to one day. I'll have to pull it out and give it to you." We cuddle on the couch, listening to music and wait for the storm to completely pass by. We fall asleep wrapped up in each other's arms. My phone rings and Mom is asking us if we will be there for dinner. Rose takes the phone and tells Mom she won't be back until tomorrow around dinner time. I can see Mom's smile in my mind.

A couple more weeks and Rose will interview in Oklahoma City and Tulsa. We will have a better idea of what our days will look like and how much time she will spend here. The job in Tulsa is about ten minutes closer, so I'm hoping she takes that one. As long as she continues to spend time with me, and she's happy at work, either job works.

We enjoy the uninterrupted evening in front of the fire. Dinner ends up being leftovers and water, but neither of us seems to mind. We are enjoying cuddling on the couch and then in bed when we both realize how tired we are. I want to make love to her again, but I don't want her to be sore tomorrow. We have our entire lives to make love and I can wait until our next opportunity.

CHAPTER 15

Over the next couple weeks, Mom teaches Rose how to cook a variety of Italian dishes and bake some basic desserts. They are both having fun working in the kitchen together and my dad and I are enjoying the end results, wonderful and tasty meals. Dad and I have put on a few extra pounds eating all the amazing food served every night. Mom talked to me, on several occasions, about how nice it is to have another woman in the house. She really misses having Lily around. Dad told me it's like having another daughter around. He loves seeing Rose every day especially when it makes his wife so happy.

When Rose isn't getting cooking and baking lessons from Mom, she is helping Anna at the clinic and spending time at the stables with me. Chestnut is responding positively to her soft voice commands and settles down quickly when Rose sings to him. Rose's presence works wonders on all of us.

Rose gets job offers from both of her interviews. She decides to take the job in Tulsa at the Woman's Center. During the interview, she saw several teenagers coming into the center. She has talked to me several times about how education and advocacy needs to start in the early teen years. Hearing the teenagers talk about sex with their boyfriends while she was there is what made her decide, on the spot, to take the job if she was offered it.

We have fallen into a pattern each evening. I spend my day working with the horses or running the weekly program, then come over for dinner with my parents and Rose. After dinner, Rose and I do the dishes and sit and talk with Mom and Dad for a while. We then head over to my house for a few hours. We cuddle on the couch and continue getting to know each other. We talk about what our hopes and dreams are for the future, including having children in a few years. It turns out Rose is on birth control, so she didn't think about using condoms with me. Sometimes the cuddling on the couch turns into a hot and heavy make out session and other times we head upstairs and share our bodies with each other, making love. I'm not pushing her, but I can hardly wait for her to stay every night and not head back to my folk's house to sleep.

"Did you call Brady about your things? We can take a weekend and go up to get them if you want," I ask her when we leave my parent's house the day she accepted her new job offer.

"He said Lily is still having a hard time with her morning sickness. He was going to drive my car down and fly back, but he doesn't want to leave her right now." She climbs up into the cab of my truck while I hold the door open for her and watch her skirt swishing around her knees. The weather has been record-breaking hot, and Rose has worn dresses or skirts most days to help her stay cool. I love seeing her in the flowing material.

"I'm sorry she's not feeling better. How about we fly up and drive your car back? We can fly up Friday night and drive back after breakfast on Sunday. That way we can spend all day with them on Saturday." I think about programs I have going in the next two weeks and know I can do it either week.

"I start work in two weeks, so the sooner the better." Rose slides over to the middle seat and rests her head on my shoulder as I drive away from the house. The radio is on the country station I always leave it on and is playing "What's Mine is Yours" by Kane Brown. She squeezes my thigh as the lyrics fill the truck. "I don't have much to move, Michael. Do you mind if I bring it to your house?" she quietly asks. I'm so surprised by her question, I pull the truck over to the side of the road. We are still on the ranch road so I'm not blocking traffic at all.

"You can move anything you want into the house. I told you whenever you're ready to move in, I'm ready to make my home, our home." I squeeze the hand that is resting on my thigh. I turn my body towards her and place my hands on each of her cheeks. Gold has taken over the green in her eyes and her cheeks are warm to my touch. "I love you Rose. Having you and your things around me would make me the happiest man alive." I tip my head down and place my lips gently on hers. I feel her fingers in my hair, pulling me down for a deeper kiss. Our breathing is coming in gasps when I raise my head. "I need you, sweetheart. If we weren't on my parents ranch, I would lift that dress, place you on my lap and bury myself in that sexy body." I turn my body towards the front of the truck and grab the steering wheel. Rose places her hands on her lap and faces the front of the truck while telling me to get us home. I hit the gas and get us home as quick as I safely can. We talk about what she will be moving. I have myself, physically, back under control when we pull up to the house.

"Michael, there's a package at the front door," Rose says as I pull the truck around to the back of the house. I'm expecting a package from Italy any day now, but I thought it would be put in the mailbox. I know I want Rose to see it as soon as it comes in, so we walk to the front of the house and pick up the package. I let go of her hand for her to pick the box up. The box is small enough, I would never have seen it sitting in front of the door. I'm glad Rose caught sight of it. "Wow! It's all the way from Italy." Rose sees my smile when I tell her to hold the package until we get inside. She doesn't think anything of it and runs a hand down my chest. "Ready to celebrate me moving in?" I love the sexual teasing she is now comfortable with.

"I'm ready to celebrate with you for any reason," I tell her as I guide her into the living room. She grabs my hand and pulls me towards the stairs after putting the package on the coffee table. When I hold her back, she pouts and stands next to me with a look of confusion on her face. "That is for you." I point to the box. "I want you to open it before we get to celebrating," I say and hand her the package. I stand in silence while she struggles with the tape. She doesn't ask me what it is or say anything at all while opening it.

"Michael!" is the only word she says before collapsing to the couch behind her. She looks up at me with tears in her eyes. I kneel in front of her and place my hands over hers, surrounding the teacup resting in her lap. The box was dropped onto the floor when Rose took the teacup out of it. The note inside is forgotten about as I watch tears stream down Rose's cheeks. "How? When?" she asks giving me the most heart-warming precious, smile I have ever seen.

"Gabriella's parents live in Italy with her aunts. She called one of her aunts and tracked down the company for me. I was able to find an antique dealer who still carries the pattern." It hits me in my heart every time she cries, even when they are happy tears like now. "I told you I would replace it. I know how upset you were when the teacup broke." I rub my hands up and down her arms and feel her shaking. "Rose, talk to me."

"I can't believe you did this for me." Rose sets the cup on the coffee table carefully. "You are sweet and thoughtful and the best thing that has ever happened in my life." I barely catch the last tear falling from her eyes as she leans forward and kisses me. "I love you more than I knew I could love anyone," she tells me as she pulls me onto the couch. Before I know it, she throws her leg over my thighs and straddles my lap. The kiss starts off tender and sweet and quickly turns demanding and passionate. She pulls my shirt over my head, breaking the kiss for just a moment. I run my hands under her skirt, enjoying the feel of her soft, silky thighs before I reach around her to unzip the dress. We can't seem to slow our hands down, running over every inch possible. Our breathing is coming out in gasps as I feel her fingers pull at my belt.

"Rose, I'll take my pants off if you'll slip your dress off," I pant. Since we've started, I'm needing to be in her now.

"Deal," she giggles as she stands up. I'm shoving my zipper down and quickly pushing my jeans down while I watch her pull the straps down her arms and the dress fall down over her hips. I shove my boots off, push my jeans past my feet and reach up to hold her hips. I don't want her to lose her balance I tell myself and I need my hands back on her. I curl my finger over the lace of her panties and pull them down. She holds onto my shoulders while she steps out of the soft material. I can see the damp lace as each foot clears the material. I smell her excitement and she sees my excitement increase.

"Now, where were we?" I tease and pull her back onto my lap.

The passion and tenderness of the moment seeps into our love making tonight and she calls my mom to tell her she won't be home.

* * *

Hanging out with Brady and Lily for the day was nice, but we are both ready to settle into *our* home when we get back to Sapulpa. We get on the road after breakfast and make it back home in ten hours. It helps to not be pulling a horse trailer. Rose's little car handles the trip easily. Alternating music every hour keeps us talking about what we like to listen too. I will be listening to more pop and rock with Rose living in the house and I'm okay with that.

We stop at Mom and Dad's to let them know how Lily is doing and get the clothes Rose has there before heading home.

"I know you have been on the road all day, but do you want to sit down for some dessert? I made Lily's lemon meringue cupcakes." Mom doesn't have to ask me twice for those cupcakes, but I ask Rose if she would like to stay. I have to start thinking of us as a unit now and not make decisions without her input.

"Cate, we would love to stay. I think we could use something sweet to end this long day." Rose heads into the kitchen with Mom to put the tea on and set the dessert on the table.

"You seem very happy son," Dad says. He is sitting in his favorite chair in the living room. I nod my head yes before he continues. "I remember, not that long ago, when you were terrified how life would work out for you. I want you to know your mother and I are very proud of you. You have your own thriving business, your own home, and a woman who loves you very much." The women let us know that dessert is on the table and we stand to head into the kitchen. I'm choked up by what my father said. He slaps me on the back before saying, "Enjoy all of the good in your life son. You deserve it." I guess there is a double standard after all. They don't seem to mind Rose moving in with me, unlike their little girl shacking up before marriage.

We discuss the ongoing mold issue the county is having with their hay while enjoying the lemony heaven. Dad is telling me that Sophia is coming into town to see if she can help as Joseph walks into the kitchen. Luca mentioned his daughter's Master's degree was in Agricultural Biology and offered her assistance. She agreed as soon as her father told her what was going on with all the ranches and farms in the area.

"Did I hear you say Sophia is coming to town?" Joseph asks as he grabs a cupcake off the counter. I can see the interest on his face even though he is trying to act like it doesn't matter to him. Sophia had the biggest crush on Joseph when she was a teenager. I know Joseph didn't let anything happen because he was several years older than her, he was in his twenties. I'm sure there was an interest on his part though. Not only would her dad have killed him, our dad would have tanned his hide.

"Yeah. She's coming to see if she can help with the mold problem. She just finished her Master's degree and hasn't started working yet." Dad tells him, not aware of Mom's new interest in the couple. Rose and I both see the look on her face and can see the wheels turning in her head. We both try and hide the smiles on our faces.

"I'm sure Luca is excited to see her again. How long has it been since he's seen her?" Joseph asks, too casually. I think if anyone asked Joseph how long it has been since Sophia has come to visit her dad and the ranch, he could tell you down to the month and year, if not the exact day she left.

"I'm not sure, but it's been a long time according to Luca. I sure hope she can figure this out. We all need some good news and healthy animals before fall calving season." Sal continues eating while the rest of us keep looking at Joseph.

"Sophia was always smart. I'm sure she can give us some kind of answer," Joseph defends her quickly. Yup, still interested. Maybe now that Sophia is an adult, Joseph will let his interest turn into something. And maybe Luca won't kill him if he does show his interest.

"I guess they will be doing the dishes at the next family dinner," I say to Rose. My heart fills with joy when I hear Rose laughing and we both continue to laugh when Mom whispers that we may be right.

Look for these titles by
Laine Faro

Now Available:

Corsco Family Series
Cannoli for the Cop Next Door
All Sizes Vet Clinic
My Perfect Love
Skittish to Love

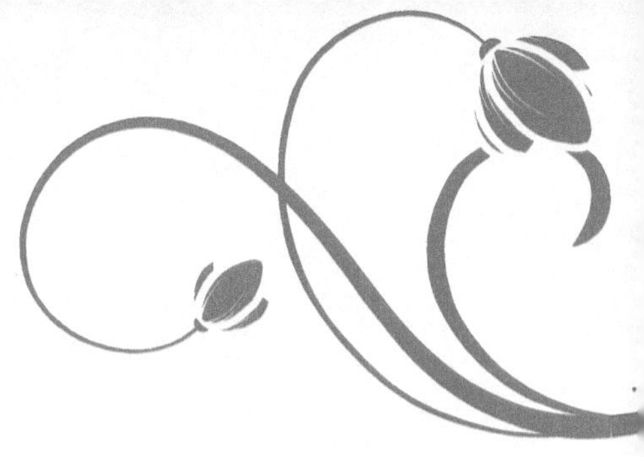

THE CORSCO FAMILY SERIES

Sal and Cate Corsco have six amazing children. Come join the oldest of their kids, Joseph, in book 5.

Sophia went to California with her mom as a child. She came back every summer vacation to visit her dad, Luca, who manages the family ranch. She disappeared for years while attending college and getting her Master's. She may be the answer to the local problem all the ranchers and farmers are having with their feed.

Joseph remembers every summer with her, especially the time by the river in her bikini when she kissed him. She was several years younger than him and he kept his distance, knowing her father would have his hide if he made his attraction known. Now she's an adult and even more beautiful than he remembered. This summer he's hoping to see her bikini, return the kiss, and hopefully a whole lot more.

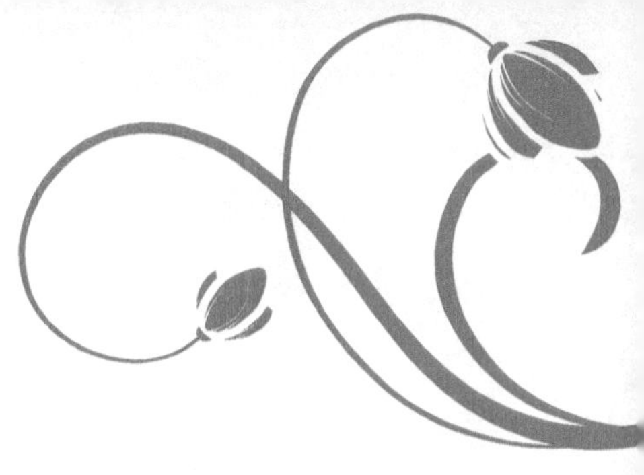

I am a victim of sexual assault and wanted to put my story into one of my characters. My exact experience is not the one I wrote in this book. It was still painful to write, but I want people everywhere to understand the statistics continue to increase for sexual assault and this is unacceptable. If you are a victim; report, speak up, get the help you need to become a survivor. It took me years of therapy, a great man in my life, and facing my assailant to become the survivor I am today.

Here are some resources for anyone looking for help:

National Sexual Assault hotline   1-800-656-HOPE (4673)
Safe Helpline (support for members of the military community)
        1-877-335-5247
End Rape on Campus
Voices and Faces Project
Not Alone (webpage with a map to enter your zip code in
        and get services in your area)